OTRANADOE!

No one stays sane for long. . . .

No one comes out alive. . . .

No one can avoid giving them what they want. . . .

"Teal Ray," the Uelson voice intoned.

Don't answer. Don't say a word. One word leads to another. . . .
"Where are you from?" the voice asked. Then it came: Pain! Burning . . . shrieking, writhing . . . animal wail. . . . And again: "Where are you from?"

That's what they wanted to know. Remember the home. Don't betray the home. Remember father. . . .

Pain, more pain. . . . Then calm . . . sweating, panting, trembling . . . no pain. . . .
But there will be more pain. There will be more. Don't say anything. . . .

So this was a Uelson prison. . . .

Science Fiction from SIGNET

* Price slightly higher in Canada
† Not available in Canada

To order these titles,
please use coupon on the
last page of this book.

Sovereign

✠✠✠✠✠✠✠✠✠✠✠✠✠✠✠✠✠✠✠✠✠✠✠✠✠

by

R. M. Meluch

Ⓢ

A SIGNET BOOK

NEW AMERICAN LIBRARY

TIMES MIRROR

PUBLISHED BY
THE NEW AMERICAN LIBRARY
OF CANADA LIMITED

COPYRIGHT © 1979 BY R. M. MELUCH

First Signet Printing, June, 1979
1 2 3 4 5 6 7 8 9

 SIGNET TRADEMARK REG. U.S. PAT. OFF. AND FOREIGN COUNTRIES
REGISTERED TRADEMARK — MARCA REGISTRADA
HECHO EN WINNIPEG, CANADA

SIGNET, SIGNET CLASSICS, MENTOR, PLUME and
MERIDIAN BOOKS are published in Canada by The New
American Library of Canada Limited, Scarborough, Ontario

PRINTED IN CANADA
COVER PRINTED IN U.S.A.

Sovereign

HIGHLAND ROYALIST LINES

(All generations after the Line Founder consist of *only sons*.)

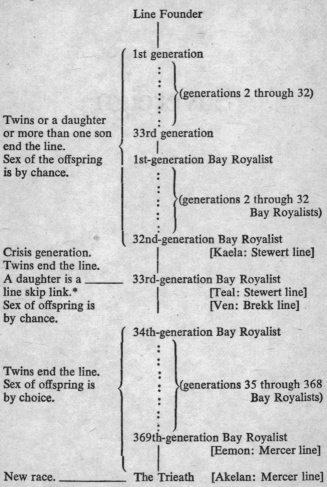

Line Founder

1st generation

(generations 2 through 32)

Twins or a daughter
or more than one son
end the line.
Sex of the offspring
is by chance.

33rd generation

1st-generation Bay Royalist

(generations 2 through 32
Bay Royalists)

32nd-generation Bay Royalist
[Kaela: Stewert line]

Crisis generation.
Twins end the line.
A daughter is a _____
line skip link.*
Sex of offspring is
by chance.

33rd-generation Bay Royalist
[Teal: Stewert line]
[Ven: Brekk line]

34th-generation Bay Royalist

Twins end the line.
Sex of offspring is
by choice.

(generations 35 through 368
Bay Royalists)

369th-generation Bay Royalist
[Eemon: Mercer line]

New race. _____ The Trieath   [Akelan: Mercer line]

*A line skip link is the daughter of a 33rd-generation Bay Royalist.
Should she bear an only son, that son would be a 1st-generation
Bay. It is possible for a line skip link to be the child of a generation
greater than 33rd, but extremely unlikely, since greater generations
can choose to have a son instead of a daughter.

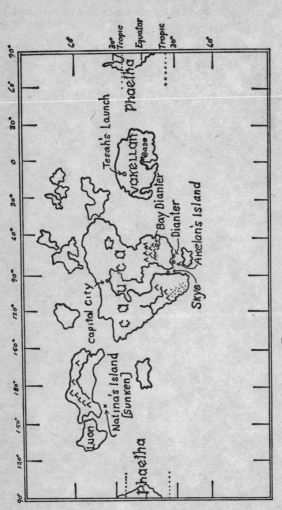

Arana

PART ONE:

Arana

I.

21/22 Beth-enea
Star Year 531 Third Epoch

Dark-red warmth and love. Wet. These were the earliest sensations he was aware of. He already had a memory, and this he would remember as the happiest time of his life, though yet unborn. The steady rhythm of the heart beating close to him, giving life to him, was a love sound. He did not know love as a conscious thought, but he felt it around him—from two people of whom he was a part. The beginning of his own emotions was return of love to those sources of love and life. Subtle shades of feelings he would not recognize until later came from the person he dwelled within: awe, wonder, happiness, love feelings like secret whispers she confided to her child. She knew he received her thoughts and emotions, though he could not sort them all. She knew she carried a son. The life she carried was a Bay Royalist, son of a Bay Royalist.

She stood on the rocky cliffs overlooking the sea. She had come to watch the Sun rise while the Night Sun set, and to watch for a portent at the beginning of the new Beth-enea. Her awkward form was bundled in waterbuck fur to protect her and her son from the bitter winds that buffeted her husband's island home. It was Cold Season winter. The southern island was colder than her maiden home nearer to the equator. But this new home would be safer when the Seasons became more severe and the invaders from the North pushed south again. She had not lived through a turn of the Star Year yet, but she had heard of the wars that the migrations of Northern people brought. She looked down the precipice to the sea that would rise to where she stood in the perihelion/periastron Hot Season. Periastron brought the worst Seasons of the Star Year, when her world swung closest and

3

farthest from the central Sun, the sun of which she now awaited the dawn.

Safe, loved, loving, and content. It was all changed by a violent *push*.

Raya felt the tiny life stir within her and at once knew she would die. She stood still an instant, frozen in disbelief. She cursed the horrible injustice of her fate and shed tears of pain and anger at her own helplessness. Clumsy with the burden in her womb and sick with advancing pain, she climbed down from the barren crags.

The cold dwarf star, a sun that lit the night, was sinking in the west while the eastern horizon had just begun to glow with dawn. The two suns balanced, like counterweights, exactly opposite each other on either side of the world. Their simultaneous rising and setting at this opposition would mark the beginning of another Beth-enea, the Time-Between-the-Cold. The stars were the Royalist calendar; and the stars told the woman she was twenty-three days before her time.

A freezing blast of wind swept down the slope, and the woman shivered alone in the frost of Cold Season winter. Though she had often traveled this way and was familiar with the bleak wilderness of her husband's home, she lost her footing and fell. She brushed icy tears from her cheeks and lifted herself from the frozen ground.

Raya broke into a blind run and fell again, unable to get up. Lying face to the sky, she watched frosty clouds rise with her heavy breath. *My son, my son, it is not time.*

A feeling of confused terror came from within her.

Little Teal, I am dying. She felt small comfort in the knowledge that she was not dying alone. She would have done without the sympathy had she the power to shield her baby from what she felt. She knew that her senses were his and that he felt the pain and fear of death even as he was being given life.

The cold Night Sun touched the western horizon, and a ray of light spilled over the opposite horizon from the east. But she did not see it.

The Sun had risen small. It was a cold distant Sun of the Cold Season. At daybreak the Sun had climbed red over the edge of the world; it shone white fire as day progressed.

Kaela laid a red mourning flower on the mound of fresh soil, and lingered there a moment. Too proud to cry, he channeled his grief into wrath toward the infant, which he refused to bring in from the cold or even to touch until he had buried his wife. It lay screaming, naked and bloody, on the hard ground where it had been born in the frosty wind. Kaela did not know how long it had been since birth—since death—but the Sun was nearing its zenith and still the infant survived. The same unjust gods that let his Raya be taken from him meant for this tiny murderer to live. He walked toward it slowly, hoping it would scream its last in the time he took to reach it. But it howled as it had all its life. It was a son, small and frail like Raya—but alive. As his warm hands touched the icy skin it shrieked louder as if touched by fire rather than human warmth. The child knew what his father felt—a son would be able to sense it. Kaela knew he could sense his fury, as he had sensed his mother's terror and felt her death. Now, from his father, he received not love but hatred; and as he was touched by him, his blood ran fire and he screamed.

Kaela carried the child to his home, his back to the Sun that had brought the dawn of the Twenty-second Beth-enea of the Star Year 531.

Day 5 22 Beth-enea
Star Year 531 Third Epoch

Dianter. At the tip of the Eastern Peninsula it was the only place that approached being a city in the entire Royalist nation. In Cold Season winter its size dwindled. Cold Season winter was not a social time, and Dianter was a social place. A place of gathering—that was all Dianter was, besides being the most beautiful region on the planet Arana. No one lived in Dianter, but there were always people there (the Northern Caucans would say there was never a person there, that the Royalists were a species of animal). It was not a town for living in. There were towns in the Royalist land, all of less than thirty people, situated in the lowlands. There were Nomad camps that wandered throughout the nation. And there were the royal lines, living by family in the highlands. Lowlanders, Nomads, and Highlanders rarely met—except at Dianter. It was a meeting place, a market place, a place to find news, a place to talk, the heart of the Royalist nation.

Bleak deciduous trees presented bare skeletons against the gray winter sky. The evergreens held on to hard, leathery needles or blades or leaves. Green leathervines adorned some of the naked seasonal trees like garlands. Grass trees fluttered in the chilling wind. They were mostly green with patches of brown and yellow. They would recover in the spring and summer, only to be parched even browner and yellower in a few Beth-enea as the severe Hot Seasons approached, then frozen in the severe Cold Seasons that followed. Akelan pitied the growing things, to have to withstand so many different seasons: summer, autumn, winter, spring of Hot Season; and summer, autumn, winter, spring of Cold Season. Eight seasons, and each of those varying throughout the Star Year. Things would be simpler with only one sun, he thought. Yet the growing things had adapted to this world and might even die in a simpler system. If his father could read his thoughts he might chide him for feeling sorry for senseless plants and for pondering pointless abstractions regarding a one-sun solar system. He looked at his father, who was talking with an expression of great seriousness to another Highland man in the colonnade. Akelan sat outside on the ground, putting a snowflower in his yellow hair. *Can you read my thoughts, Father?* Akelan concentrated on this thought.

His father suddenly scowled and broke off his speaking.

You can, can't you, Akelan thought.

"Akelan . . ." the man said to the boy seated in a thicket of snowflowers. He stood staring at him from the colonnade.

Akelan laughed with his clear boyish voice. "Don't be alarmed, Eemon, my father," he said with adult reassurance in his high tone.

Eemon turned away from the man and stepped from the colonnade. His youthful face was aged by care over his unusual child.

"I'm still a person. I'm your son. Why are you afraid of me?" Akelan said as Eemon sank to kneel beside him on the hard ground.

"You know what I'm thinking," Eemon said, disbelieving. He put a hand on his son's knee. *Just a child at the beginning of adolescence. He is my son. There is nothing to be afraid of.*

Akelan smiled with love and distress. "You knew what I would be before you sired me. You made me what I am. Why are you frightened?"

Eemon took him in his arms. Holding him, he was just a

boy; he could tell himself that. "Doesn't it overwhelm you ever, my son, that you are so very different from everyone else as to be not quite human anymore?" He cradled him as if still a helpless baby, not the powerful Trieath he was growing to be.

"I am different, but I'm human. . . ." A plaintive tone began creeping in as he felt himself being cut off from someone he loved very much.

"You are the new race. You will have children, and your race will eclipse ours till there is only yours left. You are the herald of the Fourth Epoch."

"But you knew that. You have known that. It has been known for countless Beth-enea, for many Star Years. It has been known—and planned and worked for—and now here I am, and you're frightened because I slipped a thought into your mind." Innocence and a child's dependence begged for his father, yet the power and strangeness of something new kept him at an inaccessible distance—even in his arms.

"Is my race so alien to you that you can't understand me anymore? Can't you understand fear of difference?" His blue-gray eyes were grave.

"I understand it," said Akelan, the boy's face somber. "It is a very sad thing."

Eemon contemplated his son. He looked like a normal Royalist boy—perhaps a bit fragile. No. He was not fragile. He only seemed to be. He had his father's light hair, a long, slightly curled, tawny mane of youth. His own was cut short with adulthood. His son could hardly be called a boy—why a boy's hair? He *was* a boy for all his differences, Eemon reminded himself, and he needed his father just as a Bay Royalist did. It was Eemon's one definite comfort: *He needs me.*

The eyes were light like his, but also bright. They could be called radiant, as was his whole being. He was so . . . alive. Life force in him was so noticeable—it was the only way Eemon could describe or conceive of that special trait. Arms around his slender form, Eemon wondered how much of what he had just been thinking the boy had overheard—overthought.

All of it, popped into his head.

Son? he thought.

Yes.

No consciously worded thought, but a feeling of awe and fear was conveyed to Akelan. A feeling of reassurance filled Eemon. He knew it was from his son.

"Stop this. Talk and let me talk," Eemon said, unnerved with thought and feeling exchange. "I can't communicate like this."

"All right," said Akelan. "I just now discovered I could do it. I was only testing myself. I'm sorry I upset you."

"Do you know what we were talking about a moment ago?" Eemon asked him. The man he had been conversing with, before Akelan interrupted by thought, came to sit by father and son.

"I don't need to see your thoughts to know that," Akelan said. "Where Ven Brekk is, the talk is always of Kaela Stewert." His bright eyes went from his father to the dark, powerful Ven Brekk. Deep brown eyes glared back at him, trying to hate him. He could keep it up in his absence, but never failed to melt in the boy's disarming presence. *He hopes,* thought Akelan, *he will be able to hate me when I am a man.* The dark eyes lost intensity. Ven pulled his waterbuck fur up over his broad shoulders. Ven Brekk was like the waterbuck, formidable and massive. A wintry wind disturbed his blue-black curls. Always morose, he was at this moment more glum than ever. He was the older of the men, old enough to be Akelan's grandfather. A Northerner of his age would be failing. Ven was in his prime.

"My son hears thoughts as if they were spoken, Ven," Eemon said in friendly admonition to the Brekk Bay Royalist.

Ven was clearly disturbed. *There is a man with a secret thought,* Akelan observed. Akelan did not probe him for it. He did not yet know if his ability was limited to reaching only his father's thoughts. One's own line was tightly linked. It could make a difference. This man was of the Brekk line. Akelan would not experiment on a man who so clearly wished privacy. He nestled to his father against the cold wind. Half of his face was buried in the fine silver seafox fur his father wore.

The two men were not talking now. Brekk's dark face was red from cold or from inner disturbance.

"What have Ven and Eemon been saying of Kaela Coa Stewert?" Akelan asked.

"His wife is with child," said Ven.

Akelan waited for him to continue. When he did not, Akelan said, "Everyone knows that." His tone was gently mocking. "Last I saw Kaela's wife, she said she carried a son."

"That woman would say, do, *anything* to keep her husband

king!" Ven said and piled abuse on the obscure little Lowland girl just because she had happened to marry Kaela Stewert. He saw her as the person who would bar his way to the crown forever and shut his sons into the obscure undistinguished rank from which she herself had risen by marriage. It was not for himself that Ven fought—it was for his sons. Did he feel guilty, Akelan wondered, because they were born twins? Akelan considered these things, but he still couldn't understand this unusual wrath at an innocent girl.

Eemon spoke. "There have been rumors that the child has already been born. There are rumors of a son."

Akelan observed Ven's face grow rigid and darker. A son. A single son. A thirty-third-generation Bay like Ven himself. But unlike Ven's, this baby line, the Stewert line, was not at its end. Akelan did not read his mind. He knew without it that Ven prayed for a daughter or twins for Kaela Stewert—and a crown for himself.

"Then why hasn't Stewert told his people who their next king will be?" Ven exploded.

Akelan barely suppressed laughter on perceiving his father's thought: *If it had been you, the whole world would know of it.*

"Hush. It could be just chatter of Lowlanders," he said instead.

"Or it could be Kaela Stewert buries a twin," Brekk rumbled.

There was silence between the men. The sound of the wind and the sea became noticeable again.

"I might laugh," said Eemon at last. "But I see you can't. Ven, you know a deception like that would be futile, even if anyone had the—if anyone could *conceive* of doing that. A single son will prove himself. None can pass for Bay but Bay. You should know that." He spoke as most powerful Bay on Arana, 369th generation to Ven's thirty-third.

"Does the crown mean so much to you?" the young Trieath Akelan spoke in his high clear voice. A Trieath could not wear the crown—the law keeper must be of the old race. The new race would have new laws.

"The law keeper must be above all others—it is according to the Law. The crown is due me as I am the most powerful Bay—"

"My father is," Akelan corrected.

"Your father"—he glanced at Eemon quickly then back—"abdicated at your birth," Ven said. "I was next, yet I was passed over as any common-as-air Lowlander—" he cut himself short, hearing himself grow abusive of those he wished to rule. His waterbuck skin slid from his shoulders. His dark skin shone with sweat, though the cold wind blew.

"Your line is dead. You had twins," Akelan said as gently as the words allowed.

"Everyone knows that," Ven said sardonically.

"But you don't seem to understand," said Akelan.

"I do not understand how the crown was given to a thirty-second-generation Bay while a thirty-third lived. Am I nothing? Is a generation nothing? Is the Law nothing?"

"It was given to the living line," he explained. "Thirty-second, thirty-third, the difference is not so great." That was a lie—meant to remind Ven that thirty-third generation was crisis generation.

"I am ruled by a lesser," Ven said with damaged pride.

Akelan sighed. He could see his point. But he could see his own side more. "The crown should go to the most powerful—is that what you tell me?"

"Yes!"

"Then go tell Kaela Stewert to give the crown back to me. Will that satisfy you?"

Ven's face went blank, then he said, "It would be more just."

It was not the crown then. It was Ven's jealous hatred of the Stewert line.

"I cannot wear it. I am a Trieath," Akelan said. "I am of the new race and can only rule the new race—which makes me sovereign of myself." He smiled. "My father passed it on as is his right to do. His last action—*as king*," he emphasized—"was to pass it to the living line instead of the ended one. Now, which of those actions do you question?" He took all blame from the hated Stewert rival and forced Ven to deal with himself and Eemon—which he was neither willing nor able to do. So he did not answer. Eemon was relieved that his son spoke for him as he searched for an answer to this hate-filled, obstinate Brekk. He could not be placated. Let him argue with the Trieath. Might as well oppose the gods.

"I am thirty-third-generation Bay!" Ven blurted out in protest, the only thing he could say.

"So is Teal."

Eemon looked at him sharply, as Ven did. There was no

one named Teal. There was no other thirty-third-generation Bay.

"Who is Teal?"

"I reached out to Kaela's home, to Skye, and heard his name. His name is Teal. I cannot hear his thoughts. He has not been in the world long enough to have a worded thought. But I can hear him. He is crying."

Day 207 26 Beth-enea
Star Year 531 Third Epoch

Teal Ray Stewert gazed out to sea with large dark eyes. He strained to catch a glimpse of the fishing birds hidden by the darkness, but the Hot Season's absence of the Night Sun frustrated the child's attempts. He only knew the beautiful and timid creatures were there from the sound of the soft splashes they made diving into the water after fish, and from the faint scent that came to him with the salty breeze. One bird rose high in the air and blocked out some stars with its silhouette. It dived and softly splashed as it slipped between the waves. Teal had only seen a fishing bird in the light once, when he chanced upon its nest among the floating reeds and a panic of black plumage exploded in his face before disappearing under the water. From then on he was determined to catch one. He had no reason for doing so except that it had never been done without a net. He did not want the bird so much as he wanted to prove to himself that he could capture one. Teal had to be best—his birth demanded it. The son of Kaela could be no less. All his young life he had spent doing what was impossible for his age. Four and one-half Beth-enea had passed since his birth, and already he had swum the West Strait from Skye to the Western Peninsula, something children of a full Beth-enea older could not do. By Earth time he was five years old, but he would not know of Earth for a long time yet. Now the only land he knew was his father's island home, Skye, and what little he had seen of the Western Peninsula. He knew the underwater terrain around Skye better than he knew the island itself. He was at home in the sea, an excellent swimmer for his age. His superiority went beyond what one would expect from his powerful lineage and breeding. He had once or twice overheard elders compliment his father on a fine son.

"He makes the fish look clumsy. He is a true Bay," one had said. But the one that Teal remembered and cherished was spoken by Eemon Mercer: "He is son of Kaela."

Why, Teal wondered, did his father never say that? That was why Teal excelled—in hopes of hearing it from his father. Kaela never claimed him. The bewildered Bay Royalist child was lost without him. A Bay son was powerful yet delicate. He needed his father. But Teal was rejected. It made him a weak link, and the harsh law of the wilderness weeded out weak links. He had felt the touch of destruction on the day of his birth. Reill. Red Madness. The Reill was the price the Royalist paid for directing evolution. It did not strike often—only when a Bay son was cut off from his father. It only happened once in a millennium, but every Royalist knew what it was, since at the time of trial, a test of maturity, the Fire Flower that induced a Reill-like crisis was one of the trials to be endured. The veins of the arms and neck turned scarlet, and it was pain—pain to drive one to madness were the trial not so short. Actual Reill killed. It crept over Teal, trying to destroy him before this abnormality, this weak link, this rejected Bay, continued the line. Teal fought it. He would live and his father would love him. He would call him son of Kaela.

The boy slipped silently into the sea and swam easily under the dark water, avoiding submerged rocks without even using his sonar, since he knew the waters of Skye, and he was almost certain that the fishing birds could hear his signal with their sensitive ears. He approached with slow caution, letting no breath bubbles alert them and no swift movement send a warning current as they dived. He could not venture too close to the surface or they would see him. He found a position deep enough to be obscured but within striking distance should one dive near him. He waited. A few minutes and he would need air; not old enough to stay down longer, he would have to abandon his quest till another time.

A bird dived near him. He launched upward and seized it. Its smooth body slipped through his hands like a fish (one could not catch fish without digging one's fingernails in, but he did not want to hurt the bird). He managed to hold onto its skinny bird legs, and he shot to the surface before they both ran out of breath. He swam to shore with the struggling black fowl. On land, he caught it to his chest and held it still.

Smooth against his naked skin, heart vibrating, it squeaked as Teal sat down on a fallen tree trunk, holding it. He stroked the slender neck and studied his terrified captive. He sat awhile, listening to night sounds, and the bird quieted. It looked back at him. The two wild creatures watched each other intently. Teal's wet hair touched his smooth shoulders. It was as black as the bird's feathers. His skin was ivory next to the dark captive.

He heard the hum of a whirri beating its wings. It was a fat green thing with tiny wings and big, ungainly body about the size of Teal's head. Theoretically it should not have been able to get that body off the ground with those wings. The chlorophyll-producing bird flew its bumblebee way.

"You're prettier," Teal whispered to the black fishing bird. Its black eyes met his black eyes. "Much prettier."

He did not think why he still held the bird. He had done what he had set out to do. Now he just wanted to hold another life close to him. His father rarely touched him but to strike him.

His father. The center of all like the sun, but always cold and distant, a sun to which he was forever at aphelion of Cold Season, never drawing within reach of its warmth.

He gazed up at the sky, black as the bird in his arms but dotted with stars and crossed by the bright path of the Milky Way. The Night Sun, on the other, the daylight, side of the world, was hidden in eclipse behind the Sun in mid-Beth-enea conjunction.

Teal released his hold. The bird paused a moment. Its long legs suddenly pushed him and launched it to freedom.

Teal returned to his father's house through the forest grown thick in Hot Season summer.

The irregular house was built on several levels on the southern cliffs of Skye. It was stone and wood and firebrick. The roof sloped seaward against the winds and seastorms. The foundations were many Star Years old, built over even older foundations of an ancient Stewert house that time finally caught and pulled into the sea with much of its foundations and the cliffs. When these cliffs showed weakness the same would happen to his father's house. But that would not be for several Star Years yet. The present foundations had been laid by Teal Vreka Stewert, first Bay Royalist in the Stewert line. Teal was also the name of his line's founder. Teal was a luck name. The first Bay was given the name as a mark of triumph and as a prayer for the continuation of his line. Teal Ray was given the name for luck in the critical generation thirty-three. If one's line lived past thirty-third-generation Bay, so they said, it would live to 369th and then to the Trieath. Only one line of all attempts had survived thirty-third, and a Trieath was finally born after four hundred generations of only sons. The Fourth Epoch would begin when all Royalists were Trieaths—Akelan's descendants. *Does it matter now, now that there is a Trieath and the Third Epoch has begun to end, does it matter whether my line continues or not?* Teal thought. How many generations would it take for the Trieath's children to spread their blood through all the Royalists? Bay and common Royalist alike? Highlander. Lowlander. Nomad? *It matters,* Teal thought firmly, *because my father cares.* If his father wished the Stewert line to continue, that was all the reason he needed. He did not consider that his father's only reason might be rivalry with the Brekks. Whatever his reason it was sound in Teal's sight.

The house came into view as a dark silhouette, colors of the stone and the firebricks and timber not visible without the sunlight. Its walls were new; Teal's grandfather had rebuilt them. Teal should have been named for him. His name should have been Teal Ein Stewert; all Bay Royalists took their grandfather's name for their honor name. Ray was his mother's name.

He climbed up the stone steps. His father was on the southern terrace reading the Laws. He was supposed to teach his son the Laws, but Kaela, instead, taught Teal to read and let him learn by himself without guidance or explanation. That was how Teal learned many things, and it went against both written and natural law. Teal walked silently out to the terrace with him. He liked to be near him; and if his father objected to his presence, he could leave. He often did.

Teal sat himself on the firebrick terrace and leaned against the stone balustrade. He shook his damp hair; it was black like his father's, silky like his mother's. He had his mother's large, gentle eyes, though black in color like his father's. He was growing to look like his mother—at four and a half Beth-enea it was already clear. His facial features would be hers, as if his naming determined his appearance.

His father's lamp was out. He was no longer reading the Laws. He held them rolled in his large hands and sat on the stone bench, deep in thought. His wife used to sit beside him, small and fragile, nestled under his powerful arm. He was a tall bronze statue, she a little ivory nymph. Teal would be small, as Kaela's wife had been. He glanced over at the boy. Doe eyes were closed, a wistful expression on delicate child's features. He could see Raya in him. Why, he thought in mounting fury, was that not Raya? What gave this creature more right to live than she had?

Teal was too stunned to scream when he was struck the first time. An instant later he realized he was in pain and bleeding and being struck again with something whiplike, whether a vine pulled from a tree or a leather belt. Tears blinded his eyes. He shrieked and writhed away the third time, and the fourth fell harder. He curled up on the floor, teeth clenched to stay quiet, trying to accept it. His father must have a reason.

Alone and bleeding and in searing pain, he raised his head stiffly. He lifted himself up on his elbows and gasped for breath. His tears began to burn like acid. He saw his wrists, streaked brilliant red where his veins ran—they were not wounds—it was under his skin and those were veins. It was Reill, Red Madness.

Blood turned fire, and the water of his tears still worse. Wanting to scream, but not daring to be found like this, he climbed over the balustrade and dropped to the ground, not bothering to catch himself or to try to land on his feet, insane with pain. Crumpling with a thud, still a conscious thought remained: he knew what Reill was and that it was a mark of shame on his father. He would not be found to shame him. He would crawl into the forest and die.

Opening eyes with disbelief. Still alive? The pain of his wounds told him so. He lifted a limp arm before blurry eyes and strained in the darkness to see his wrists were white. The Red Madness had passed. *Why did I live?* Reill kills. It was still within him; he felt it sleeping and he knew it would flare again. Kill next time? There would not be one, Teal was determined. He would not die like that. He could not live to endure the unendurable again.

Insects buzzed around his wounds. He flailed white arms to drive them off. Some of the wounds broke fresh. A short-haired scavenger's eyes glowed red in the underbrush. Teal tore some leaves and threw them at the creature. They fluttered down around it. It crouched, puzzled. Finally, seeing that this was not going to end in a meal, it slunk away.

Teal ·lifted himself from the damp soil slowly. Life fragrance of the sap exhaled from the torn plants. The boy staggered through the forest, crushing living things, and tramping and rustling like a Northerner. He found the cliffs and dropped like a dead weight into the sea. Beth-enea ago it would have dashed him on the rocks, but Hot Seasons were getting hotter and the water higher every successive Hot Season.

Instinct would not allow him to inhale water, though he wanted to. The fierce stinging of salt on wounds turned to numbness. He broke through the surface and breathed deeply. *Swim the East Strait,* he thought. He knew he was unable, and so started out. At his slow pace he indulged in a fantasy of his death, almost enjoying the torment. Some predator fish came to the blood but would not attack a person, no matter how young, knowing even one Bay Royalist to be a deadly match. They hovered hungrily and followed, hungry company to a dying child.

Teal grew too tired to move and floated on his back, gazing up at the stars. He saw the cloudy band of the Milky Way and wondered what it was, and how far the lights, the stars, were. Then he swam again, but inaction had stiffened his limbs, and he could not resume course. He was too far to even turn back to Skye, and thought triumphantly that he had sealed his fate. He wove another death fantasy. He let himself think of his father, though something warned that he should not. *He never touched me to love me. He never owned me son.* And this for some reason brought the tears. *He doesn't even like me.* He sobbed and shot to the surface, coughing up water. *He must love me. I have to be someone great.* He soon found himself thinking, *I can't die now.* Panic quickly followed the thought. Now he was trying desperately to reach a goal that he himself devised to be impossible. His strength gave out and he sounded a shrill sonar distress whistle. A quick fantasy had his father come to the rescue, but a real fear set in: his father coming, then on seeing who it was, turning back. He shrilled again, sinking, waves gently lapping over him. He thought he heard an answer as deep blue oblivion surrounded him.

II.

"Why wander so far from home, son of Kaela?"

Teal looked up at gentle blue-gray eyes and fell in love with all his five-year-old heart. The beautiful godling was bending over the child on the ground, caring for his injuries, pain in his eyes. Bright sun haloed yellow-maned head.

"I'm Akelan."

The Trieath. First of the new race, what all the breeding had sought to achieve through four hundred generations of only sons. Some people were already figuring how the fifth change was to be achieved. It was on the minds of all, ingrained in the being of every Royalist: the betterment of the people. It was their chief concern. But not to Teal. Not because he was young, but because he was the misfit. The mistake. He lacked the selfless spirit of unity because he lacked what every Bay had, and had to have to live—his father's care. Teal's only concern was to be loved.

Cool hand on his forehead. "It's a wide strait for such a young one. You dare too much. Not even Kaela's son must do that," the god said.

Teal sat up. His lashed back stung, but it was healing with the rapidity of his people. He was awed and nervous, and instead of saying what he felt—or throwing his arms around Akelan's neck—he said, "I have to go home. I shouldn't be here."

"Here" must be the Eastern Peninsula. The sea stretched to the west. He was on a grassy knoll above the beach. He started to stand, intending to start his journey home. Akelan laughed and held him down. "I'll take you home. It's too far for you."

The little boy allowed himself to gaze on this divinity. Not a boy, not a man. His long hair said he was unmarried and not yet an adult.

"What happened to you?" Akelan asked, touching his back next to a long, angry wound.

17

"I don't know," Teal mumbled.

"Tell me," Akelan coaxed.

"I don't know," the child insisted stubbornly. So like his father. He did not need to tell him; Akelan knew. He watched over him and listened from a distance. He'd heard his distress long before he whistled.

Akelan touched his hand to the fine, black, baby's hair.

Teal was shocked to see tears in beloved eyes. Akelan was crying soundlessly. He took Teal, pulled him in close to him, and held him, weeping.

Teal could not understand. He stroked his hair with his tiny hand. "Don't cry."

Akelan started to sob at that, and Teal fastened his arms around his neck and clung to him. Teal had never known what it was like to be held by anyone or touched. What Akelan felt for him . . . he knew the feeling from somewhere. He wished Akelan wouldn't cry. . . .

Akelan did not want to take him home to his father, but he could see no alternative. He considered talking to Kaela, but Kaela might kill his son instead of being persuaded. He was certain he could not stand the shame. What to do then?

"I'll keep an eye on you," he told him. Teal fell asleep in his lap, thumb in his mouth. Akelan had never seen a Royalist child do that.

At last Akelan swam the boy across the strait and placed him on his home beach. He knelt before him and kissed him. He had never been kissed. Akelan sensed it and hurried back to the sea before he started to cry again. Kaela was the only one who could save or kill his son, and so he left Teal to him.

Teal stayed on the shore, looking out where the young god had gone, afraid to go up to his father's house on the ledges. He felt something new, touching, a gentle touch, a kiss. Something old—love—that's what it was. And something strange and unidentified—hope.

Day 100 30 Beth-enea
Star Year 531 Third Epoch

Teal learned much by the time he was eight Beth-enea, ten Earth years, of age. He had learned to sleep at sea, ending the danger of drowning, barring underwater accidents. He was familiar with the Royalist part of the Eastern and Western Peninsulas and the Royalist island continent. He knew there was a vast land to the North inhabited by the Caucans, who were their enemies. He learned there were other Northern people, but he only knew them as names: Phaethons and Vakellans. He learned there were Northern-blooded people living in his own land, the Mountain People, who kept to themselves, cohabiting the same country in peace. He learned of sex with a Mountain girl who did not understand his language. He tried to make her stay with him, but she ran away, leaving him hurt and bewildered. He learned that the Brekk line was the Stewert's rival and that the twins Thoma and Igil Brekk hated him for being single-born. Twins ended the Brekk line. Not even a daughter, a line skip, but twins. He had not yet learned of war but he had learned it was soon to come. The raids had started. The first wave of invading Northerners was expected that Beth-enea. As Hot and Cold Seasons grew severe, the Caucans would move down the Eastern and Western Peninsulas into the Royalist land where winter and summer offset the Hot and Cold. Hot Season was perihelion. Cold Season was aphelion. Severe Hot and Cold Season was near the time of peri-astron of the two suns, when the Night Sun drew close, too far for its heat to be felt, but close enough for its pull to influence Arana, distorting the world's orbit to extreme.

What Teal learned was mostly on his own. He was independent—unwillingly. His father never told him what he was expected to know, and it was up to Teal to find out for himself somehow.

He knew the Northern people were different. He had read it in the Laws, but he did not understand how different or where they came from: "Millennia ago the new people came from the sky. They came and lived in the North, this infant people. We stayed in the South, where our home has always been. The new people grew and splintered and became Caucans and Vakellans and Phaethons. Some took to the mountains, others the islands, until they peopled the North; and every turn of the Star Year they turn their eyes South. Still the sea is ours." He tried to remember the coming of these people, epochs before his birth. It was a vague image from race memory. Line memory yielded nothing. Kaela had cut him off. The coming of the new people was like a dream not quite remembered, hovering at the fringe of consciousness.

From the sky? The gods lived in the sky. He touched the silver holy symbol he wore around his neck. It was a rosette, like the path of his world orbiting the central Sun. The Northern people could not be gods; gods did not make war on their worshipers. He studied the delicate silver pendant. He liked it because his father used to wear it. When Kaela stopped wearing it Teal wondered if he would mind him taking it. To his surprise, Kaela spoke, as he rarely did, seeing it glittering at his throat: "Yes, I guess they are friends of yours." The gods? Teal wondered. He did not have any friends that he knew of.

The dark eyes searched the morning sky. It was spring between Hot Season and Cold. Thick mist rose from the forest and the sea.

From the sky?

He saw the bright planet Canda, Land Sister. Were the Northern people from Canda? He had heard stories that Land Sister supported people just like Arana, Water Sister.

The sky grew light and Canda faded as a candle's light in the sun.

Spring was a time of many rituals. It was Teal's time for the rites of the end of boyhood. It began the middle period of becoming an adult. Teal felt he had missed boyhood altogether. He was not ready, but the time of trial had come.

Never awkward and chunky as Northern boys, he had lost all traces of boyishness and was sleek and streamlined, not feminine, not masculine; the middle period.

The rites were easy. He had put himself through worse. They took place at Dianter, where twelve other Highland boys were to undergo the trials at the same time. Lowlanders did not have rites, and Nomads had their own ways. Thoma and Igil Brekk came to watch him fail. If for that alone, Teal knew he must succeed. He suffered a gash on his arm capturing his seafox, but it would heal scarless, as if it had never been.

No one died this time. It was a good sign. The rites seeded out the weak. Teal knew he was defective, a weak link, but he survived the Reill (it was still there—he felt it always), and he lived through the rites, which included Fire Flower. The Fire Flower brought on a Reill-like crisis. It was to remind one of debt to his father and to appreciate life, for a Reill victim did not live to this age of trial—not till now. Teal did not withstand the Fire Flower as well as one would expect of Kaela's son. And his reaction at the end was also inexplicable. The Fire Flower washed off with water, unlike real Reill, which caused water to feel like fire during a crisis. For some reason young Teal was terrified of the cleansing water. But he lived. Teal held the rosette in his hand; someone was watching out for him.

The other rites he not only survived, but he came out proud and praised.

Some men eyed him, but they chose other boys. He was hurt and lonely. He learned a man could not take a boy his superior—and thirty-third-generation Bay was superior to all but three people. The knowledge eased the hurt but not the loneliness.

Thoma and Igil Brekk hated him. No, just Thoma. Igil was only a mirror. Teal guessed that Igil had not an original thought or feeling within him, but merely twinned his brother. And Thoma hated Teal because he could not hate his brother, whose existence made him a common birth, not a thirty-fourth-generation Bay. He would have been Bay were he single-born. A daughter of a thirty-third Bay could be a line skip—her son could be a first Bay. Twins ended the line. The Brekk line had gone suddenly from second most powerful Highland line to lowest. Thoma and Igil could not even have a middle name, the honor name. They could not even refound the line to win an honor name. But Thoma could not hate his own twin. So he hated Teal Ray.

Young versions of their father, Ven Brekk, Thoma and Igil were dark and muscular, blue-black hair cut short as if they were adults, but they were not; they were not many Bethenea older than Teal, nor were they married. Teal's black hair flowed down his shoulders, midway down his back in boy's style.

Teal found himself at the Nomad camp. Bronze victor's bands on his arms, he was honored by the Nomads. They brought him to celebrate the Festival of the Sisters: Land Sister, Canda, and Water Sister, Arana. The Dianter inscriptions carved into stone tablets in the Old Language of the First Epoch told the story of the once close sisters, and of Canda's abduction by the jealous god, Night. Night married her, and the only time Canda was seen again was as a light in the arms of the Night sky. It was the story of the planets clouded in poetic Nomad mysticism.

Night fell at Dianter and the planet Canda shone brighter than the brightest star. According to the tablets, she used to be larger than the Night Sun and visible in the day, long ago when the sisters were close.

The Nomads danced the story just as the Old People had Epochs ago, ending in celebration and sharing in the marriage. The ritual stirred memories—memories too long ago to be within a lifetime—memories of their ancestors.

The Nomad girls dancing as Canda and Arana were dressed in blue maiden's dress. Night was the largest of the Nomad men, wearing a cape of black feathers. They looked like fishing-bird feathers. He blacked his face with charcoal as the ancients did. The rest of his body was naked, sun-darkened. The other dancers were dressed to portray the other roles, Darkness, Storm, and others. A naked young man carrying torches was the Night Sun. The fire they danced around was the Central Sun.

Night swooped down on Canda and ripped her maiden's belt from her, and bore it, and her, away from Arana and the Central Sun, while the Night Sun blazed in fury. He fell on her and had her there. The dancer was probably a virgin to that time, but there was no way of ensuring it, she being about Teal's age.

Teal lost the thread of the ritual, intent on one dancer only.

Heat. Nomad woman danced by the fire. He saw heat, from the fire, from the woman. He felt heat from the air, from within. A bronze chest band hugged her ribcage below her breasts, a bronze snake rising from it, nestled between her bare breasts. Her brown body gleamed with sweat. A full skirt obscured her glistening form from her slender waist to her calves. Teal felt tense and tight in that region of his own body. Shame at sexual response was unknown to Royalists, but painfully acute to Teal Ray. The red flush in his cheeks was a brand of shame as he discovered what her snake's pose mimicked, but his color could be mistaken for heat.

Another dancer steered the woman to the young Bay she had captivated. She wondered why the Bay had not claimed her himself instead of waiting for her to be led to him. A look assured her there was no mistake; the dancer had seen rightly. She led him to darkness to celebrate the marriage of Night, away from the dancers and away from the fire. He still felt heat.

Day 22 32 Beth-enea
Star Year 531 Third Epoch

The wars began. They began late because of internal struggles within the Caucan land. But at last, united under their new messiah, the Caucans swarmed south in unheard-of numbers, not merely out to occupy the more hospitable climate of the South, but to destroy its native inhabitants, the Royalists. They burned the Lowland villages; and the Lowlanders fled with Nomad camps into the Highlands. Then the Caucans formed hunting expeditions to exterminate the "dangerous beasts." The Caucans had a new leader, Gordon Tras. He would rid the world of the Southern menace, using technology against the savage animals.

Royalists had no factories to make weapons as the Caucans had but they were stealthy and could steal what they needed from their enemy. And they had fire. The cleansing fire blazed with double fury on Caucan gasoline and explosives. Caucan ships came down the straits between Eastern and Western Peninsulas. They sank in the vicinity of the island Skye, victims of Caucan mines diligently collected from the North and used against their makers. Teal had helped plant them.

But there was nothing to be done about the planes. The flying ships were new—the Caucans had not had them a Star Year ago. The Vakellans had had them before—faster and better ones—but the Vakellans never made war anymore. Vakellans sent up ships that left the world. But these were Caucan airships they had developed themselves to attack from the sky. Crude flamethrowers caught some of the low ones, but the Royalists were for the most part defenseless against them. They could only flee—which was effective. The planes were useless without targets, and all they could find was virgin wilderness. Houses were few and far between, carefully hidden and virtually unfindable. Ships and planes rendered weak weapons, the Caucans came by land, over the barrier mountains, south into the Royalist land. They spent sleepless nights waiting for the natives' stealthy attacks on their invading force—or else they slept and never woke. But they could not turn back. At home it was winter. All over the planet it was Severe Cold Season, but in the South it was summer and moderate with a few light snows that never stayed. Home was deadly except the part on the equator, which was warm, but would be even more deadly come Hot Season. Gordon Tras told the Caucans to destroy the animals and to civilize the land before that time came.

Teal had not lived through a periastron war before, but he had heard and read of them enough to know that this was unusually harsh. His racial memory gave no indication that it was to be this bad; and his father, who had seen the last one, was clearly disturbed.

"It's Tras," his father said in a rare moment of speech. He was king and put aside personal hatred in his nation's need. "He is a leader. The Caucans never had one. We are to be the common enemy to unite his people. Kill him, and they will be a clutch of whirris without a clutch sire." His father was prepared for a long journey into a cold country. He wore a hunting blade at his waist and carried a long waterbuck skin. He was going north. He took the crown from his head. It was just a thin gold oval with gold spikes radiating out like the corona of the Sun in eclipse—when Canda used to eclipse the Sun. The crown was very old, old as the Dianter tablets. He left it on his bed in his own small room. Teal had never been in there. "Don't let Brekk have it," Kaela said and strode out the door, a tall god framed in light in the doorway. Teal stared after him.

Don't let Brekk have it. So much in so few words: *If I should not return this is for you.* Teal knew his father did not love him. He knew he hated him. *But he hates Brekk more.* It was something. Teal shivered.

Teal crept into his father's forbidden room. Four walls, two tall windows, and a porch with a skylight. A waterbuck seemed to leap from the frescoed walls to escape the white griffinbeast. The crown lay on his sleeping place. The bed cover was the one woven by his mother—no one ever told him, but he knew. He knelt and placed the silver rosette in the center of the crown and said a prayer over it to charm it for safe return.

Skye was not a safe place, situated at the narrows of the straits. He woke to planes. He fled from the house, praying they had not sighted it. They did not bomb the island, which made him wonder why they had come. Ships. They must mean ships were coming. This was the van on wings. But he saw no ships. He dove into the water and sounded a sonar distress. It was answered by a Claren signal and another Highland Royalist call—followed by a warning. He detected sonar—not that of a Royalist or of another sea mammal; a strange unfamiliar sound. He found the source. Submarines. These too were new. But they were easily taken care of with Caucan mines.

His father returned unharmed and unsuccessful. Teal knew enough to stay away at this time and set out for the Western Peninsula to fight. The invaders were all men. Teal wondered if these Caucans had any women.

A little Highland girl with a Caucan machine gun waited in the underbrush. She was younger than Teal and the weapon was almost half her tiny size. A wreath of flowers on her head and clutching steel to tender naked skin, she waited.

The Caucans acted worse than beasts, though they called the Royalists beasts. They were atrocious to the Royalist men and unspeakable to the women that fell into their hands. Killing made Teal physically sick, but he found it easy after witnessing what they did. The little girl with the machine gun also was enraged and nearly took him down with the Caucans. He slapped her and she cried. She dried her tears and licked the bramble scratches on her thin arms and the dirt from her hands. It was the kind of thing that convinced the Northerners that Royalists were really beasts. But the "beasts" had no word for rape or mutilation, the concepts being unknown to them. A new word had to be invented for what the Caucans did.

Teal followed the fleeing Caucans into the mountains. He wondered if their war was against Mountain People too. They were quiet people, of Northern blood but much like Royalists in their pacific isolationism. Teal felt rage at the thought that the Caucans might dare to hurt them.

Teal climbed up a tower tree to have a look around him. It was night. The Night Sun shone more faintly than Teal ever remembered, it being farther than it had ever been in his lifetime. All was dark. A Caucan fire flickered up on the moun-

tainside. Teal slid down the tree and crept up toward the
Caucans, uncertain of what he was going to do. He would decide once there. Someone sighted him and threw a rock at the
movement in the bushes. He sprang backward and fell down
a steep incline.

Winded and hurt, he lay at the bottom of the slope. The
Caucans would come looking. They had not been certain
what he was or they would have fired. He felt too weak to
move, needing time to lie still and recover. If he tried to slink
away in this state, he would be heard and gunned down. So
he risked being found, mock dead, with his dagger in his
hand hidden under a clump of yellow-green scrub. Someone
did come. Teal took a deep breath and held it.

He did not flinch, prepared for the light that flooded his
closed eyes, the lamp focused on his face. Then the heat of
the light traveled down his body. He heard a noise like the
lamp being set down and someone taking two steps toward
him. He felt body heat now and heard the rustle of clothing
of a Caucan crouching beside him. He smelled him—male
Caucan, but he knew that already. He could not smell gun
smell. . . .

At his touch the knife flew out from cover and eyes
opened. Then he froze.

The Caucan met his gaze, calm, not at all shocked, in fact,
expecting. He ignored the knife at his throat and slid his
hand beneath Teal and his fingers went down his spine,
searching for a break. He was a healer.

Teal lowered the dagger. "It's not broken," he said. But, of
course, the Caucan could not understand. So Teal sat up and
shook himself. Pulled muscles hurt. He looked at the healer,
and the healer looked at him. Northerners aged quickly, and,
though he was middle-aged, he looked old to Teal. His
slightly graying hair was receding; set in a bed of wrinkles,
his eyes were gray, gentle and calm, with an air of mischief
and look of weariness. His form was obscured by shapeless
clothes that the Northerners wore despite jungle heat. Teal
was naked but for his knife belt. He was, though he did not
know for no one had ever told him, beautiful. This man told
him, but he could not understand Caucan. He gave Teal a
piece of candy. Teal accepted hesitantly. On impulse, Teal
shot a popweed at him. The puffball of a seed flew out and
bounced off the man's forehead. He smiled and almost
laughed. He goosed Teal, who was so startled he yapped like
a puppy. Wide eyes turned to the chuckling man. He was

playing with him. This too was new. Teal started to growl, and the man made a motion to stay quiet, which he understood. The healer rubbed his sore shoulders, and Teal relaxed to the point of falling asleep. He'd found someone to be nice to him.

He haunted the area as long as the Caucans were there, waiting in popweed ambush when he could catch the healer alone. He forgot about fighting. The affair continued awhile, till finally the Caucan bought his way out of Gordon Tras' army and went home. He left a confused and desolate lover behind him.

Teal was suddenly keenly aware that he had not seen Skye in a long time. It never occurred to him that his father might think he was dead. What Kaela discovered upset him worse. A trickle of blood ran down the back of Teal's leg.

Slammed against the wall so hard the plaster fresco cracked, Teal tried not to cry out. "What man has had you?" Kaela roared.

Unless it were Eemon or Akelan Mercer he was in trouble. No one else had the right but Ven Brekk, and if it were Brekk Kaela would kill him.

Teal did not answer. Kaela slapped him hard. "Was it Brekk?"

"No."

"Who was it?"

Teal could not talk and paid for silence under a whip.

He slunk away into the forest to bathe in a stream.

III.

The only remedy for the boy's state was marriage. Kaela sent him out to find a wife before he totally disgraced the line, and before he did something foolish—typical of a crisis generation—such as impregnate a Northern girl and destroy his line. There was no telling what the boy was capable of. He'd already shown his lack of discretion.

Thirty-third-generation Bay was crisis generation, the point at which all the changes from old race to new race began to come together and become manifest. It was also an unstable generation, neither new (though "Bay" meant "new") nor completely old. The changes took their toll. Many a line ended at thirty-third Bay. Once past thirty-third, the danger of the line ending was past, and even chance no longer held the reins of their directed evolution, since all Bays greater than thirty-third generation had the power to choose the sex of their offspring—and chose a son. That was one of the changes. But continuing past thirty-third was difficult, so rare as to only have happened once—in the Mercer line. Many lines ended at thirty-third, the Brekks' being only one of those many. Thirty-third-generation Bay Ven Brekk was the last Bay of his line. After sixty-six generations of breeding— thirty-three to Bay and thirty-three more—they'd come to nothing. Kaela Stewert did not want the same happening to his own line. Teal must sire a son, a thirty-fourth-generation Bay. Not that it mattered for evolution's sake, for his people's sake, since the Mercers had produced the Trieath. But for pride. Because he was a Highlander. Highlanders were the leaders and the breeders, the ones who caused the changes, the fathers of the new race. Lowlanders bore daughters and

28

common sons. Lowlanders were the people, the followers. One son, that was the Highland way, the only way for change. If more than a single son was born, the changes did not occur. Although the physical characteristics were unchanged by the birth of brothers and sisters, the line ties were weakened and diffused; the mental and emotional links branched off in divergent ways, many taking energy from a single source. A Royalist was affected by those of his own blood, by someone who came to be in the same womb or from the same father. For a Bay to suddenly gain a brother or sister would be like putting a cold molecule next to a heated one—like a drain of consciousness, a sharing of line memories and strengths, a splitting and splintering of the line. An end.

There was only one Highlander who could have more than one child and not destroy his line. That was Akelan Mercer, the Trieath. He was the first of the fourth race. The changes were set and totally ingrained in him. He could have daughters and sons like a Lowlander and they would all be Trieaths. And each of those children could breed like whirris, mating with lowest- or highest-born alike, and their children would be Trieaths. Till all Royalists were Trieaths and the Fourth Epoch would begin.

Teal could not breed like that. He needed a wife, one who had no twins in her family history like Ven Brekk's wife. Ven Brekk had himself to blame for his line's end. Any Bay who married a woman whose father was a twin had to be touched with madness. It was line suicide. It was to be expected from the crisis generation, the thirty-third. Kaela warned Teal not to be so careless and sent him off.

A wife. Teal didn't know where to look. He felt a desire for the Nomad dancer. A sense of being alive was associated with her memory. But he'd lost her. She'd left him afterward, and there was no finding Nomad camps, not in wartime. So he went to the Lowlands. His requirements were simple: anyone who would be nice to him.

He came to a village: ten buildings and a central path and a common well. It was a typical Lowland town, built under dense evergreens, out of planes' sights. It seemed deserted, no one stirring except for a little child-woman Teal's age, trying to coax her white, fluffy pet down from the roof of the well shelter. Intent on the mewing, squeaking animal, she did not notice Ray. She might have run had she seen him, for though it was an honor to marry a Highlander, it also meant leaving home. When she finally did see Teal, he was climbing up the shelter to rescue her pet. She wouldn't run now. Ray got the ball of fluff down and took it and its owner home to Skye.

Kaela made no comment on his choice, but wondered where—how—he had found a girl so like Raya. For the resemblance, they could have been brother and sister instead of husband and wife. Tiny, fragile, doe-eyed, dark-haired, she was named Lia. Teal and his child-bride were given part of the house, and they played at being man and wife. Lia cut Teal's hair to the length of an adult's. Marriage made one a man no matter his age.

Days were spent playing and eating, and nights loving and sleeping; that was life with his wife-playmate. Nothing warned him that this time of wonder would soon end.

Laughter on Skye was almost a forgotten sound, but it came rippling back. Lia gathered up all the popweeds she could find and had a popweed battle with her husband.

Lia's white ball of fluff gave birth to a lot of little white balls of fluff.

"It must have happened on the day you took me," said Lia, holding the entire litter cupped in the palms of her hands. "That's a good sign. Do you believe in signs?"

"Of course," said Teal, holding the mother, white fur against his cheek.

And Lia was soon pregnant. She sat on the rocks, dabbling her feet in the salt waves. She wore a thin white shift loosely draped over her thin form, which was beginning to show the life within. She baffled her mate, who was totally in awe of her; she growled when he wanted to make love; she cried for no reason while insisting she was happy.

Baby-fine dark hair curled loose and soft around her neck and touched her shoulders. She wore red flowers in her hair. Red was the Stewert color, and she was now a Stewert. She liked the purple ones, but her husband warned her she must never wear purple; it was the Brekk color.

A warm breeze swept over the sun-baked rocks. The Hot Season approached with perihelion/periastron. Jungle growth sprouted in the forest, tangles of vines, tropical fruits and large brilliant flowers. A pity the time was so deadly while it was so beautiful. The last of the leathervines were dying in the heat, shriveling skeletons clinging to heavily foliaged trees, their seeds in the ground, awaiting the return of the cold.

Lia made a wreath of jungle flowers, red ones, and

crowned her husband when he joined her on the rocks. He licked her ear. He looked at her closely, troubled. He had not realized she was *so* pregnant. She laughed at him and cradled his head in her lap.

"Can you tell if it's a son?" Teal asked her. It would be a thirty-fourth-generation Bay. Another only son in the long line of only sons. Perhaps Kaela would accept him if it was.

"I don't know," she said in her high, thin girl's voice.

"They say you can tell when you carry a Bay." He nuzzled her.

"I don't know what it's supposed to feel like," she said, playing with his black hair. "I feel magic."

"Don't worry. It doesn't really matter."

"I'm not worried." She giggled. "You are."

His black eyes looked serious. He looked up at her face. She was intent on arranging the red flowers in his black, silky mane. His gaze dropped to her small breasts, hardly concealed by the thin cloth, then to the slightly rounded abdomen which he laid his cheek against. "I wonder why we even continue this line now that there is a Trieath. What does it matter if there is a thirty-fourth-generation Bay? I feel useless. Do you feel like that—outdated?"

"Why?" She was obviously unconcerned.

"I guess it doesn't make much difference to women. The male carries the seed of change. But still it's different for women now too. Akelan's daughters will be Trieaths the same as sons. Women will at last be men's equals in the Fourth Epoch."

"Men will at last be women's equals," his child-wife said. Teal met this blank-faced and puzzled. She smiled down at him. "Don't you see, you silly male, for all your pride in your lines and being Bay Royalist and seed of change, how inferior your sex is? That is why you have to change. Eemon Mercer had to have four hundred generations of breeding in him so he could sire the Trieath. His wife had no breeding and she bore the Trieath. Any woman in the Royalist nation can bear a Trieath. There is only one man who can sire one."

What Lowland, feminine nonsense was this? Teal growled, "But you need a man—that man, Akelan. A woman can only bear a Trieath by Akelan Mercer."

"Well, he can't very well have children without a woman either," Lia countered.

She missed the point. "But when Akelan has daughters,

any Royalist man will be able to sire a Trieath by them, so there goes your argument."

"No," she laughed. "That is what I'm saying: at last men will be equal to women."

Teal growled. This woman could not understand.

Looking back, Teal wondered if they would have eventually fallen away from each other from inability to talk had they reached adulthood together.

Day 204 33 Beth-enea
Day 1 1 Beth-enea

Star Year 531/532
Third Epoch Perihelion-Periastron

Death time. It was winter at Skye but hot and humid like a rain forest. In the North it was summer, and all was dying under the rays of the central Sun that had never been so large in Teal's life.

Periastron and perihelion did not come on the same day, but came close. The Star Year turned at mid-Beth-enea. On the Dianter tablets the first recorded date was when periastron and aphelion came at the same moment. It was a sign from the gods, and was the earliest recorded historical event in the Royalist nation. It had not happened since.

Severe Hot Season arrived and the Northerners swarmed south in migrating hoards—women with them this time—to escape the heat. Gordon Tras of the Caucans said they had to claim the land and civilize it, not live in fear of wild beasts.

Kaela and Teal had to go back to war. Teal was forced to leave his very pregnant wife. Kaela was glad to get away from Raya's mirror. She looked just as his wife had the last time he saw her alive. Teal built her a little shelter deep in the jungle. "Stay here. Don't go to the sea," he commanded.

The sea had risen to the cliffs, almost to the house, in the icecap-melting heat.

"And don't ever go to the house. Never. Wait till I come back for you." He saw he frightened her. He gave her a

present of little white fluffy creatures like her pet—in fact, all
of them that he could hunt up. She laughed to weakness, her
little house full of white fluff. "You stay here and take care
of them, and I'll be back before you know." He would not
leave her alone in childbirth.

Teal went to fight. He picked up a little of the Caucan language, mostly hate words. He could read parts of long
printed speeches made by Gordon Tras condemning his
people to death as killer beasts.

Despite superior weapons and vast numbers, the Caucans
were at a disadvantage in the jungle of the Royalists' home,
fighting animal stealth and human intelligence. Their planes
bombed their own men in overzealous haste, thinking they
had *finally* found a target. They began to show some sense
when Gordon Tras stopped believing his own propaganda.
Though he called the Royalists animals to the public, he realized that it was just a story to remove the Caucans' reluctance
to fight. At last taking into account the intelligence of his
enemy, he began to find out about them—about their breeding, what a Bay was, what Highlanders, Lowlanders, and
Nomads were, that their king lived at Skye, and that Bays
were their leaders. He realized he had been attacking the
whole nation, scattered as it was, when he should concentrate
on a few people—the Bays. He also learned that the king's
heir had a wife with child—possibly another Bay. That had
to be stopped. It would be the easiest to take care of. How
elusive could a pregnant woman be?

When Teal suddenly screamed for no apparent reason and
doubled over as if his guts were spilling out, Kaela recognized what had happened. Something similar had happened
to him once. Teal and his father returned to Skye faster than
they knew they could.

Lia had gone to the house, and she was dead. What was
left after a soldier performed an abortion met the horror-
struck eyes of her husband. He ran out into the jungle and
struggled to live through a Reill crisis, unseen.

His father left her for him to bury. Though she had been
far along, there was no knowing what the child would have
been once the Caucans were done. He did not care. He
buried them, then hid himself and went through another
crisis, certain he would die this time.

He dragged himself to the shelter he had built for his wife.
It was full of lost, lonely, hungry balls of fluff. He seized two
of them, one in each hand, intending to plunge them into the

sea. They cheeped and mewed in his rough grasp, and he
started to cry wildly instead. He let them all go and collapsed
on his wife's bed, red darting over his wrists and neck.

He woke in his father's arms, being carried away from the
burning shelter. He did not let him know he was awake or
Kaela would have put him down. Ear against his chest, he
heard a heartbeat that his own heart had matched. He
breathed in the same rhythm as if he were an extra append-
age grown on to his father. He was borne up the incline to
the cliffs but not to the house. He was set down, still sham-
ming unconsciousness, in a patch of soft grass. Kaela walked
with heavy footsteps up to the house.

Crackling sounds and the smell of smoke came to disbelieving Ray. His father returned and lifted him, heading
down the hill. Teal could not maintain stillness and stirred.
He lifted his head and looked back. Cleansing flames con-
sumed his father's house. Timber roofs collapsed and caved
in as firebrick walls crumbled.

Kaela set him on his feet. "It can be rebuilt in the spring,"
he said, nothing else.

Teal stared a long time. His father left him, to return to
war. Teal took to the sea also but swam south.

Instinct or guiding power, he never knew for certain what
brought him to that particular island; around the southern tip
of the Eastern Peninsula headed toward Dianter, he stopped
there. He climbed a beach of yellow sand to yellow rocks. An
outcropping of green sprang from the land around a deep
blue pool of fresh water. Yellow-green grass sprouted bravely
over dry yellow ground under the scorching sun. Teal rested
on yellow rocks, feeling the sun's rays on him. And heard
music—soft melody from strings of a rillia and a voice neither man's nor woman's, perhaps the divinity of this island. It
might have been weariness and lightheaded imagining, or the
voice of death calling. He lifted himself and followed the
sound. He crossed soft, yellow-green, living carpet, and
crawled over yellow rocks to the source.

Akelan did not look at him or pause in the song. Teal lost
the words and even the melody. Only beautiful sound flowing
through empty self was he aware of. He sat down on the
rocks by Akelan to listen and watch.

Gray eyes focused on something unseen. Subtle change in
expression with the music played on Akelan's face with a
look of quiet joy. Short, yellow curls in a golden halo with

the sun's brightness crowned the divinity. Teal came to find a god and found one.

Akelan's fingers lightly touched the strings of the rillia, and it sang and echoed. The rillia became a living thing in his hands, smooth polished white wood, resonant and mellow. Teal lay at his feet like a pet, eyes fixed on loved master, till they would not stay open, and he slept, soaring skyward on notes of a sung prayer.

A rosette, a circle, a fish, a cross, the Sun.

He opened his eyes. Akelan was singing. The sun was setting.

Akelan stopped, and the last note vibrated and rippled out on the air. He reached down to Teal and brushed sand from his cheek, which was rough from its grainy imprint. Black eyes looked lost and confused at the setting sun.

"You sleep like a newborn," Akelan said.

Teal in his daze tried to think. He shook himself and sneezed. He remembered there was a war going on while he'd slept in limbo. "I shouldn't be here."

Akelan laughed. "That is exactly what you said last time!" His smile took the place of the sun for the confused Teal. "Stay and tell me why you should always be elsewhere than you are." He gave him something to eat, and Teal remembered how hungry he was. He had slept a long time.

"Did you sing . . . all that time?" Teal asked.

"I did."

"What was it?"

"A song. A prayer." Gray eyes met his. Teal dropped his eyes to Akelan's feet. The rillia lay there. He could wish to be a rillia. Frightened of answering questions, he asked one: "Why are you here? The people are fighting."

"I cannot fight."

Teal looked up. No trace of fear or cowardice showed in his face or his voice. Shame at daring that thought caused Teal to lower his eyes again.

"My father went to fight," said Akelan.

"So has mine," said Teal softly. He nearly jumped at the touch on his neck. Akelan held the silver rosette pendant in his hand, fingers brushing against his throat. "You can have it," Teal said quickly.

"It is a god thing. You should keep it."

"I don't have any gods," said Teal. He suddenly yanked it from his neck. The silver chain broke, and he hurled it into the sea. "Those gods kill wives."

"That is grief madness," said Akelan. "Come, sit with me."

Teal sat beside him, and Akelan put an arm around his shoulders. He ran his hand across Teal's back where there had been wounds last time they met six Beth-enea ago. He had healed smooth and scarless as Royalists did. No scars showed on the outside.

"Gods give life. You must not demand more and be angry when a gift ends. Gods do not kill," said Akelan.

"No," said Teal. "There aren't any."

"You cannot accept the old gods of the Nomad rituals," Akelan guessed.

"None of them."

It was pointless to continue this way. "What was your wife like?" It was evident that his wife was newly gone.

"Pretty."

"What did she look like?"

He had him talking, then laughing, then crying. Tears for an ocean on Canda; weeping children were told they would sink the continents, and that the reason Arana had oceans and Canda didn't was that there were no people on Canda to cry them.

"It's all right to cry," Akelan said, holding him. "You're supposed to. Don't try to get angry instead." He got him to forgive the gods, and to forgive himself for leaving Lia alone, but he could not shake him from deep-rooted wrath at the Caucans who did it and at Tras because of whom it was done. Teal was more like his father than either of them recognized. Akelan talked with him long into the dark night of Hot Season. The Night Sun rose just before dawn. Only then did Teal realize how long he had been there.

"I have to go."

"You said that before," Akelan said. "Where are you going?"

Teal would not answer, but burning face betrayed him.

"You go to kill men. Stay with me."

"What would be said of me if I let my wife die unavenged?"

"That you follow the Trieath."

So Teal stayed and listened, and Akelan got him to accept a god, but never guessed or probed to find that he was the one.

Day 176 1 Beth-enea
Star Year 532 Third Epoch

The Stewert line was dead. Ven Brekk waited for a lull in the wars to contest his claim to the crown again. Spring came, and the Caucans fell back to regroup for another attack. The Royalists breathed deeply and licked their wounds.

Ven Brekk came upon Teal Ray Stewert with a circle of people at Dianter, listening to Akelan Mercer. Ven still could not hate Akelan. And it would be impossible to fight someone who would not push back. Teal Stewert he could hate.

Akelan was talking about the right to take a life. Ven hoped Stewert would not be convinced by the Trieath that it was wrong. He did not want to slaughter someone who would not defend himself. That would leave Ven an uneasy king. Still, a Stewert could always be counted on to try to kill a Brekk, he told himself.

Ven did not dare break into Akelan's circle to offer challenge, so he withdrew into the hills, threw back his head and sounded the shrill Brekk challenge whistle. He waited. Surely Stewert heard him. His throat tightened to think he might be challenging a pacifist. He steadied himself and challenged again and again and again. Then the Stewert answer came shrilling. Alarmed birds took shrieking to the air. Cries of warning from beasts and the whistles of challenge sounded and echoed in the hills.

Teal followed the call and found the Brekk rival in the ancients' place, the rocky gully called the Womb. Dark and deep, here were the first laws inscribed in the Dianter tablets. High midday sun splashed through the foliage on to the rocks below. Teal descended into the cool, shaded glen, sounding return challenge once more. Gray dampness met his white hands as he climbed down the slippery rocks.

Each saw that the other was not alone. Two pairs of eyes like those of a scavenger beast glared down from a ledge beside Ven: Thoma and Igil. Akelan had followed Teal Ray. Others peered down to watch, supposing themselves unnoticed. Unlike Ven's sons, Akelan did not hang back on a rock but bounded down and stood between them.

"What challenge, Ven?" Akelan said, face very pale. One who had never known fear for himself was terrified for two loved ones. "Has he wronged you? What wrong? I rule it invalid. I will not have this fight."

"No wrong that it is your right to call," Ven answered, avoiding the eyes that would accuse him of murder. "We must fight. It is the Law."

"What law?" His voice went shrill, not condemning but pleading. Whatever birds were left in the glen after the challenge whistles went screeching skyward at Akelan's cry.

Ven turned to his sons. They parted to reveal a tablet they leaned against. Akelan sprang and climbed up like a tree creature. The tablet bore one of the old inscriptions: should there ever be two of equal claim to the crown, they will fight till a clear superior stands.

Akelan spoke very softly in a hiss to the Brekk beside him. "How long did it take you to find this, Thoma?"

The dark eyes attempted wide innocence, but guilt was in Thoma. He looked to Igil, searching for and finding support.

"Why have you done this to your father?" Akelan said softly.

Hate and fear and grief narrowed Thoma's eyes. "It is his right."

"But you are not doing it for him—don't try to tell me you are. You haven't convinced me, and you haven't convinced yourself. The only one who believes you is Ven, who is willing to risk death for your false pride."

Thoma said nothing, but glared back as defiantly as he was able. He should have been king. Cheated of this by the carelessness of his father and the birth of his brother, he could at least be a king's son. Otherwise he was nothing. It was his father's fault for making the foolish choice of a wife who gave birth to twins. He goaded his father to fight to restore some of the pride and honor that Thoma felt was due him. He never considered that if Ven had married someone else, he himself would never have been born at all. He considered what he wanted to consider. So Ven would fight for Thoma's pride, to make him a king's son.

"I pity Ven the cruelty of his son," Akelan said and crawled down, feeling damp, cold rock and spongy moss beneath bare feet.

Ven and Teal had faced off. Left to themselves with no outside influence they would not hate; they would not fight; they might even become lovers, Akelan thought. Thirty-third generation, crisis generation, would do anything for love, and so Teal and Ven would try to kill each other, one for father, one for sons. Looking at Ven, Akelan could not even see his hate for the Stewert. Ven did not hate Teal. It puzzled Akelan. His hate simply was no longer there. He was not fighting for himself at all. He was fighting someone he did not hate—just for Thoma. Maybe, then, he could be dissuaded. It was less to ask Ven to withdraw a challenge than Teal to refuse one. "Ven, Teal is a child—"

"Not according to the Law," Ven said. Teal's marriage had made him a man.

So Thoma had thought of that too. "Damn Law!" Akelan cried. "Ven, if you take advantage of that, you are lower than I ever knew any Royalist, any *Caucan* was capable of being!"

Ven would neither listen nor look. Akelan could not sway him. But Teal was young and lonely; maybe he could persuade him not to fight, for love of him. Akelan seized Teal by both hands. Enormous black eyes flew wide. The child was terrified—not of death, but of his father. There would be no dissuading this one either. "Teal, don't."

Teal shook his head and tried to pull away.

"Teal, he will kill you. You are equal bred, but he is an adult. You cannot fight an adult. You will break like a girl." He pulled him in like a lover and held him. He felt Teal's lashes flutter against his neck, beating back tears. His body was rigid and very aware of the Brekk watching him. Akelan whispered, "Come with me. There is no reason to stay here." He spoke gently. "You shouldn't be here, child."

As soon as he had checked his tears, the boy was pushing against him, so Akelan let him go. What had he been asking, anyway? For a Bay to choose Akelan before his own father. He should have known the impossibility of the request even if the Bay were Teal Stewert. Akelan withdrew.

Thoma and Igil had moved down from their vulture's eye-view. Ven gave his purple cloak to them. He gave it to Igil.

They faced each other naked, weaponless but for their own wits and strength. Rocks must stay on the ground and water in the stream—breaking skulls and drowning were allowed with those restrictions. After that it was tooth and claw and whatever it took to defeat the opponent.

Teal quickly analyzed his challenger; he had the bulk and weight and strength. New-cut hair offered no hold. *He will try to break my neck, since that is what he defends against.*

And Ven's first move was to grasp for Teal's long hair. Teal ducked under his high attack and landed a fist in his abdomen. Ven had thought he was prepared for that, muscles hard and tight—but he had not anticipated that kind of power from such a delicate-looking adversary. Momentary shock gave time for another blow, and Teal darted out before he could be caught. Once in his enemy's hands, Teal would be done. Ven gasped and cursed himself for leaving himself open, for underestimating the Stewert Bay. Pride hurt worst. Ven fought like one of two minds; part wanting to crush, part seemed to want to lose. Teal circled, and Ven sprang suddenly as if on a wild buck. Teal dodged and kicked him as he came down. Ven grasped his arm, and Teal sank his teeth into the other's hand. Ven would not let go. He got an elbow in an abdomen that would not take more. Humiliation at what he had expected to be a quick victory flooded him, followed by blind rage. He threw Teal to the ground and pinned him there, grinding his face into the dirt. Physical pain was too mild. He wanted to hurt and hurt mortally. Degradation he learned from the Caucans. Cackling laughter from somewhere screamed in Teal's ears. *If my father were here . . .*

Ven found himself thrown off, landing hard, not thinking to break the fall. Teal moved in and Ven was assured of his victory; at close quarters it was a test of superior strength, which he knew he had. But the demon he had released by sheer force dragged him, fighting bulk, up the rocks. For the first time Ven felt fear as the ground rushed to meet him. All was spinning for Brekk. A small foot and slender ankle stood before his eyes, to be broken at a breath, but he had not the strength to try. A drop of blood traced down the back tendon to the heel. Teal stood over him, clear superior.

Teal limped to the spring, a pool of icy water wept by the rocks of the Womb. He bathed himself and threw water on his face so no one would know he wept.

Thoma and Igil were caring for their father. Thoma, muttering, seemed to think he had thrown the fight. Why would Ven Brekk give victory to Teal Stewert . . . ?

Akelan was on the ledge, calmly obliterating the Dianter inscriptions.

Teal climbed up and knelt by him. Akelan stopped and looked in surprise. "You are alive."

"I won."

Akelan turned around to see Ven on the ground. "Is he alive?"

"Yes, didn't you see?"

Akelan breathed a prayer of thanks, then said, "No, I wasn't watching."

Teal rubbed his arm as if there were dirt on it. "You didn't see any of it?"

"No."

Teal let out a breath he had forgotten to exhale. "What are you doing?" his strained voice asked. Akelan had picked up his iron tool again and was hammering with a stone. "I mean, why?"

"Three Epochs ago," Akelan said as the chips fell, "someone sat here where I sit, chiseling just as I, no better than I"—three Epochs his inferior the inscriber had been—"setting down laws for his people. They were meant to serve for all time—as one of the First Epoch viewed time. People change. So laws must. They are not bonds. I free you."

He had chiseled around and left the histories. His eyes glistened. "It is sad to have to erase the hand of our first fathers, the legacy they left us. But no longer will anyone be able to point at a rock and say, 'I must fight.' "

Teal climbed down and bathed again. In spite of Akelan's disapproval, he felt a breath of self-worth and maybe . . . pride? It was a fragile feeling and Teal couldn't risk breaking it by telling Kaela. He wouldn't tell his father he'd won him the right to keep the crown.

That too must have been god-inspired.

Day 188   4 Beth-enea
Star Year 532   Third Epoch

Teal had become a young man. The house at Skye had been rebuilt, and Teal lived there with his father. Kaela did not beat him anymore, not because he was too old or because of Teal's victory over Brekk (which he was unaware of), but because Teal had lost his wife and the score was even. But they never talked. He had not forgiven anything.

Teal was often at Dianter, sitting at Akelan's feet. Large crowds gathered to hear what Akelan had to say. He spoke of peace. But the wars had not stopped. They had not even slackened, for while the Royalists listened to Akelan talk of peace, the Caucans heard Gordon Tras say they must prepare for the future and capture the South before the next Star Year brought the killing periastron again. They must do it for their children and grandchildren.

It was a moderate winter day with a brisk chill hanging in the still air. A crowd of Lowlanders, Highlanders, and Nomads listened to Akelan Mercer. Teal was seated quietly up front and did not know his father had come until Kaela spoke.

"You," he addressed the Trieath, "are the best thing that ever happened—to the Caucans."

Hush. A piper bird twittering. Eemon Mercer drawing up for a challenge on his son's behalf.

Kaela stood at the edge of the crowd, as king, crown on his head. Teal tried to make himself small and invisible.

Akelan was unperturbed. "Because I tell our people not to fight?" he asked Kaela.

"Yes, and because they listen, and now our land is *half* of what it was only four Beth-enea ago!"

The people stirred and began to listen to their king.

"And the *last* Lowland village has burned—not because we are going to stop them but because there *are no more*. There are no Highlanders or Lowlanders; we are all Nomads." He threw the results of Akelan's teachings up at him in a strong voice.

Teal felt the tearing inside and wondered if this was what Akelan had felt watching Ven and him face off for challenge. The deep, resonant voice and the high, clear answer pulled him in two directions.

"What would you have me do, Kaela? Become a Gordon Tras and send my people to a slaughter?"

"You preach peace, and we get overrun, because Tras is screaming war on the other side. We already *are* a peaceful people. You are making us fit to slaughter. We don't need you. *Go tell your peace to the Caucans.*"

Sympathy was with gentle Akelan, but war weariness, running, and lost homes said Kaela was right.

"You are right," Akelan said quietly and stepped down from the white marble bench he stood on. He sat. "I will go this night. Will you come with me?"

Almost a bitter smile on his dark face, Kaela answered, "I have been." He had gone once to kill Tras.

"Come with me," Akelan said to the crowd. "Who will?"

No one.

"I will keep your grave," Kaela said, offering to honor his death.

Akelan smiled. "I yours, should I outlive you."

"I hope you do," he said sincerely, but in a tone that clearly doubted that possibility. Kaela withdrew, and Akelan called for companions again.

"Father?" He turned to Eemon. Eemon looked tired and grieved, as if he were burying his son. No doubt it was what he was envisioning, though Akelan did not enter his mind to see.

"Akelan," Eemon spoke. "You have no offspring—"

"Father, I'm coming *back*," Akelan interrupted. "Come with me. Someone come with me." He got no answer. "Then I will go alone," he said resolutely. He sent them all away.

Teal stayed at his feet. "No one will come," Akelan said sadly, half to Teal, half to the sky.

"I'll go," said Teal.

Akelan looked down. "Why didn't you say when I asked?" Akelan smiled sadly.

"You knew I would."

"I don't know *anything* about you." Akelan ruffled his black hair, short in front, trailing long down his back in the manner of widowers. "You don't believe a word I say; you fight when I say peace; you claim no gods, but listen to me forever talk of mine. You, as a pupil, are my most glorious failure."

"You don't want me."

Akelan slid off the bench and knelt down by him. "Teal, I even get the impression you don't expect to come back."

His gaze fell to the ground.

"You think you are coming to die with me."

Eyes on the ground, he spoke in a scarcely audible voice. "You don't want me."

"I would not leave you for a hoard of believers." Akelan kissed his forehead. "Come, it's late. I have to talk to Gordon Tras' people."

Teal followed, unable to do otherwise. Akelan was wrong in supposing he had no god. He had one and would follow him until he was no longer there to follow. But his wandering would continue farther than he could imagine, to places he did not yet know existed.

IV.

A circle. A Caucan church with a circle emblazoned on the heavy, wooden doors opened to a circular worship sanctuary where the Royalist Akelan spoke to the Caucans about his country, himself, and peace. Akelan learned to communicate quickly. He spoke clearly and fluently, drawing the language from the Caucans' minds. Teal sat and listened to the foreign words come from Akelan and watched hostile stares of Caucans melt to confusion and at last to sympathy, and even to love. The church grew too small, and Akelan moved outside and drew a great circle and invited all the Caucans to come within. A great crowd stood outside the circle, but soon there were more within than without. Some watched him as if he were a talking animal, an oddity from the wilderness for them to come and gawk at, but most of them were listening, however reluctantly at first.

The circle soon had to be enlarged. A thousand people had come into the boundry. Teal had never seen half that number of Caucans at one time except in war. The great crowds looked to him like armies. It was new to see them gather in peace.

Gordon Tras' police came to break it up, but, on arrival, could not figure out how. To shoot the animal right there would have angered the crowd, so the officers waited for the Royalist to anger the people or to lose their interest. And they also listened.

Akelan went to many places and filled many circles in Cauca, for Cauca was a big land with many people. Akelan traveled, and Teal followed.

Wherever they went they began meeting with a filmed speech of Tras being played in the center circle of every town. The Caucan leader was attempting to counteract the corrupting influence that he saw infecting the country like a disease. So Teal finally got to see his enemy Tras as a recorded image. He was a smallish man approaching middle age, ruddy-faced, flushed with the excitement of his speech. Black hair, tied back in knots as Caucans wore it, was falling in wisps as he shook his head for emphasis. Pale brown wild eyes rolled in frenzy as he exhorted the people to save themselves. Deep voice boomed and shook the soul and reached out and grabbed the audience. He was persuasive, eloquent, and alive. He had the presence, like Akelan, the power to focus all attention on himself among a crowd of thousands. But Tras was an image on film. Akelan was a warm, living presence, and the people listened to him.

Teal learned that Tras, not the Caucans, was the evil. He knew he must kill Tras for his father, for his people, for his dead wife.

Despite Tras' vehement opposition, Akelan picked up some Caucan followers, three young Caucan musicians who dared defy the voice of Tras to join Akelan. The three were good company and Akelan was glad of them. They were a good influence on Teal, merry and jovial with a Bay Royalist who knew too much hate. They slowed down Akelan's progress across Cauca, lacking the stamina of ocean people who were used to swimming great distances and traveling on foot when Caucans would use beasts of burden. But their spirit was great, and it quickened the warming of people to Royalist Akelan when they saw him accompanied by people of their own blood.

It was from Wings, one of the Caucan musicians, that Teal first heard of Earth. He was explaining to Teal, "You can tell an upper-class Caucan by his name. They usually have Earth names."

"What is Earth?" Teal asked.

"You've never heard of Earth?" Wings was surprised.

"I have heard the word," said Teal.

"It's a . . . place." Wings could not think how to convey the concept of another planet to him. "The country of Vakellan discovered it. The Vakellans keep Earth time and use Earth languages and dress like Earth people. Since Vakellan is the leading country, the Caucan upper class is trying to keep pace and is switching to Earth ways too."

Teal took this in and considered it with great seriousness. He was too serious.

Wings looked out for the young Royalist when he could. Teal did not yet understand that he too had the presence. He still did not know of his own attractiveness, a compensation granted by nature. Teal needed people; his beauty was a means to attract them. He possessed two opposing "gifts"—the Reill to destroy him, and the presence to save him. Yet he could wish to either live or die, rather than be torn in some middle state like constantly dying. He drew his knees up to him, hugged his legs, and rested his chin on his knees. Sensitive, fine features bore an expression of pain. Dark brows drew together but did not meet. Smooth, white forehead creased in thought. He was too serious.

The five had paused to rest the night in a field as they often did. Teal was restless, not owning to himself that he was jealous. He ran off to explore the area on his own while Akelan talked with the three Caucans, discussing the meaning of the Circle.

Teal bounded across the field like the frightened doe, feeling the freedom of running. The open land was as endless as his energy. He did frighten a doe and raced her. Were it a hunt he could have caught her, but, having no need, he let her escape.

The only restriction on him was the clothes he wore, a concession to the inhabitants of this foreign land. The full, baggy pantaloons were intolerable, but he was told he must cover himself. He wore breeches of soft animal skin, not tightly form-fitting, but showing that he was obviously male, which was daring for the Caucans, and a sign of barbarism. So he wore a tunic over that. His sex sufficiently ambiguous (more so because of his smooth Royalist face), the Caucans accepted him as possibly human, though uncivilized.

Wings had given him the tunic, which was red, as a kind of friendship offering.

"How did you know my color was red?" Teal asked, referring to his Stewert line color.

The young man shrugged, missing Teal's meaning. "I thought you'd look good in red."

He did look good in it, but it made hiding difficult, as he wanted to do when he found himself on a Caucan estate. The land here was altered as Caucans loved to do, making nature obey them. Trees stood in ranks, and every blade of grass was the same length. A tremendous house stood in the middle of the ordered grounds.

Teal met a girl here and made love to her on a three-legged bed. He wanted to lie with her and hold her afterward, but she fiercely ordered him away, suddenly harsh after tenderness. He ran back to their camp, more disturbed than before.

Everyone was sleeping. He stole soundlessly by the three Caucans. He woke Akelan and offered himself to him. Once married one is not a boy, yet he offered himself like a boy, and Akelan was too close to Teal's age to accept. Akelan could not understand, but saw him to be distressed and felt him trembling. He held him, and Teal accepted that—it being all he really wanted.

The journey through Cauca continued and the circles grew bigger. Then Akelan was invited to Phaetha by the leader of that country. So the five of them started toward the coast to go to the island country Phaetha. The Caucan musicians insisted that they come too. "Quite frankly, our lives aren't worth much here," said one. "Gordon Tras has an army of assassins."

"My wife met one," Teal said hollowly.

"You were married before?" The Caucan looked at him strangely. He'd taken Teal for a child. "What happened?"

"I left her alone and Tras had her killed."

"God," was all Wings could say, brown eyes wide and awed. When he found his voice he said, "You mean we killed your wife and you're here saying peace?" He put his arm around Teal.

Teal decided he liked this Caucan. He did not know his real name. They called him Wings because he could pilot an airplane. "I did my time in Gordon Tras' army. Flew a tin can full of bombs. Never found anything to drop them on down there—I thank God, now. I was always so afraid one of those things would go off in my plane, so I was real anxious to unload them. Some pilots got overanxious and unloaded 'em on our own army. I should have realized then how stupid the war is." He wore a tunic with a big circle embroidered on the back. "I'll tell you, I'm pretty anxious to get out of this country. I'm surprised I haven't been arrested yet. And I'm real surprised you and Akelan are still alive." So was Teal. Especially after Teal awoke one morning to three panicking Caucans shaking him, demanding of him how long he could stay underwater. Brushing leaves from his hair and sleep from his eyes, Teal answered he could stay submerged for the Aranan equivalent of half an hour. The three Caucans' ruddy faces turned ash-gray. Teal then noticed Akelan was not in the camp.

"Where's Akelan?"

They pointed to a pond a distance off behind a screen of trees and undergrowth, and said that he'd been under longer than an hour, fleeing a gun-bearing agent of Tras'. The agent had since left, assured that the Royalist had drowned. Teal didn't wait to hear details but bolted for the pond and dived in before his companions could stop him. He swam to the blur at the bottom of the deep pond. The shock of the cold water opened his eyes. He was awake, alert, and panicked, drawing near Akelan, who floated calm as death at the bottom, pale, almost bluish, in color. Tears blending with the water, Teal reached out and expected to touch a body as cold as the surrounding water. But Akelan's skin was still warm. The motionless figure moved. Akelan's head turned and he grasped Teal's hand and gave it a squeeze. He hadn't run out of air and drowned—after an hour and a half. He even seemed to . . . breathe? He rose to the surface with Teal and spit out a tremendous amount of water, coughed, and breathed deeply. His face flushed red.

The baffled Caucans on shore greeted him as one returned from the dead—as a god.

Akelan laughed. "Just because you can't understand, don't make a god of me."

"But Royalists can only stay under a half-hour—" Wings protested.

"You've got your facts wrong. No magic. It's just me." He grinned and the three laughed in relief and squashed him in embraces.

It was less easy for Teal to shake the belief in miracle, since he *knew* the limit was half an hour. The answer was simple—Akelan was a god.

A fish. The priest-king of Phaetha was a young, energetic man with a dancer's body beneath the white flowing robe with blue border in the pattern of fish. He wore it for the ceremonial welcome of the "priest-king of the Royalists," as he called Akelan. Akelan did not correct him, sensing he used the title loosely, fully aware that the Royalists had no such position. The king greeted them at the boat (which they had had to drag Teal aboard; boats were evil).

After the formal greeting, the king was informal and friendly. He shed the robe. He wore trousers like the Vakel-

lans', soft shoes, and a fine, colorful creation for a top such
as the Phaethons delighted in—the more different the better,
hardly functional, purely decorative. The Phaethons were
small and agile people with flowing movements, dancers one
and all. Their motions as they spoke were not merely expressive gestures, but essential parts of their message.

The Phaethons were a peaceful people and needed no per-
suading as had the Caucans, but they were no less interested
in the mysterious Royalists and came out in great numbers to
listen to Akelan. His gatherings were held indoors, there
being Phaethan buildings large enough to contain them. All
the buildings in Phaetha were large, comfortable, and cooled
by Vakellan air conditioners. No matter how hot it got out-
doors, indoors was livable; in the same way, they could heat
the coldest winters.

"If you can control the air, why do the Caucans want to
move into our land?" Teal asked the priest-king while Akelan
and his followers were staying at the palace. The language
was much easier to pick up than Caucan.

"Because Tras wants his war," the priest-king said and
sprawled himself in an oversized three-legged chair of exotic
design. "Tras is an idiot—no, I shouldn't say that. He has
united Cauca, I will give him that. From then on, he has not
made a right decision.

"I hope you realize," the king said, shifting his attention to
Akelan, "I probably saved your life. You were mad to have
crossed that border. God must have told you to go there, because someone was obviously looking out for you. Well, God
told me to get you out of there, and I did."

Akelan smiled, both amused and appreciative.

"I am surprised Tras let you alone as long as he did," the
priest-king added. "He will have to make a move soon. You
have begun to threaten him directly. There have been two assassination attempts since your coming."

"But I—" Akelan began. "Oh, why don't they listen? I
speak *peace!* Teal, they are all like you," he said.

Teal looked up quietly from the floor, where he sat
crosslegged on a fish-shaped rug of blue and green.

A thought struck Akelan. "Teal, that wasn't . . . that
wasn't you, was it?"

Teal's eyes were on the carpet. He tugged at his pant leg in
nervous gesture. He was barefoot and shirtless. Black hair
made his back, already pale from lack of sun, seem white. He
wore black slacks, as did the priest-king.

"Teal?"

"Only the first one," said Teal.

The Phaethan priest-king howled with laughter, and Wings was chuckling so infectiously that Akelan could not get angry. Teal's gaze was still on the floor, and he was the only one not laughing (Akelan had succumbed momentarily). Akelan gave in and simply said, "I love you, child," and cuffed his sulking head.

The priest-king was as inquisitive as a child and asked all about Akelan and the Royalists.

"I heard a prophecy, I guess you'd call it. Could you explain it to me?" he asked at one point. "It's a Royalist prophecy, I believe. 'There will come one who has seen the face of hell, and he will make way for him who has seen the face of God, the one who will be the father of the new race, the Trieath, through whom we shall be reborn by the blood of the one who wears hell in his eyes.' " It was an ambiguous in the original language as it was in translation, and had aroused the priest-king's curiosity.

"That's a Nomad saying," Akelan explained. "The Nomads tend to be very mystical. I really don't know what that one means."

"But you are obviously the one who has seen the face of God."

Teal could tell them what hell looked like. *By the blood . . . Will you kill me, Akelan?*

Teal had heard the prophecy before—the Nomad girl who had danced by the fire for him had told him. Strange how a girl who made him feel so alive reminded him of his death. She made him aware of his own mortality.

And Akelan's immortality.

For after grasping the warm hand of what he expected to be a corpse at the bottom of the pond, Teal knew he was divine. So firm was his conviction that Akelan could not help but perceive it, and sat him down to straighten out the misconception. They sat out on the palace terrace overlooking the sea. There were three-legged chairs to sit on and no one else there to choose which they wanted, but Akelan and Teal passed them up for the steps. Teal looked at Akelan with adoration. This would be difficult. Repeating "I'm human" over and over had no effect on his devout believer, and Akelan finally yelled at him, "Staying underwater indefinitely is not a miraculous feat if you've got *gills*."

Stunned, Teal watched his god turn into an amphibian.

Akelan not only had slits that were gills behind his ears, but webs between his fingers that, though normally retracted and invisible, now appeared and made his hand look like a duck's foot, or a frog's. Teal was on the verge of fleeing, fainting, or screaming.

"I didn't want to tell you. I can't stand that look of yours, Teal. It's me. Just me."

Teal pulled away, and Akelan on reflex reached out for his arm, but he stopped at Teal's horrified reaction to the webbed hand. "Here, Teal, touch me—it's just my hand."

Teal only stared, frozen.

"I'm human, Teal, just as you are, just as the Northerners are, just as Lowlanders are. We're all different, but all human."

Teal hesitantly touched his hand, avoiding the strange and alien membrane.

"Go on, touch it and I'll take it away," Akelan said.

Looking delicate as the membrane inside an egg, it was tough as a fish's fin. Teal touched it once and shrank away.

"Okay, child, okay," Akelan said and drew them back like a cat its claws so that they lay unnoticeable between his fingers. Now that he knew they were there, Teal could still see them, though he couldn't before.

Teal seized Akelan's now-human hand and held it, trembling. Akelan, with his free hand, stroked back the boy's hair, which was falling into wide, black eyes. "Hey, I'm me, just as I always was."

Looking lost, Teal cried out, "What's human?"

"What I call human," Akelan said, "is someone that first of all has intelligence—he has to think and be able to create. Creative thinking is something that makes you human. And he has to laugh and cry—or at least feel like it—and love and feel. A person has to feel and have emotions. And a human has to need other creative, intelligent, sentient humans. That's about it."

"What about two arms, two legs, a head, and a body to connect them?" Teal offered.

"What about the Northerner who gets his legs blown off in war? Does he cease to be human?"

"How about being *born* with—"

"The last queen of Phaetha was born with no right arm."

"Those are defects and accidents," Teal tried to explain. "You're trying to say it has nothing at all to do with what you look like."

"You're trying to say that if I had fins instead of arms I wouldn't be human."

"All right, forget the two arms, two legs—they have to be able to—barring accident or defect—to have children by other humans."

"I'll accept that," Akelan said.

A cross. At Phaetha, Akelan received a gold cross on a chain and an invitation from Leader White of Vakellan to visit her country.

"I knew she would take you from me!" The priest-king threw a mock temper tantrum. "Leader White gets what she wants. She's a charming lady."

He crowned Alekan with a delicate coronet made of small gold and lapis fishes.

Teal was almost glad to get out of the hospitable land. He preferred facing the enemy by Akelan's side to being sat in a corner while people fawned on the Trieath.

The Vakellans sent an airplane for the Royalist. It was not a "tin can" such as Wings had piloted, but a jet, something Teal had never seen. Climbing higher and higher, Teal wanted it to keep going up instead of leveling off. Wings put a paw around him. "Scared?"

"Is this a ship that leaves the world?" Teal asked Wings, looking down to the ocean through the wisps of clouds.

"No, this is just a plane. We're going to Vakellan, not Canda." He laughed.

Teal turned to him. "Can a ship take you to Canda?"

"Yeah, the Vakellan ones can. Do you want to go or something?"

"Is it a world, just like Arana?" Teal asked.

"A lot like. There isn't much water. I don't think a Royalist would like that much. It's mostly land. And it's colder."

Teal turned his gaze back out the window. They raced to meet the blinding sun. Teal hoped that the plane would somehow *slip* and leave the world. He could not know that he would leave soon enough.

Almost everything "Vakellan" was actually "Earthen"—the plane, their religious symbols, their language, their dress and customs. The language was hard to learn, being a conglomeration of Old Vakellan, English, Russian, Chinese, and Alpha Centaurian, with a few Uelson and Caucan words thrown in. It was no trouble for Akelan as a telepath, but Teal was baffled by the inconsistencies. So he listened.

Akelan spoke at length with Leader Vensar White on Vakellan culture. She sat with her five guests in her drawing room. Only one of them understood her. Akelan had to translate for the rest.

Vensar's hair was artificially curled and tinted, and Teal wondered if something were wrong with it. He watched and observed, and only spoke once—when they began talking of Vakellan's space fleet and ships that left the world. Vensar was explaining that the fleet was a world effort, that they had members from every country on Arana—except the Royalist nation.

"Why?" Teal asked.

Vensar smiled and shrugged. "None of your people ever volunteered. My brother Hollingsworth is admiral of the fleet; he asks me the same question. Why?"

Teal did not give her an answer. He stared upward, at the stars, through the skylight.

Teal learned the language well enough to ask a Vakellan woman to marry him. A Vakellan would not love before marriage. It seemed a good idea to Teal—she wouldn't get up and run off or send him away afterward if she were his wife. He missed living with a woman.

"No," was the answer.

Black eyes blinked. "Why?"

She tried to smile. She knew what she said would hurt no matter how gently spoken. "Teal, you will marry *any*body. I have to be someone's number one and only. Do you understand?"

"No. Not at all," he said. He looked like a child she wanted to comfort more than a man she wanted to marry. She *did* want to marry him—an adventurous, foolish, romantic part of her did. A level head rescued her.

"Then I'm afraid you'll just have to accept without knowing why," she said, feeling unspeakably cruel. The words would not soften. "I'm sorry."

Teal returned to his group looking like a lost dog.

Akelan caught himself before he blurted out, "Didn't your father teach you anything?" Of course he hadn't.

Wings looked after the zombie he found in their company during the stay in Vakellan. Teal stared blankly, seemingly unaware of what he saw or where he was led. Wings did not have any idea if anything penetrated, if his mind were as numb as his body seemed to be. He did not leave him alone. He dragged him to the churches with the group, even though he suspected him to be more out of reach of a god than ever.

5/6 Beth-enea
Star Year 532   Third Epoch

The crowd at Dianter welcoming home the Trieath from
his journey to the land of death at the turn of the Beth-enea
was jubilant in spirit and lavish in praise and love. He was
not triumphant, for the wars continued well past their usual
time, but he was alive; and that was a miracle. The Trieath
lived; he would have children; the fourth race had not been
ended in a foreign land. They crowned him with snow flowers and gave him a cloak of Mercer white. They welcomed
kindly the foreign followers who dared what his own people
would not—to leave their homes to follow Akelan.

Frail and looking 150 years old, Eemon Mercer was led to
the son whom he'd given up for dead. Years fled in moments
as Eemon left off his grave vigil. The people crowned him
along with his son.

Teal avoided the welcome. The returning heir to the Royalist crown crept down to the beach, not wanting garlands of
red flowers for the future Stewert king. He did not want
honor. He did not feel like rejoicing. He was sick and jealous,
and wanted to be left alone. He left the people to crowd
around Akelan where he stood on his white bench outside the
colonnade.

Teal watched the breakers roll in and smack, white and violent, against the rocks. Little sea creatures were left behind
as the waves rolled back, scurrying, deserted, on hard, cold
grayness. Then the white assault smashed in again, hitting the
sea creatures, swirling them up and pulling them back, or
breaking them against the rocks.

It was Cold Season Spring and the air was brisk, though
the sun shone brightly. It was a clear day, and the Royalists'
sensitive ears were the first to detect the approaching sound,
though it took Wings to identify it. "Tin cans. Planes. A
whole damn squadron."

The Caucans finally found a target.

V.

Teal wakened from his walking sleep when the bombs began to fall. He had to find Akelan. When the planes came, Teal had been on the beach, and his own escape into the sea would have been easy, but he would not leave his leader.

Had he known what lemmings were, he would have made the comparison between them and the crowd of Royalists herding into the sea. Some did not reach the deep water in time, and the froth that washed the beach after a bomb hit offshore was red. In horror and sorrow at the loss of life, Teal reserved some small comfort knowing Akelan was not there. Just as Teal would not leave him, Akelan would not abandon his Northern followers who could not escape by water, not able to swim beyond a crawl. Akelan would be with them, making a slow overland escape.

Teal ran inland to the gathering place. The colonnade was a pile of rubble, column drums thrown and smashed around the grounds as if a giant had picked them up and hurled them in a rage. There was a crater where the white bench Akelan used to stand on had been. Teal ran blindly, calling out for him. He heard Northern voices and flew through the wood toward the Highlands. He caught up with the three Caucans. Wings grabbed him. "I thought you'd had it. Come with me. We can get through. I know how these birds leave their droppings."

"Where's Akelan?" he cried as Wings pulled him along with their small company.

"Come on!" he insisted, and Teal shrieked, *"Where's Akelan?"*

He did not wait for the answer, certain he did not want to hear it even if they would give a straight answer. He tore back, crashing through the whipping brush as if rabid. A bomb dropped close by, and he was thrown off his feet and rolled down an embankment. He found Akelan—what was left. He recognized him by smell. He did not look like Ak-

55

elan anymore. He was dead. Teal knelt in blood, trembling, praying another bomb would fall right there.

A tiny voice spoke. "That has to be Teal."

"Akelan!" Teal tried to shout, but it was a whisper. He looked for his eyes but they were not there.

"Teal, go away." A small movement of lips under mud and blood was his mouth.

"You were playing dead so I'd go away. That's what you did to Wings!" he said. He stood up and screamed, *"Wings!"* He knew they were too far off. *"Wings!" Oh God! Where is your god now? I wanted to believe you.*

"Teal, go—" The tiny voice broke off. Teal dropped to his knees searching for life signs. He found none. He bolted for the Highlands. *"Wings—"*

He heard the explosion and felt it in his face. He screamed, put his hand to his face. A wet mass. Eyes . . . eyes . . . sockets full of gelatin. Teal screamed again. More explosions were the only answer.

Burning with fever, screaming, reaching for Akelan and not finding him. Screaming all night long—or was it day? He groped, blind, and trembling too violently to hold himself up. He put his hand in something wet like mud, but it was sticky and didn't smell like mud. It smelled like blood. *Akelan. Akelan. Akelan.* He realized he'd found him. He threw his head back and whistled the Royalist distress call, not so much as a call but a desperate cry. . . .

The rarefied air he breathed on waking was cold. It told hi   o longer Dianter. He was in the Mountains. A searching hand met the rough blanket warming him, then stone wall next to him on his right. A cave in the Mountains then. He smelled something vile, yet soothing, along with cave smells; it was a medicine smell such as the Mountain People made. A cave of the Mountain People. They must have picked up after Dianter. Teal heard a sound and turned his head toward it. Light. Puzzled, he turned his head in the direction of the wall. Dark. Delirium, perhaps. Light and Dark. He had lost time sense. Inner clock said many days had passed, but he could not remember any of them, as if he had shut down for that period. It was only a momentary waking, and he felt the shutting down this time. Almost as if the waking had been a dream. *Of course I am dreaming: I have no eyes.* Light and Dark.

A rosette, a circle, a fish, a cross, the Sun. The image was so vivid that Teal's eyes flew open. Dim light was too intense to bear, and he shut them. Eyes? Disregarding the pain of the bright dimness, he opened them again.

It was a small cave, with a coal fire for heat burning in the corner hearth. Scent of woodsmoke and of coal mingled with the medicine smell, stone, moss, and a breath of new plant growth from outside where a piper bird twittered. Light came in through the narrow opening in the rock, illumining rough walls and a floor polished smooth from the tredding of many feet over the stones for many Star Years. He saw the gray, handwoven blanket and the gray wall he had felt. He saw his thin white hand and arm. He saw. He shut his smarting eyes. *They have given me back my eyes.*

He attributed his new sight to Mountain magic, since he knew little of the people—and almost as little about himself. It never once occurred to him that his eyes could have grown back. He had seen blinded animals, and in his travels with Akelan he'd met blind Northerners; from them he assumed that once eyes were gone there was no regrowth. He'd never seen a blind Royalist. Perhaps, he thought, the Mountain People took care of those too. His father never mentioned such things. Kaela hadn't taught him much.

Next time he looked it hurt less. He looked and saw a person dressed in fur, leaning over him, putting a wet cloth on his face. He was an ancient man, wrinkled as Royalists never get, with leatherlike skin. The Mountain People were said to live a score Star Years sometimes, so much older than the long-lived Royalists—and they were of Northern blood. Sunk deep in the old man's skull, ocean-colored eyes looked on Teal from ocean depths. He mopped salty sweat from his Royalist patient's brow.

An attendant accompanied the old man. A hood shadowed the aged face of Eemon Mercer. His gray eyes were the color of a winter sky and as bleak. Emaciated, he crept as silent and insubstantial as a shadow. He held a bowl of water for the old Mountain man. He had the patience of a beast of burden, his life the heaviest burden of all. Proud Mercer's shoulders bowed. Frail, almost ethereal, he wasted away and served the gentle people. He crept out silently, careful not to spill the water. Teal wept with his new eyes.

As soon as he was well they let him go. The Beth-enea was thirty days old. Where had the thirty days gone? He tried to think. Eemon's image clung to his brain. Teal fled home to his father.

Like a cape storm, his father's eyes carried that fury, but it was all chained behind a face as immobile as the stone walls of the Mountain cave. Kaela did not ask where he had been; Teal stank of Mountain medicine. Teal was shocked to see his father as thin and worn as he was. He still held his tall frame erect. More than pride, it was defiance. He wore no crown.

Teal never addressed his father. He did now. "Where is your crown?"

The look answered, the fury of murdered pride. Brekk had claimed it.

"I'll reclaim it," Teal said. He had won it once lawfully in challenge.

Still no reaction. What was it?

Teal tore himself from the look and stumbled out onto the terrace and sat on a stone bench. All around him was new and built by his father's hand. It was the same design as the old had been, but was more magnificent. The facade facing out to the terrace was a mosaic, the center of which was a fiery lithra, a proud, regal, wild creature. The frescos within were as brilliant, living and breathing. More than ever this was his father's house. His soul was within the firebrick walls. It was not just the home of the Stewert line, it was the place of the Royalist king. Teal had to retrieve the crown from Brekk.

He donned a gold dagger belt and a waterbuck skin that would not inhibit passage through the water. Teal left the many-leveled house on the southern cliffs, dove into the sea, and made for the West Peninsula and the home of the Brekks.

Ven was not shocked to see him, and made no contest. He even placed the crown on Teal's head.

No, this isn't right. It's for my father, Teal thought, but he could not take it off in front of Brekk. He turned, crowned, to walk out of the Brekks' cliff dwelling, when purple-mantled Thoma appeared at the exit, blocking his way. The shadow, Igil, was not far off.

"Let him pass," Ven told his son.

"I will, Father," said Thoma. "But the Brekk crown stays."

"The Brekk crown is where it belongs," Ven said wearily.

Teal had never seen Thoma surprised till then. He tossed his blue-black curls like a bull its horns. "Father!"

"Let him pass."

Thoma could not. His pride would not have it. He lashed

out at his father with a verbal assault. "A fine king who gives his crown to any hermaphrodite who asks. A king who took a wife knowing her seed gave twins—a woman any Bay would avoid as he would a Caucan—"

"Thoma," Ven rumbled.

Thoma was visibly daunted, not measuring up to his front.

Ven stared down his willful son and stunned him with a roar. *"You would not be a Bay were you single-born!"*

Thoma could not let that pass no matter who spoke it. He was going to challenge his own father; Teal saw it coming. Teal felt the crown on his head and intercepted as Thoma opened his mouth. "Your wrong is invalid. There will be no fight here," he said, and passed by a stunned, cowed, and dangerously vengeful Thoma.

Teal went home, apprehension mounting as he drew near the majestic house rising up the cliffs. Some vague foreknowledge told him to be afraid.

He approached his father, holding the crown in his hands.

Kaela made no move to take it, leaving Teal wondering what to do.

"I brought this back to you," Teal offered.

"You brought it to me?" Kaela spoke in a quiet, harsh voice. "You mock me. Do you want a challenge?" Kaela would have beaten him, but Teal was king—though Teal did not yet accept it.

"I . . . I brought this—" Teal stuttered in confusion.

"You said that."

Teal could not prevent tears. They splashed onto his cheeks. "I don't understand—why won't you take it?"

"You think because you are king, you may mock me. I will show you you cannot." Kaela spoke evenly, coldly.

"I *don't!*" Teal screamed back, shocking himself. "Why won't—" His voice broke, all his faculties betraying him into breaking down before his father. Nature was scheming without his consent to arouse pity.

Determined not to be affected by any softer emotions, Kaela grew more harsh. "You won *yourself* the crown," Kaela said in a voice beginning to strain. "Are you abdicating? If so, it goes back to Brekk. Are you giving it to me to bear to Brekk for you? I assure you I will not hand it to him again." It had destroyed him the first time. Teal had not realized that this was what his actions meant. He had won the crown by opposing Brekk. It was his, not his father's. He knew now why he had never told his father he had won it

Beth-enea ago back at Dianter. Something had told him not to. Now he was kicking the fallen.

Teal dared to look up at the noble face. Black eyes had sunk, cheeks were dark hollows beneath high, prominent bones. It was intolerable for him to be beneath his son. Teal could not give up the crown without giving it to Brekk. He could not keep it without being his father's superior. He saw one way out. He neither gave it up nor kept it. Maybe Teal would still officially be king, but if he was not in the country and not making decisions, the person he left behind to make the decisions would be, in effect, the ruler of the Royalist nation, until, if ever, the king returned. He laid the crown at Kaela's feet and left Skye without a word or a backward look.

Day 98   6 Beth-enea
Star Year 532   Third Epoch

Homesickness became a chronic ill, like the Reill never leaving. He called no place home, living in the sea like a fish, occasionally coming to land on deserted Northern islands on a warm day to dry out in the sun. He saw no people. He dreamed of Akelan and his father, Wings, his wife, and the Nomad girl long ago. Mad with loneliness, he came to a Caucan shore once and met a young Caucan man who wanted to take him to bed. All he wanted was to be held and feel the after closeness. Instead, the man laughed. Soul searing, Teal would never forget it. He wanted to run. Run away from this, from memories, from everything. He ran, leaving his pride far behind for the scavenger beasts, and headed for the most distant place he could call to mind. He looked up at the stars.

"You want to enter the Vakellan Space Academy," the man said with a halting voice. He ran his fingers through sparse, graying hair, betraying nervousness.

"Yes, I want to go to Canda," Teal said, eyes aimed squarely at him.

He stuttered, and Teal persisted. The man was sweating. It *was* hot on the equator, but the room was air-conditioned. He did not know what exactly he was to do with this Royalist who rose out of the harbor, strode into the main building, and informed them he wanted to be in the Vakellan Space Fleet. He avoided staring at the young man, standing naked as he was born. He looked up and out the skylight. "I . . . think Hollingsworth White should be the one to talk to you. Do you know who he is?"

"Yes, Vensar's brother. He's fleet admiral. That will be fine," said Teal.

The man was startled. He had called Leader White by her familiar name. Was he sure the top was high enough . . . ?

Teal was expecting another graying Northern man, but Hollingsworth White was young; his given age was thirty-four. He looked just like his sister Vensar, but his hair was its natural color, unlike Vensar's. It was brown. His features were almost boring in perfection and proportion, but his expressions were uniquely his own. He lifted one dark eyebrow at Teal's entrance, then the other followed it up into his forelock. "Teal Ray?"

"Yes."

Hollingsworth White was not afraid to look at him. "I'm Fleet Admiral White. Sit down."

Teal obeyed without thinking. It was that kind of command, that kind of commander. He did not think to hesitate.

Admiral White took a shoed foot off his desk. "You want to enter the fleet." He rested his chin on large, folded hands, head bowed, and he looked at Teal through the tops of his eyes.

Teal folded his legs under him on the chair, curled up on it like a wild creature. "Yes."

Admiral White did not merely accept him, he dared him. Teal met his challenge. He was in love again.

"Doublefine, eh?" White said in Alpha Centaurian dialect, one Teal would know well.

And so the Vakellan Space Fleet acquired its Royalist member.

Teal was tested and drilled and found out how much he did and didn't know.

"Holly, he's not a dumb animal. He learns fast. He doesn't miss a thing. He watches. He scares the hell out of me," the woman who administered the test said.

"Not an animal as the Caucans would have us believe," Holly said, reviewing the results. "My sister said as much."

"I didn't say he wasn't an animal; I said he wasn't a dumb one. There's something . . . *very* animal about him."

"He didn't hurt you?" Holly looked up from the results.

"No, no . . . it's just the way he *is*. He washes his hands as an animal does its paws. Naked and shameless as one too."

Holly chuckled. "He's a good-looking kid," he said, and she blushed. "How old do you suppose he is?"

"I don't know."

"A child?" Holly mused. "He looks like one in ways, but he's not. He doesn't carry himself like one. I don't know either," he said and looked back at the results. *He does seem very bright. Maybe it's true they are a higher form than Northerners. What would Pauli say about that? . . . I wonder why he came. . . . Did you ever see eyes like that? . . . Now, son, when you're commanding a crew, remember . . .* He'd already claimed Teal as one of his kids, and begun planning his future like an overambitious father. *Doublefine, eh? Never remind them you're best—just be it.*

Teal was taught Earth languages and the Earth concept of time. Earth seconds, minutes, hours, days, weeks, months, and years. "We keep Earth time on this base," Holly explained. "It's what this part of the galaxy uses."

They sat in Hollingsworth White's office, a large room that was three-quarters window, overlooking the surrounding desert, the harbor, and the landing pads. The atmosphere was informal, thick carpet underfoot, and green growing things every place one could be set.

"Where is Earth?" said Teal.

Holly frowned, and Teal was concerned that he had said something wrong. "Here, come along," Holly rose and motioned for Teal to follow. He almost touched his shoulder, but did not know if the Royalist would consent to being touched. Teal never touched anyone, and Holly took his decision from that.

Teal was afraid he was being taken to someone else for an explanation. He wanted to hear it from Holly.

Teal followed him out onto the observation deck with silent grace. For one unaccustomed to shoes, he adapted easily. Flexibility would naturally be a trait of a people who had been able to return to the water when faced with a scarcity of land. He looked odd but attractive in shirt, pants, and jacket. Clothes, especially in hot weather, were foreign and totally unfathomable, but he endured it. He would not cut his hair short as the Vakellan men did, though. His was relatively short in front, tapering down his back, and a few long feather wisps almost reached his waist. Holly wondered what, if anything, it signified. With no others to compare, it was impossible to tell what traits were Royalist and what was Teal. Holly wanted to ask him many things, but he was answering questions now.

It was night, and the stars were out. Holly pointed to a bright star and explained that it was actually the four suns of the Procyon system, which lay between their own and Earth's. "On the other side of Proycon is Sol. Sol is a sun like the Central Sun. Earth, a planet like Arana, orbits it. It is twenty-five light-years away. Procyon is fourteen—meaning it takes light fourteen years, Earth years, to get from Procyon to here. You are seeing Procyon as it was fourteen years ago. Do you understand?"

Teal paused, his forehead slightly disturbed by wrinkles of thought, then smoothed. "Yes," he said.

Holly believed he actually grasped the hugeness of it. The concept of such distance was only an abstraction to Holly.

"The Earthmen travel faster than light. It was for a long time thought impossible—as was flying itself, for that matter."

"Can the Vakellans travel that fast?" Teal broke in.

Holly smiled. "No. Earth is one of the few worlds that can—they and their colonies—which is what makes them so important. Another world that has attained faster-than-light travel is Uelso. I can't show you its star either, but its general direction is that way." He pointed to the ground. "On the other side of this planet."

"We are between them."

"Yes. And they are at war." He did not have to explain the implications. The child caught on quickly. "Gereny is another superlight world, and they are the Third Power of the known galaxy. But they are too distant and too isolationist to concern us. Earth and Uelso aren't far at superlight speeds, and they are *not* isolationists. We're much closer to Earth than to Uelso. Uelso would like to conquer us and rob us of our worlds—and attack Earth, using us as a base. Earth would be our ally, but is a dangerous friend. Many of Earth's sublight protectorates have been swallowed up by their benefactor. They tried to move in on us not long ago. They built an installation on Canda without even asking our permission.

But they forgot that our primitive bombs destroy as well as modern ones. Now they're back to the diplomatic approach. They have some sense of honor or decency that prevents an outright attack and conquest of a helpless sublight world. It's not their outward force but their corruption that is to be feared. So we have refused their petitions of friendship. However, they protect us. It's in their own best interest that we not fall to Uelso. We are too weak to defend ourselves yet, but we are learning. We learn from Earth. We monitor them more skillfully than they can know. That is why you must learn of Earth. Vakellan has adopted much of Earth's culture. My name is an Earth name, an English one. The Earthlings are people as we are—we Northerners. My people are different from yours, more than physically. We have a different psyche. We came from an aggressive, adventurous stock. We are a people composed of individuals. Yours are not. You have a common goal, common duty. You've never felt the need to push outward. You have stayed in one place countless thousands of years and evolved. Yet *you* ventured out. Why?"

I am flawed, Teal thought but did not speak. Holly did not press it and continued. "You know my people are not native to Arana." He guessed that Royalists would know that.

"Yes. Royalists are," said Teal.

"Do you ever wonder where we came from?"

"The Dianter tablets said from the sky. Is it from the stars then?"

Holly was intrigued. Royalist history went back that far? How far was that far he could not guess. "Yes. According to theory, we are of the same stock as Earthmen. The Uelsons are another species entirely. Earth has some allies that aren't human or humanoid at all." He stopped and tried another question. "What are the Dianter tablets?"

"Our ancient laws. They are hundreds of thousands of Star Years old. They are engraved on the Dianter tablets. They were. The Caucans bombed them, and they aren't anymore."

"You mean you had a recorded history of our coming?"

"Yes," said Teal.

Holly felt the historical loss, senseless destruction, and the hatred the Royalists must bear the Caucans.

Ray's eyes were fastened on the expanse above him. Holly noted his customary faraway gaze. "Why do you want to go to Canda?"

His gaze was constant. "It was as distant as I knew. I would like to go farther now."

"You're farther from your country now than any Royalist save the Trieath ever was."

Teal drew inward at the mention of the Trieath. He made no reply. It occurred to Holly that it was because he had not asked a question. He leaned on the rail. A cold breeze of desert night chilled him.

Teal's gaze shifted to another point in the sky. He suddenly appeared very young, whether an effect of his smooth face or because he actually was a child.

"How old are you?" Holly asked.

"I was born at the dawn of the twenty-second Beth-enea of the Star Year five hundred and thirty-one," Teal answered.

"Do you know what that is in Earth time?"

"No."

Holly worked it out. Twenty years. "Is that young or old for your people?"

"I am young." He would still be a child had he not married.

"You will have to learn to think in Earth time," Holly cautioned. "Doublefine, eh? Are you picking up the Earth languages?" Teal answered in Chinese.

He learned rapidly. So rapidly that Holly told his teacher, "Well, give him Uelson and see if he can still think straight." *Why am I doing this to him?* The child was obviously brilliant; why was he trying to trip him up? He had not said a word of praise to him regarding his achievements. He did not seem to need it. Teal was defiant. If he was expected to fail, he was certain to succeed. He was soon ready to enter the academy, and he took it by storm—as directed by Holly. It had been an off-handed well-wishing that Teal took as command. He excelled. The other cadets were afraid of him, although they admired him, and a few hated him.

Teal got himself a rival, a Caucan named Pauli Calvin, the absolute antithesis of Teal Ray. He was a slow-moving intellectual genius. He was sixteen years old, the youngest person in the academy. Pauli was physically clumsy and unattractive, even ugly, with a face marred by blotches kindly called freckles and pocked by adolescent acne. He was careless of his appearance, and his personality inspired little affection. He had red, butch-cut hair and pale green eyes, narrow shoulders, and a pudgy, pubescent form. His genius earned him special notice from Hollingsworth White, who spent a considerable amount of personal time with him and had him listen in on Earth radio signals. Teal now knew jealousy as a distinct, identifiable feeling, and set out to outshine and to destroy this other object of special interest. Physically and emotionally oriented Ray clashed with the human computer, and the two weren't rivals but mortal enemies.

Teal was more popular with fellow cadets, growing aware of his ability, like Akelan's, to draw people to him. Teal liked most of his fellow cadets, but never dared express it. And he could never let Holly know what he felt toward him.

White did not know what to make of Teal and consulted his sister Vensar, who offered information on the Royalists. But it gave no insight about Teal. "The Caucans think they are uncivilized because they have no leaders except one whom they call king. They have no courts, no police. They don't have them because they don't need them. Their king is the man to consult in a dispute—one man for an entire nation. But their natural law is harsh. The Royalist's is a survival of the strongest culture. Brutally so." It could explain his striving to be best—but not his single-minded obsession, or his frightening intensity. White never had what he could call a light conversation with Teal, even when he thought one was starting.

"Holly is a girl's name," Ray observed.

"Yes, my first group of cadets took to calling me that."

"Mine's a girl's name."

"Get ribbed for it? I do."

"I tried to kill someone who did." That being Thoma.

Holly worried about the boy and his unnatural seriousness, unaware that Teal was blindly jealous, sensitive, in love with him, and trying his best to please him. Holly was someone to worship and someone to be proud of him. He wanted desperately for Holly to be proud of him. Someone to be a son to. An only son.

VI.

"Ours is the Diakyon Solar System to the Earthlings. What we call the Central Sun, they call Diakyon A; and our Night Sun is Diakyon B or the Pup Star," Holly explained to Teal. He often spent time with a few special people. He unashamedly kept favorites, and Teal hated all the others. Pauli was one. Another was an island nymph called Natina. All his favorites were young and bright and were referred to, in the fleet, as Holly's children, a name Teal gloried in. Teal was the newest of them all, and it hurt to hear the others talking to him as old acquaintances discussing important affairs with him. Teal had never had brothers and sisters, and he was unable to compete, still learning the basics that the others already knew—such as the composition of his own solar system.

"The Earthmen call Arana, technically, Diakyon A I. Canda is Diakyon A II; Gola is III; and Malc is IV. That's technically. They use our names for convenience. A word on our names: Canda, Arana, and Gola, as you probably know, are Royalist names."

Teal nodded, a Vakellan (and Earth) motion of assent. His hands were clasped between his knees, and he listened attentively to whatever Holly said. Of course he knew the names were Royalist; Arana was Water Sister, Canda was Land Sister, and Gola was Distant One.

"Malc is a Vakellan name. Your people didn't have a name for it because Malc is too far out to be seen with the unaided eye. I imagine the reason the Royalist names stuck for the other three is that you named them first.

"Our solar system is unique in that it has two planets capable of supporting human life, Arana and Canda; however, we are only indigenous to Arana. There are no native Candians.

"Canda is a planet where there should not be one according to a phenomenon the Earthmen discovered, which

67

they call the Titius-Bode relation. At first, they dismissed it as just an interesting occurrence in their own solar system. Then they found out that it was not unique to their system, but rather, it was a rule for the distribution of satellites around a central body, dependent on the central mass. In Earth's solar system, the relation fell apart when applied to the outer satellites but only because their central sun lacked sufficient mass to influence those more distant bodies. Give me something to write on."

Teal found some paper and gave it to Holly, who wrote:

$R = A + B \cdot 2^n$ where R = distance from central mass (in astronomical units), and A = distance of first planet (in astronomical units), and B = distance of the second planet minus the distance of the first planet (in a.u.), and $n = -\infty, 0, 1, 2, \ldots$

"Given Sol, or their planet Jupiter, as the central mass, the relation gives a rough estimate of where the satellites will be. Our sun is more massive, and their relation gives a much more accurate prediction, though still imperfect."

He wrote:

$R = A + B \cdot 2^n$ $A = 1.1$ a.u. $B = 3.7$ a.u.

Planet number	n	name	R	actual mean distance
1	$-\infty$	Arana	1.1 a.u.	1.1 a.u.
2	0	Gola	4.8 a.u.	4.8 a.u.
3	1	Malc	8.5 a.u.	8.49 a.u.
4	2	Night Sun	15.9 a.u.	15.85 a.u.

"You forgot Canda," Teal said, seeing Gola called planet 2.

"I didn't forget Canda; the relation did," Holly said. "It simply should not be there. It should not have been formed where it is, one and a half astronomical units from the Central Sun. And the theory is that it was not. When the solar system was formed, Canda was not formed there in its present orbit. It could not have been. The theory continues that it was once a moon of another planet, or that it was a captured world from outside the solar system, or that it was once part of a double planet with Arana. The clue for the latter idea is the Royalist names, Arana and Canda—Water

Sister and Land Sister. Do you have any idea why your people called them Water Sister and Land Sister?"

"The Dianter tablets call them that," Teal said. "They tell of Land Sister being snatched away from Water Sister, and of a time when Canda glowed huge in the sky."

Holly was elated. He slapped his hand on the white desk. "That all but proves it! Arana and Canda were once a double planet."

Teal was pleased to see him in that state. "I remember seeing Canda in the sky, big as the sun," he said.

"You remember?" Holly questioned.

"My race—I see what my ancestors saw."

Holly couldn't credit this entirely. He came from a splintered, individualistic people who could not understand group memory. He passed it over as something Teal had been taught to remember. "Where are these tablets?"

"I told you the Caucans bombed them," Teal said. "There are countless copies everywhere, but the original is gone. The Nomads celebrate the Festival of the Sisters in the spring and live the record."

Holly was still excited. "I have to tell the Science Academy," he said. "Can you remember exactly what the tablets said?"

"I know it by heart. Everyone does," Teal said.

Holly had him write it down and translate it. Teal basked in the attention and sensed he had given something of value to White. He was soon upset when Holly hit the intercom and called, of all people, Pauli. "I have to talk to you later," he told Teal's archrival.

Teal contained hurt fury and sat in the chair by the white desk, plotting to kill Pauli Calvin. He wanted to storm out of the room but could not be sure Holly would call him back. If he should not, Teal felt he could not live. He did not dare find out.

Holly continued talking about the double star system, Teal listening, transfixed by his voice.

"Earth is a very different place. None of us has ever been there, but it's easy enough to speculate from what we've heard and what we know. Their world is less massive than ours is, as is their central sun. One of us going there would seem somewhat stronger; we would weigh less and could lift more massive objects. The biggest difference, of course, is the seasons. They have one sun, and their orbit's eccentricity is consequently less than Arana's, which means they have no

Hot Season and Cold Season. They have the four seasons
only. Their time unit, the year, is thus very convenient, being
a cycle of seasons. For us, it is better to think in terms of the
Beth-enea—opposition of the Night Sun to opposition; aphelion to aphelion. For longer periods of time, we have the Star
Year, an orbit of the Night Sun around the Central Sun,
roughly equal to forty point six Earth years, or thirty-two and
a half Beth-enea. The Earthlings' longer time units are arbi-
trary divisions of ten years being a decade, or one hundred
years being a century, or a millennium being a thousand
years. Most of their measurements are in divisions of ten. But
for shorter time units, they have months, which were originally based on a lunar cycle, and weeks, which are units of
seven days stemming originally, I believe, from ancient religious beliefs. Earthlings, especially women, are influenced
by the lunar cycle. Earthlings' lives are dominated by the
cycle of night and day—which is slightly shorter than ours.
They have what is called the circadian rhythm corresponding
activity to night and day. We have no such thing—two suns
making for little periodic regularity."

"My people have a cycle with the Star Year," said Teal.

"That's forty years; how does that work?"

"I don't know. I haven't lived that long." He would learn
terribly when the time came.

"That's very interesting. I wonder if Pauli knows anything
about that." He perceived Teal's reaction to the name this
time. *He hates him because he's a Caucan,* he guessed.

When Teal was dismissed, he missed the usual pat on the
back or squeeze of the shoulder that Holly's other children
received as a matter of course, and he was stung and bewildered. He tried not to dwell on it—it was a small thing, he
told himself. Brooding over rejection availed nothing—that
only brought Red Madness to the surface.

Day 15   9 Beth-enea
Star Year 532   Third Epoch

Teal was twenty-five years old and a captain in the Vakellan Fleet. He had traveled to Canda in a spaceship. There

was not much there, and he decided that it wasn't what he wanted after all. But he liked the ship. He liked to fly.

Although he had advanced swiftly, he was not proud. Holly's other children had done brilliant things. Natina had developed the Vakellan "sky-snooping" system. She had been responsible for giving Arana a communications system so sophisticated that even Earth did not have one to compare with it. And Earth didn't know it. Earth's fastest method of communication was via messenger ship. Light radio was rendered useless over distances of light-years. Arana could transmit, and, more important, receive at ultimate velocity—instantaneously. Natina had not developed it herself; she was not a scientist. She was a telepath who could receive at ultimate velocity, and she had stolen the idea from the hub of the galaxy. She spoke of gaps between moments and an absence of space. Teal, though very good at abstracts, could not accept this. Pauli chastised him, "Just because you can't bite it doesn't mean it's not real." Teal had once proved Pauli's arm was real.

Natina was Teal's greatest rival for attention, though he did not bear her the wrath he held for Pauli Calvin, who was another of Holly's gifted ones, working at some very secret project for him. Natina was Holly's constant companion, or so it seemed to ever-jealous Teal Ray. There was no way to compete with her and her sight. She would tell what someone on Earth was doing at that moment that would be significant to Arana later. Her predictions were short-range, extending a few years. Farther than that, she was building assumptions on assumptions, and her certainty declined at a geometric rate. But within the years she was accurate, she was infallible at predicting future events based on what she saw of the present. At least she'd never made an error yet. This made her irreplaceable to Holly, and Teal could never hope to give him what Natina did.

Teal could no longer stand the strain of feeling alone and sought solace where he could find it. He got himself into severe trouble for making love to a shipmate. At home it was acceptable; here, the taboo was strong enough to get the girl discharged from the fleet. Teal was retained, either in consideration of his origin or through some intervention by Holly. Teal was terrified to find out. He was dragged before a stern-faced board of inquiry. He was too shocked to protest this ill-treatment because of being nice to someone. It made no sense to him. But if Holly considered his action wrong, it was wrong. Teal tried to answer the board's questions without breaking down in tears . . . and daring not look at Holly White. He did not have to see his face to see disapproval, disappointment, hurt, and shame in his eyes. He was dismissed and walked out the door.

Blinded by tears, he guessed at the corridor. And crashed into the wall, sinking to the floor. Holly came out and gathered the crumpled, sobbing wreck off the floor into his arms. Teal clung to him and cried for he didn't know how long, like a five-year-old pulled out of the water by the Trieath. When he calmed he had matched Holly's breath rate and heart beat—like everything else, he could not control it. Something within him made it happen, and Teal was just beginning to understand what made him do the things he could not help. It was the Bay Royalist fighting for his life. A Bay needed his father, and all the things he did were the Bay crying out for his father. His breakdown in the hall was meant to bring his father to his aid—and it had worked on his substitute father, Holly, who reacted with compassion to his misfired instincts.

Holly took him to his room and talked with him a long time. When he spoke sternly, the tears started afresh. Holly thought it was an act, then reconsidered. The child was in genuine torment.

Child. Holly knew he was no longer a child, but that was how he felt toward Teal. And in many ways Teal was still a child.

"Teal, I want you to know why I was so angry with you."

He blinked huge eyes that were ready to cry again.

"When you were brought in, I was just telling the two board members with me why I thought you would be the best person to take part in a project we have been working on. . . . I still want you for that position."

Wide eyes grew wider and a timid voice asked, "What is it?"

"First I want a promise of obedience. We have rules here, believe it or not. Doublefine, eh?"

Teal's gaze hit the floor, and Holly regretted his harshness. It was unnecessary. Teal nodded with downcast eyes. What was meant for his father was taking effect on Holly, who felt a spell had been cast on him by the Bay Royalist's son.

"I'll show you what it is," Holly said. "There's a car outside to take us there. It's a project all my kids have been working on, and there's a place for you."

It was a long drive through the desert. Teal wondered why they didn't take a plane, but soon discovered the secrecy surrounding the project. It was so secret that Teal had never been aware that it was a secret. Before it had been "just a project."

It was underground and it was a ship. A superlight ship.

"She's better than anything the Earthmen have, or the Uelsons. She's smaller, faster, more agile. We stole the principles from all over the galaxy. She's a warship, and we have to use her soon. Natina says the Uelsons are preparing for all-out war."

Teal stared at the ship while Holly continued. "The Uelson target is Earth, but Earth's fate is ours. Earth will be surprised. Other allies will come to aid her, but Natina says that Earth will fall in the first hour of battle unless aided at that weakest time. We have to give Earth that time."

Teal scowled. "Can't the Earthmen be warned?"

"Natina says they won't listen. We'll try, but I know as I know Natina that they won't listen."

"One ship against the Uelson fleet?" Teal said.

"For a short time. We can do it. They have nothing like this. On our own, it would have taken at least a hundred years to develop this, probably more. Notice she's not a cylinder. She has artificial gravity, not centrifugal force. None of the three so-called Powers, Earth, Uelso, or Gereny, have this yet. She carries a crew of only ten. Her name's *Tesah* and she needs a captain."

Teal's head snapped toward Holly.

"Are you going to take a look, captain?"

Teal hesitated and then climbed down from the deck to the *Tesah*. Holly followed. "She can be launched with a standard booster, just like our sublight ships. Come to the lab, I can have Pauli explain it—"

Teal halted. "I'd rather not," he said. "I mean, I'd rather hear it from you." Then a thought daggered through him. "*He's* not on the crew, is he?"

Holly smiled. "No. He was one of the designers." Holly showed him the ship, the weapons, the controls, and the solo pods, which were ten person-sized capsules. They were lifeboats. "God knows why you need them. If you have to evacuate this ship, you're dead. All these pods have is two hours' worth of life support, no radio but auto-distress, no monitor. Natina insisted *Tesah* be equipped with them—nothing she *saw*, just a feeling. I don't understand Natina's power, but if she says her feelings are to be reckoned with, I'll trust her word. She's never before predicted the specific events surrounding one ship in battle. Maybe we'd be tempting fate not to have them."

Holly, Teal noticed, had tremendous faith in all his children.

"You'll have intensive training and test flights. You've experienced what can happen at close to light speed, the time dilation and difference of perception, but superlight is a whole new universe, with new laws of physics. According to sublight physics, you can't even reach light speed. On paper it's impossible. But you don't fly ships on paper. In actuality, of course, it's not impossible; the Earthlings do it, the Uelsons do, the Gerens do, and light does.

"Superlight is not hyperlight. Hyperlight (which *is* possible according to regular physics) refers to the combined velocities of two objects moving away from each other faster than light. For example, when two rockets take off in opposite directions, each traveling at seventy-five percent of the speed of light, an observer will see them separating at one and a half times the speed of light, but neither rocket actually passes the light barrier.

"Superlight, on the other hand, is the actual crossing of the light barrier. Traveling at this speed is very . . . *lonely*, because you are totally isolated; you can't be perceived by a sublight observer, and you can't just slow down again by cutting your engines, because the energy required to move your ship approaches infinite near light speed, whether *accelerating to or decelerating to*. Once past the barrier, it takes more energy to *slow down* than to speed up. The faster you go, the less energy it takes till you reach cruising velocity, two and a half times light speed, which requires zero energy, just as zero velocity does. Then, faster than cruising velocity, the trend reverses again, and it requires more energy the more you accelerate, on up to ultimate velocity, which is instantaneous travel.

"The danger is that once your ship is crippled at superlight and you can't get the energy to recross the barrier, it's over. You go on forever at cruising velocity, undetectable, out of touch with all sublight parties . . . except us sitting here on Arana with Natina seeing, unable to help. So you take care."

"Then in battle, how do they recover crippled ships if they can't decelerate?" Teal asked.

"Use your head," Holly said.

"Did I say something stupid?"

"You're not thinking."

Teal thought. "I don't know. What did I miss?"

"Battles must be at sublight."

"Because weapons go at sublight," Teal remembered, feeling foolish. "You'd run into your own weapon."

Holly nodded.

"Oh, I am stupid."

"No, you've just never flown a battleship. I have to get you thinking in warship terms."

Teal met his crew, positions numbered One through Ten, all of them Holly's children. They were from different countries, as cosmopolitan as the Vakellan Fleet. Teal was Ten. Natina was Seven. She represented her tiny Northern island/tribe/nation. She was a Water Nun. Her powers of perception, which reached across the galaxy, she attributed to "the Sea." "The Sea gives me the Sight. If one sees enough of the present, the future is no mystery." Slender, liquid-eyed, childlike to behold, she was the oldest. Her Sight had a blind spot or two, as Teal discovered. "You can't see that which is closest to you." Which meant, just as Teal couldn't see the bridge of his nose, her vision blurred around the one she loved—or was infatuated with, for the feeling was not returned. What was closest to Natina was the man who held position Eight. His name was Vanguard. He'd tried to lay Teal down behind the computer bank, but Teal was cold and aloof—not out of consideration for Natina, not because he didn't want to. He wanted to respond to anyone. He was afraid. He thought Vanguard loved him but Natina whispered to him, "When there is a storm at Sea, you cannot see beyond your own bow."

Teal frowned and sifted her metaphor. "He doesn't love me?"

"No," she said.

"Then why—" He broke off from embarrassment and because Natina knew what he meant.

"I don't know. I will never understand that either." She looked sad.

Teal wished Natina could talk as well as she saw. Like Nomads, her explanations often clouded rather than clarified. As to how she saw what she saw, she simply said, "The Sea told me." Holly was the one who really told Teal. "What she means is that all life—as we know it—is connected by a common bond, that being water. She plugs herself into the universal whole—all water—the Sea—what you will—and she *sees*." Then, by worshiping the Sea, was the Water Nun revering all life?

They drilled. Passing the light barrier never became easy. It was a totally disorienting experience. It always came sooner than expected, like blacking out for a split second, a few frames missing from a movie film; suddenly, one was *there*, faster than light.

Leadership came easily. Teal had never thought it would. His ability surprised him. Teal had the power to lead people. He spoke and they listened. He ordered; they obeyed. He moved; they watched. He could inspire love, respect, or fear; there was no neutral reaction. He kept his distance from his crew—especially from Vanguard—appearing lofty and reserved to cover sensitivity. Vanguard was the only one not fooled. He was intrigued by Teal and loved to play games.

There was an alert sooner than expected. Vanguard reported Uelsons coming to Arana.

"This is not the time," Natina said to Holly. "This is not *Tesah*'s time. You can handle this, Holly."

Holly did. The division of three Uelson warships that swung into orbit was met by sublight missiles, destroying the flagship, which had disdainfully not bothered to dodge the primitive weapons. Until it happened, they would not believe a sublight missile could harm a Uelson warship.

The Uelsons protested loudly over light radio, "We are on a peaceful mission."

"With armed peaceful weapons on peaceful warships," Holly shot back, his children ringing the radio to listen.

"We use these ships for all purposes," the oily voice returned.

"Well, we're peaceful too—you just didn't get out of the way of our gun salute," Holly said. Vanguard had to leave before his snickering was picked up. Teal was petrified— they'd destroyed a Uelson warship. What was to prevent them from opening fire? Natina was calm. She appeared to be listening to a voice only she could hear.

Earth ships appeared, and the other two Uelson ships slunk off, tails between their legs, back to Castor Base.

An Earthman, Admiral James McCreedy, radioed Arana, "Is all secure? Do you require assistance?"

"Get those goddam war machines out of our space!" Holly barked in English.

"We offer protection—" McCreedy began.

"Then protect us! Where the hell were you when we were shooting down superlight warships? You vultures are here for what's left!" he hollered into the radio. Natina was giggling silently.

Holly ordered a sublight missile fired at the Earth ship, not intended for destruction, but as a sign of hostility. The Earth ship, not as fatally proud as the Uelson flagship, avoided the missile with ease and went home.

Holly turned to Teal. "They saved us, you know," he said. Teal noticed he was shaking slightly. "But I have to treat them like that. It's sad they cannot be trusted. We can't even tell them we're their ally."

Natina verified his statement, then began to predict, "We will have two more Earth visitors soon. We mustn't turn them away. They will come in a broken ship. They are hardly more than children. We cannot let them die. One saved us once, and the other will save us come Armageddon. He must live. His name is Orestes."

Teal heard this with skepticism, but the two Earthlings did come, though Teal never saw them. Few people did. The two visitors were quickly sent back to Earth in an Earth ship so they might see as little of Arana as possible. They were the only aliens ever to land on Arana. And one of them was called Orestes.

This made Teal see Natina in a new light. He approached her with trepidation, fearful of the knowledge in her gentle, luminous eyes.

"What do you see in my future?" Teal dared ask.

"I can't see you at all," Natina said.

Teal's anxiety divided and doubled, and he stared numbly. "Nothing?"

"You won't let me. I can't see where you're going because I can't see where you've been. I don't even know where you *are*. I try to look and it's like touching a flame, and I have to look away. I don't know. All I see is a blank. A big, red blank."

She saw. She didn't recognize it, but she saw red and pain. What terrified Teal was that it was *all* she saw.

The time came at last. Natina announced, "The Uelsons are mobilized. Here it comes. It will be called Armageddon I."

Holly bid them each a hasty goodbye/good luck.

"Afraid, Natina? It's far from the Sea." He held her hands.

"I'm not afraid to fly." She smiled. "The Sea has assured me I will die in the Sea."

Holly kissed her.

Teal was slinking aboard, quietly. Holly grabbed him. "Don't run without looking back," he said. He decided that whatever his aversion to personal contact, no child of his was getting away without a hug. He embraced him, and was surprised by Teal's far from cold, though startled, reaction.

The child adores me. He could not comprehend how he could not have noticed before. Teal's infatuation—perhaps he deserved a more serious word—love?—explained why he had suffered so much when he had thought he had lost Holly's esteem. There would be time enough to straighten out misunderstandings when he returned.

"I saw a rosette, a circle, a fish, a cross . . . but I have no god to whose worship those belong," Teal said.

"My god go with you," Holly said.

The gods abandoned me quite some time ago.

"Goodbye, son. And don't come back while the Uelsons are still a threat." He smiled and let him go to the ship. He never dreamed Teal would actually obey that order.

PART TWO:
Earth

I.

October 1, 2182 A.D.
(Day 200 10 Beth-enea
Star Year 532)

It was called Armageddon I. Armageddon meaning it was a great war; I meaning both sides would live to fight again.

Earth was surprised. Only a skeleton fleet was available to defend the home planet. The bulk of the defense fleet was speeding out toward the Sagittarian arm of the galaxy, where they thought the Uelsons were preparing to attack. Arana tried to warn them, but the message was taken as a Uelson trap. When the truth was learned, a messenger ship was sent after the fleet. Left to her own resources, Earth had no chance of surviving for the time it would take to overtake her defense force. But Earth was not alone, and the *Tesah* intercepted the Uelson war fleet before Earth knew it was there. *Tesah* gave Earth time to get a skeleton fleet into space.

Teal had been warned the ships were mammoth. They were also used to hitting mammoth targets, not small ships the size of *Tesah*. The little ship dodged and fired, weaving among the enemy ships.

The Uelsons attempted radio contact.

"They want to know who we are, and why we're attacking without provocation," Vanguard said. "Should I answer?"

"No response," Teal ordered. "They mustn't get any clue about where we're from."

A red glow appeared around a Uelson ship, a burn in the energy field.

Tesah's advantage was that she fought a visual battle—that she *could* fight a visual battle. The big ships' instrument tracking was efficient only against other big ships. They had no weapon or defense against a small ship which had the

81

power of one fifty times her size. They also could not hazard a shot, for the ship weaved among their own, and they feared destroying one another. "Why should that stop a Uelson?" the crewman at the monitor said. Later it didn't, as *Tesah*'s destruction became imperative whatever the cost.

A Uelson ship lost control, narrowly avoided collision with a comrade ship, and sped out of control in the general direction of Earth. Before it could be caught in the planet's gravitational pull, a Uelson scavenger ship sank its teeth into it and towed it back. Scavenger ships were slow, massive, unarmed garbage ships that salvaged their own debris for reuse, and to keep it out of enemy hands. Uelsons were noted for leaving nothing behind.

Teal was aware that scavengers went to Uelson Castor Base—formerly Earth Base Sixus, the site of a massacre roughly ten years before. Twenty-four thousand Earthlings on the Sixus settlement were slaughtered, the Earth base razed, and a Uelson base erected. It was now the Uelsons' primary attack base, the closest one to Earth. If the Uelsons won this encounter, what had happened on Sixus would happen on Arana and Canda—and Earth, but that was secondary to Teal.

"Teal, another fleet just sublighted and is moving in. I don't know whose—"

"The Lokins," said Natina. "An Earth ally. There should be another fleet coming about now."

The monitor looked. "Yes . . . what the hell are those?"

"Kalixjhans."

The Kalixjhan ships looked odd because they were not of human design. The Kalixjhans were fish. They were not friends of Earth but aided her for the same reason Earth aided Arana—self-defense against the Uelsons, to whom Kalixjhan flesh was a delicacy.

"Everyone's fighting for Earth but Earthmen," said the monitor.

The Kalixjhan fleet moved like a school of fish, tightly knit in close formation with never an accident.

Teal looked to the serene Natina. She wasn't surprised at all by the appearance of the two fleets. He felt a moment's resentment. Why hadn't she told him? She would have told Holly, of course, but Teal didn't seem to be worth telling. Instead of a captain in command, Teal was feeling very much like a puppet. So very much like a puppet.

Suddenly the Earth ships and the Lokins became . . .

clumsy. Their shots went wide, they misjudged distances and speeds of vessels.

"What happened to them?" Teal demanded.

"I'm picking up some kind of interference," the monitor said. "It's from the Uelsons. It's jamming the tracking instruments. It's totally a visual battle now."

"But the Earthlings can't fight visually," Teal breathed.

"Neither can the Uelsons." Natina smiled, knowing a secret.

Teal shot her a hate look and thought hate at her.

An Earth ship jumped. The monitor screen showed it first there, then, in the next instant, five ships' lengths from there. It was as if it had superlighted for a few meters' distance. A shot was fired at it from a Uelson ship—and went through it. The specter ship glided on untouched, as insubstantial as space.

"An illusion," the monitor said. "The Earthmen were ready for the Uelsons' jamming signal then."

"One was," said Natina, again secretive. "This visual battle will end as soon as the Uelsons realize they have been outwitted."

"By whom?" Teal asked her on impulse. She smiled slyly but did not explain.

Earth ships disappeared and reappeared elsewhere—their images did. Shots came seemingly out of nowhere, the only clue to the real location of the Earth ships. Now the Uelsons were the blind ones.

"It's light refraction," Natina told Teal, who was ready to kill her for her silence. "What you're seeing is the light reflected off the ship, but refracted to where the ship is not. This is Orestes' doing. One of the two Earth visitors I told you of."

"If we can't see where the ship really is, how do I know I'm not on collision course with one?" Teal spat at her.

"Because it has stopped now. They're back to using tracking instruments, and the trick won't work. It can delude eyes but not sensors that don't need light to see."

"Interference gone," the monitor reported as the jamming signal was turned off. The battle resumed as before, and the refraction had stopped with the interference. "They didn't get much use out of that secret weapon."

"Wouldn't it be sad if someone decommissioned ours so easily," someone said.

Natina's face went pale. "Someone has. Oh dear God,

someone has." She attacked the controls and piloted the *Tesah* out of battle.

"Natina!"

Her gentle face went hard, and she took command. "Everyone into solo pods—she's going to go—"

Teal seized her. She shouted over him, "There's no time! Too late! Why did I not see?"

Teal looked at his stunned crew awaiting his order. He was suddenly past caring whether they listened to his word over Natina's. "Go."

The eight crew members scrambled into the solo pods, and Natina and Ray followed. She took his arm. "Revenge us. You're the only one who will be able to. It was Vanguard. The Sea has tricked me." She sealed herself into the metal tube. Teal climbed into the last pod, and all ten shot out of the ship. There was no light, no sound but his own breathing in the pod. It was dark and close, like a womb, but all was hard and fearful. He could not see the scavenger ship approach him, or see *Tesah* explode behind him.

Darkness.

Strange room. Metal walls. They called this place Otranadoe.

Otranadoe:

No one stays sane for long. . . .

No one comes out alive. . . .

No one can avoid giving them what they want. . . .

"Teal Ray," a Uelson voice intoned.

They had taken his Earth-style dog tags and spoke to him in English.

Crouched animal-like on the floor. *Don't answer. Don't say a word. One word leads to another. . . .*

"Teal Ray."

Silence.

"Where are you from?"

Something struck him in the darkness. *Pain. . . .*

"What is your name?"

They knew his name. Don't answer anyway.

Pain! Burning . . . shrieking, writhing . . . animal wail. . . .

"What is your name?"

They knew. They wanted him to speak. The first step. Don't give them the first step.

A pin prick of pain like a dart or a needle . . . fire from within . . . wretching, burning, howling. . . .

"Where are you from?" *That's what they wanted to know. Remember the home. Don't betray the home. Remember his father.*

Pain . . . pain . . . frightened animal shrieking . . . wretching, clawing.

Calm . . . sweating, panting, trembling . . . no pain. . . .

"What is your name?" stern voice, more gentle.

There will be more pain. Muscles tensed, waiting. There will be more pain. Don't say anything.

So this was a Uelson prison.

October 4, 2182 A.D. (Saturday)

"It sure as hell did look like sabotage. I can't believe they overtaxed themselves. No one would be that careless with a ship like that." McCreedy flicked cigarette ash on the floor.

"I wish we knew who they were. I'd like to thank them," Father Michaels said solemnly.

"I wish we knew who they were so I could sleep at night!" McCreedy pounded his wooden desk top so hard his coffee spilled, adding another stain. "Everyone and his dog bailed us out of that one—we had *fish* fighting for us. But that *one* damn ship made me scared—really scared. I don't go for this anonymous Savior from outer space. I want to know who done it and why. I don't believe there's some benign power looking after us—I mean other than Jesus Christ, and you can't tell me this is the Second Coming—"

The father chuckled.

"What I'm saying is that I don't think this was any act of charity, sending a supership to save Earth while she had her back turned. Someone had a reason for it, and it had to benefit *them* somehow. I want to know what's in it for who! I don't want to wake up tomorrow and find a super-race landing on Earth in a *fleet* of superships saying, 'Pay up, Earth.'" He lit another cigarette with his old one and looked to the priest for comment.

"A fleet of superships," he echoed and rubbed tired eyes. "Why do you suppose, Jimmy, they only sent one?"

McCreedy shook his head. "It's all they could afford; it's

all that was necessary; it's all they had; it's all they felt like," he tossed out for consideration. "I don't think I'm getting warm. We could have *asked*, if those damn idiots on Pacific Defense hadn't blown our one refugee to atoms. One of their solo pods—get this—splashed down in the Pacific Ocean. Was it recovered? Are you nuts? Pacific Defense did not check to see what it was before they totally demolished it. *That* has me terrified too—what if our saviours who sent the supership think Earth is hostile because we atomized one of their people—if they're even people—and decide to attack us?"

The priest shook his graying head. Jim McCreedy was a spring wound tight with the pills that had pulled him through forty-eight hours of Armageddon I. His eyes were light brown rimmed in red, tired, yet forced open. He gnawed on what was left of his ruined fingernails, between drags on his cigarette. He hunched his four-starred shoulders and pulled his tan admiral's jacket around him. He was twenty-nine, the youngest admiral in United Earth Fleet history. He was too young to be so old, the father thought, having passed one hundred himself.

"The *Uelsons* know where that ship was from," Jim said, shifting in his chair. "If they didn't buy one of the crewmembers to sabotage it, then they'll find out from one of those two solo pods their scavenger ships picked up and ran with. Either way, the Uelsons will know, and we don't."

"Do we have any good guess as to where it's from? I heard the Diakyon system."

Jim snorted, picked up his cold coffee, and put it in the Slave to heat up again. "I'll believe it was the Second Coming first. I've been to Diakyon. Their fleet admiral is a real nut in command of a fleet of antiques. Diakyon's fleet is entirely sublight. That's like expecting a preindustrial culture to produce a rocket. There really aren't any good guesses. That's what's so damn frightening."

"Admiral of the Fleet Johnson thinks maybe it was from Earthling descendants of men lost in the early Star Age—"

"You know what I think of Fleet Admiral Johnson," McCreedy said wryly. "I'm sure they're *American* descendants too, right?" He scratched his head, covered with tousled hair of a nondescript brown. "The only reason he got that job was that he was the only male, white American near the top. They couldn't give it to Doshi—India doesn't have a big enough stake in UEF to get their man in; and they couldn't give it to Van Mare—she's a woman. Don't think the best person gets it in this Enlightened Age—that's a lot of shit. Do you know what has been used to drag me down in this Enlightened Age? 'McCreedy's a half-breed alien,' 'McCreedy's a Canadian,' 'I hear he's queer.' Goddam! Sorry, Father."

Father Michaels smiled and rose slowly. He walked behind McCreedy's chair and rubbed his shoulders, which gave about as much as solid iron would have. "They put you on the board, didn't they?"

"Yeah, I'm a real big shot now. They had to—"

"After your brilliant leadership in Armageddon I?"

Jim snorted a laugh. "Yeah."

"Will you be leaving Chicago Base then?"

"No. You don't get rid of me that easy. This is still my base," he said and ground out his cigarette. The Slave sucked away the ashes through a metal slot.

"How did you manage to stay on the board and be base administrator at the same time?"

"Easy. I'm obnoxious. They don't want me to come to Luna as all board members do. The only way to keep me away is to leave me in charge here. Being unbearable pays off. Ow—"

"Relax." The priest rubbed McCreedy's shoulders and they began to untighten.

"God—save the queen," he lamented his muscles. Then he sighed, and his head dropped down, chin on his chest. "That's wonderful." He kicked off his shoes and curled bare toes in the carpet. He stretched his short, muscular doglegs. He had a doglike quality; thick build, broad shoulders, sharp, almost canine teeth, and fierce, yellow-brown eyes. His numerous enemies capitalized on the effect. "Dog" was a common epithet for the Uelsons, who originated from the area designated by the Canis Major and Minor constellations. Few people ever saw Uelsons, as McCreedy had, and knew they were not doglike. Nor were they tall and formidable. They were small humans, with weasel-like rather than doglike features, with skin like a newborn mouse's; and they stank.

"You ought to get married," the priest said.

"To who?" Jim laughed.

"If you'd station more women on Chicago Base, you might meet one you liked."

Jim shrugged. "I don't have time for a goddam wife."

"You could use some mellowing."

"Yeah, that's all we need when the Uelsons come hoarding

in—a mellow admiral. Damn—is there any sedative I can take to counteract these greendots? I gotta get some *sleep* someday."

"No pills, Jimmy. You just relax yourself."

"Oh hell."

"Go to bed. Try not to brood over the battle—"

"Say two Hail Marys and call me in the morning. . . . Sorry. Cheap shot."

"And here. I have something for you." He brought forth a small, very old box.

"What is it?"

"It was given to me a long time ago—when I was young." He stopped and smiled inwardly. "A long time ago—on the condition that I give it away. So I'm giving it to you with the same condition."

It was a tiny silver pendant of the Madonna and Child on a short, delicate chain. Jim opened his mouth and forgot to close it. When he spoke he stuttered, "Why me? Why now?"

"One does things while one can. It's yours. Give it away when you feel you should," he said. While he could. While he was still alive—at one hundred, one's mind turned that way—but more important, and possibly more pressing, while Jim was still alive. The signs of an early fated life were on him. "Go get some sleep. The world will keep."

Jim pocketed his remaining cigarettes and jammed his feet into shoes that seemed to have shrunk in the past few minutes. He left his zoo of an office, stumbling over a telephone on the way out.

Jim summoned his car and punched the program for home. He left the base and its artificial daylight, and drove into night.

The three steps to his threshold demanded all his reserve strength, and he suddenly knew he had been through Armageddon. He put his hand to the metal panel by the door, which was programmed to open to his touch. It slid open with mechanical reluctance, and he stumbled in and collapsed on the couch, not making it upstairs to bed.

He could not help but dwell on the battle. He relived it. The Kalixjhan fleet swam before his closed eyes. The bright nova of the *Tesah* exploded. The Earth fleet returned from checking the enemy ruse, and drove off the Uelsons, whose scavenger ships swallowed up two solo pods from *Tesah*.

He was wide awake.

The alien solo pods were taken to Uelso. What then? The

aliens talked, in which case Earth could expect a fleet of Uelson superships to drop in anytime. Or the aliens maintained loyalty to Earth as they had in battle, and they were taken to prison and didn't talk. In which case they were better off dead.

March 11, 2183 A.D.

Screaming, bleeding, acid, beatings . . . pain . . . pain . . . pain. . . .

Same voice every day. "Teal Ray."

He did not answer. Every day.

Pain.

"What is your name?"

They'd just said it. Don't answer. Pain! Piercing, stabbing pain. . . .

"Where are you from?"

Never! Never! Never! Don't betray the home.

Wishing for death. Kill me. Kill me. If there is a god . . . How long can this last?

"Where are you from?"

Always the same questions. Same pain.

Origin unknown. ID: English. Solo pod: Earth design. Physical type not Earth, Lokin, Uelson, Geren, Aranian, Zharaghan, or of any protectorate of said worlds. Unusual characteristics: extremely large lung capacity; easily adapts to changes in pressure; advanced, well adapted to upright position; vocal range from low guttural sounds to high-pitched, whistlelike scream, spanning from Geren lower limit to Kalixjhan upper limit. Though definitely mammalian, has Kalixjhan characteristics worthy of note. Eyes adjust to minimal light (nocturnal?). Unusually sensitive auditory perception. Extremely high pain threshold—immeasurable. Has not given desired response yet. Regenerative powers: characteristic of unfamiliar life form. Regrows extremities. Heals flawlessly at rapid rate, leaving no scar tissue.

Teal had thought that the Mountain People had restored his eyes after Dianter. He was soon to learn he had done it himself. He was immobilized in a room stinking of antiseptic. He saw the scalpel coming at his eye and screamed.

April 2, 2183 A.D.

Teal sat on a rotted, lichen-covered log in an Alpha Centaurian forest, shaking. He kept his wounded eye shut and glanced about him anxiously with the other. He was naked, not having had time to think about clothes. It was raining steadily and Teal was cold, but that was not why he was shaking.

He twitched with remembered pain. He sniffed the air for anything remotely Uelson. He would catch the scent of Uelson antiseptic, would jump, then reseat himself, realizing it was himself he smelled. The stink had soaked into his skin and was a long time wearing off. He did not seek shelter from the rain.

He could not believe he had gotten this far. He didn't know how he had known what to do. Like being possessed, something just took over and he escaped from escapeproof Otranadoe.

It had begun when someone left his torture-chamber door unlocked. Not knowing what he was going to do on the other side of it, he bolted through. He spent several days hiding and running through the prison, then he hijacked a ship and sent it through the annihilation field that surrounded Otranadoe. The ship disappeared in a white blaze. The Uelsons thought that he had gone with it, and so called off their search for him.

"Always use weapons that leave bodies," a Caucan assassin had once told Teal. "Then you know whether or not you got your target."

Once "dead," Teal stowed away for three days in the freight compartment of a supply ship until it embarked for the planet Uelso. From there he stole a stolen Earth Voyager ship and piloted it to Earth colony Alpha Centauri. He tried to enter the atmosphere at the wrong angle and bounced off into space. Rattled, he turned around and tried again more successfully. He had never flown a Voyager before and could not figure out how to land it, so he sank it into the ocean and swam back up.

Now he sat in the alien forest, rain trickling in rivulets down his back. He was terrified. Finally sure that he was not

being followed, he was still frightened by the strangeness of
the world he found himself in. The trees were different, the
insects were different—they looked like tiny monsters. There
were too many suns in the sky, so he was not sure if it was
supposed to be day or night—if there *was* a night here.
He was glad that the rain clouds blocked out all those alien
suns.

He had caught a rabbit to eat, but it made him sick—partly because he had not eaten in a week, partly because he did
not know what it was and it looked so strange.

He spoke to see if he still remembered how. He said "help"
in five languages.

He was becoming very aware that he was cold, sick, and a
long way from home. He had to do something before he
started screaming. He was, he thought, mad.

To the Uelsons, to his home, and to the rest of the galaxy,
he was dead. Teal felt as if he really *had* died and was just
now coming back to life. What had happened during the six
months of his captivity? What had happened to his ship
Tesah? He'd never known. How had the war come out? He
didn't know that either. Was his home still there? Or had the
Uelsons destroyed it? The thought of being the last Aranian
left, alone on a strange world, brought him close to panic.
Coming back to life after six months was hard. He was not
sure he wanted to.

He had only ten more years to live anyway. The Uelsons
had put a death collar on him, a device that took ten years to
kill although its real purpose was to induce despair.

Ten years to live a new life. What to do with that. How to
begin. He had no idea.

He could not remember sleeping. That was the first thing
to do.

He curled up on some wet leaves and shut his eye. He
would make some plans tomorrow—whenever that was.

July 23, 2183 A.D. (Thursday)

"McCreedy, are you going to clear my ship or aren't you?
First I'm homesick, now I'm sick of home. When do we get
off this rock?" The big man paced around the clutter on the
admiral's office floor.

"Kury, sit down," McCreedy said.

Kury pushed some things off a chair onto the floor and sat heavily, growling.

"Kury, I know you," McCreedy began with a wry grin on his face. "Tell me truthfully, did you send this to Fleet Admiral Johnson?" He pushed a piece of paper across his desk. Kury took it in his big hand and read it. It was a computer record of a telegram.

Kury gave a guffaw, face wrinkled in smile lines. "Wish I had. Damn. No, that ain't me, mannie."

McCreedy took it back. "I thought maybe that was a pseudonym of yours." He scanned it over again and looked to the commodore. "Who the hell is Ray Stewert?"

"Some new guy. Give me a cigarette," Kury said and reached for McCreedy's pack. "Quiet bastard. Hell, that's funny. Is he up shit creek now?"

"No." McCreedy smiled slyly, baring pointed teeth. "Anyone who tells Admiral Johnson to fuck off and signs his name deserves a medal. I stood up for him. I told Johnson it was a transcription error. So who is this guy? Where's he from?"

"Don't know. Canuck, maybe." He winked a devilish brown eye at McCreedy. "Really, I couldn't even tell you what nationality he is. No accent at all."

McCreedy was mildly alarmed. "None?"

"He ain't Uelson; don't worry about that." Kury sat back. "Big eyes." Uelsons had little, beady, weasel eyes. "Real big—and black. Pretty. Desk captain. Young bitch."

"Oh, is he one of these new tyrants?" McCreedy said, sounding disappointed, stretching.

"Doesn't seem to be. He acts like an old hand at command. Not hard, but in control of his subordinates and a first-class bitch to his superiors if they deserve it. He ain't afraid of brass either."

McCreedy smiled ironically, "No, not if he sends a fuck-you telegram to Johnson. Is he rich?" The rich could afford dangerous words; it was no great feat for them.

"Listen, I don't know," Kury said. "Why don't you ask *him* all this? *He* could answer it." He was showing impatience.

"Hang on, you'll get your ship off the ground, Boris." McCreedy used his forbidden, hated name.

"I'll fly it up your ass," Kury said threateningly.

"I will call you what I like, you commie spy. You will address me as sir."

"I'll fly it up your ass, sir," Kury rephrased. "There's something obscene about a twenty-nine-year-old admiral."

"I've been told." McCreedy searched his desk, then glanced around the room. "Hand me that radio." The Russian picked it up and tossed it to the admiral. Kury had been born in the Ukraine, but both his parents were Russian. He changed his mind about his nationality every other week. Today he was Russian.

"GC, clear Commodore Kuryin's ship for liftoff as soon as you get a hole in the sky."

"Yes, sir," the ground controller responded.

McCreedy switched the radio off. "Getellotta'ere."

"Thank you, sir." Kury rose. He slung his jacket over his shoulder. He turned at the door. "Oh yeah. Stewert—he's got a Uelson dog collar on his neck."

"He *what*?" McCreedy nearly lit the wrong end of his cigarette.

"A whatsit—Uelson death collar. One of those gadgets that takes forever and a half to kill you—"

"Yeah, yeah, I know what it is," McCreedy said impatiently. "How—?"

"Ask *him*. 'Bye, sir." Kury turned on his heel and was out the door.

It was an orderly office he came to, but not one in which the envelopes stood up and saluted. McCreedy mistrusted a too neat work area. The captain was absent. McCreedy got a light from the Slave, and the captain appeared in the door.

He was short, like McCreedy. His slenderness gave an illusion of greater height, but his eyes were on a level with the admiral's. He paused a moment, then came in and sat at his desk in a businesslike manner with no trace of apprehension. Four stars did not frighten him.

Kury was right; he was pretty, and his eyes were huge, with long dark lashes more at home over a woman's eyes. Black hair was cut very short as if in an effort to counteract feminine features, high, delicate cheekbones, straight nose, slender build, and smooth white skin that looked as if it had never seen the sun. His jacket was slung over the back of his chair, his shirtsleeves were rolled up above his elbows, and his shirt neck was open. His tie was tied around a lever on the Slave in a bow (which Jim could not look at without a chuckle tickling his lips). A closed neck and a tie would have been uncomfortable with a Uelson death collar. It looked like a dog collar with diamond-shaped metal studs, but they were not metal, and they were not studs; they were stakes on the inside and they grew over the years. It was practically indestructible; cutting a collar so close to someone's neck could prove as fatal as the collar itself. McCreedy had seen them on the very few Sixus survivors. It was not his most vivid memory of Sixus. He remembered shoveling bodies onto death cars.

"Yes, sir?" The captain looked up at him.

"You're coming to the rec with me for a cup of coffee."

"I already had my break, sir," he said.

"Take another one."

Stewert rose slowly and stepped out the door. "Musa, take the desk," he called, then turned his attention back to McCreedy, and accompanied him to the officers' rec.

McCreedy felt his attention entirely on him, nerves picking up impulses and impressions. The man almost visibly sparked, totally aware, totally alert, with a very quiet facade that McCreedy saw as so transparent he wondered why no one else noticed this live wire, dangerous and irresistible as an electric current he'd closed his hand on.

"I stuck my neck out for you, mister, and I want to know why," McCreedy said over coffee. With his fingertip, he traced a groove in the wood veneer on the table.

The captain knew what he was referring to, and answered frankly, "Because I don't care if Johnson is God's son, he has no right abusing my kids when they're *trying*. They're new, they're fresh out of the academy, and dammit, they don't fuck up on purpose, so he can just leave them alone."

"And fuck himself, as you so subtly put it," McCreedy finished for him.

"Yes."

"What exactly happened?" McCreedy asked.

Ray took a breath and wondered where this interrogation was leading. "One of my kids sent a message to Luna on the wrong transmission code—double zero one. It landed straight in Johnson's office, as double-oh-one's will. Well, you'd think the kid was a Uelson spy. Johnson said he could be sent to prison for abusing the UEF communications system, et cetera, et cetera, ad nauseum. So I told him to fuck himself."

Although Ray seemed to be speaking without restraint, McCreedy noticed tremendous care and control. Ray was aware of small topaz eyes studying him.

Except for height, the two men were physically dissimilar.

Everything about the admiral's build and features was doglike. Ray was the reverse, slender, androgynous, though he carried himself in a masculine manner—through conscious effort avoiding jungle grace.

"Why weren't you in Armageddon I, captain?" Admiral McCreedy asked.

Ray did not change expression. "I was on an Alpha Centaurian exploration ship at the time," he said.

"Where are you from originally?"

"New York," Ray said. There was something in the way McCreedy asked that meant it was not an idle question. Ray came to learn that James McCreedy never asked idle questions. "Why?"

"You have no accent whatsoever. Didn't even pick up any of the Alpha Centaurian colonists' 'Wot tyime is et? Aoh, fyive o' clock? Doublefine, eh?' " he mimicked the dialect. The last phrase sent Ray's nerves dancing, and his senses blasted off and left him.

Ray chastised himself, remaining stone-faced in his turmoil. He should have known better. A perfect accent was a clear giveaway of foreign origin. McCreedy was watching him closely.

"How old are you, captain?"

"You've read my file."

"Why aren't you a soldier?"

"Why should I be?"

"You're being evasive."

"You're playing games with me, admiral."

Their eyes met, and Ray dropped his gaze. He noticed a tiny pendant around the admiral's neck. Madonna and Child. That was another thing that made Admiral McCreedy unpopular besides his disposition, his half-alien descent, and his Canadian citizenship—he was Catholic. Roman Catholic? New Catholic? Old Catholic?

"I want your opinion as a nonsoldier who isn't a coward—"

"How do you know I'm not a coward?" Ray asked as much as challenged, both of them watching and feinting and parrying.

"You risked your career for one of your kids," McCreedy said. "Doublefine, eh?"

Ray shivered inwardly.

"I know what the soldiers think. You tell me. Diakyon."

Ray did not even blink, though he could not have been more jolted by a cup of coffee in his face.

"The Diakyon system presents a sticky situation. There are a lot of people—soldiers—who wonder why we don't just move in and take over Canda and build our defensive military base, and damn the Diakyonites. You *know* what happened last time we tried that. So we tried the diplomatic route—we offered protection in return for a base on Canda. We got a return offer from Arana: they'd *let* us protect them in return for agricultural aid to Canda."

"Who said that? Hollingsworth White?" Ray asked.

McCreedy nodded and thought he saw a smile touch the solemn lips.

"What would you say, captain?" McCreedy shot at Ray. "What do you make of the fleet admiral's offer?"

"Does a fleet admiral have authority to make an offer like that?" Stewert said warily. Why was the man asking him this?

"Apparently so," McCreedy said. "Or are you saying he's going above his power? Bluffing, perhaps?"

"I haven't said anything yet. I asked a question."

"I see," said the admiral. "How would you react to that offer? Would you suggest we accept it—if you had the power to suggest?"

Ray thought. "Unless you can outfox the man, I'd accept his terms."

"You think we should try to outfox him?"

"My first impression is that he could dance circles around any ambassador we'd send."

"Then you would advise accepting his terms."

"With the information given, yes."

Cautious. How cautious. Conditions on everything he says. Leaving an out; an escape. Is he afraid of being trapped?

Teal was making some observations himself. Jim McCreedy had connected Ray with Arana. He'd just met him! He suspected something. No, goddammit, he *knows*. He *knows!* He just hasn't realized that he knows yet.

II.

January 2, 2184 A.D. (Saturday)

Thinking he would never recover from his American New Year hangover, Teal poured himself another cup of coffee and sank into an armchair, red-ringed black eyes gazing out the window at gray Chicago. Inside he felt blank. Slowly the thoughts began to creep in and demand sorting. First off was a solemn vow never to touch champagne again as long as he lived. Second was wonder at why people did that to themselves on purpose. He sighed and shrugged it off as another inexplicable difference in their cultures. The subtle differences between Earth and Aranian psyche were the most disquieting; little habits and behaviors and ways of thinking he could not pinpoint nor clearly recognize left an uneasy awareness that he was indeed a stranger here. He operated on a different plane, at a different pace, with different thought patterns, with different emotional reactions. These people were further splintered by nationalities—over one hundred nations, compared to Arana's ten countries, including the island tribes. And he was convinced that Americans were insane.

He wanted another cup of coffee but could not expend the energy to stumble over to the Slave to get it. The dependence on mechanical monsters was a trait of Earthlings, but it was deceptively easy to grow accustomed to—even for Ray, who had done everything for himself, including catching his own food. The pace of life was deadly, but Ray felt a need for it and for the pressure, without which his internal strife would explode.

There was an incredible distance between people, especially in Chicago. People were less emotional than he was, though they thought him cold, for that was what he would have them think. The bond was missing between father and son, which Teal at once pitied and envied. Honor, too, counted for little.

In concrete differences, Teal discovered companionship in

animals—in the dog. McCreedy had given him a dog for Christmas. McCreedy was also responsible for the hangover, for which he was less than grateful.

Then there was his strength as an alien coming to a world less massive than his own. He was careful not to show any more power than his small frame intimated. Especially to McCreedy, who was already too close.

It was the subtle, only unconsciously perceptible differences that drew McCreedy to him. As distant as people were here, Ray felt the need for a chasm. He had built his wall of stone, and Jim was a trickle of water wearing down the boulders. He was so very different—and at the same time, so similar. Teal sensed a kindred spirit trying in a roundabout way to make contact. Teal was frightened of touching, of letting down his guard; he could still hear Caucan laughter. And yet he knew Jim was afraid too.

A wave of loneliness swept in from a cold sea, and with it, a wash of homesickness. But home would be just as lonely as Earth—perhaps worse because of a failed mission and broken honor. How could a sole survivor—captain—return with his head up? He had to atone for the deaths of his crewmembers and to atone for his own living. Of all the living who did not deserve to be, he felt he was the most guilty—adding another reason not to let anyone close to him. He had mourned eight deaths countless times. The ninth he was certain still lived— in luxury, he fancied. There was another solo pod reported captured by the Uelsons. One of the dead had told him whose it was. "It was Vanguard," Natina said before the Sea claimed her as she said it would. A solo pod was reported downed in the Pacific Ocean and annihilated there. Teal wept openly for that death alone. Her sight failed her when fate was closest to her, or Vanguard would never have been aboard *Tesah*. Hadn't she admitted, "When there is a storm at sea, you can't see beyond your own bow."

The phone rang, and his setter, Peritas, barked.

"Shut up," he mumbled. The dog obeyed but the phone wasn't listening. He punched the answer button. "Stewert," he snapped.

Kury's image faded in. "Hell, you look like shit." The rugged face broke up in smile lines. He looked older than he was, but the eyes were young and merry. Teal hardly knew him and then only as "sir." The sudden joking familiarity was unexpected and put him on guard.

"Sir," Teal answered in a gravel voice, lower than his normal register on Arana. His dog laid her head in his lap and whined, sensing her master was still sick. Teal patted the silky head. His chair wobbled slightly. It wouldn't happen with three-legged furniture, he thought with irritation and tried to keep it still.

"Hey mannie, you have another party last night?" Kury needled.

Teal sniffed and maintained an indignant silence. The commodore felt the frosty wind emitting from the disheveled face on the screen and began acting more like his superior officer. "Captain Stewert, you've been flying that desk of yours for almost a year, and according to your file that's the sort of thing you've done most of your career. You're a captain in the military division, albeit communications." He spoke depreciatingly, considering communications only the bastard son of the military, belonging more to the diplomatic division (which had its own communications also). "That means you are of a rank to command the big ones. But you ain't never gonna be given one with a blank flying record."

Teal feared where this was leading. Kury was about to do himself a favor and believe his own story that it was for Ray's sake.

"Now, I have an opening for a Second on my ship . . ."

Second was a commander's job. Teal guessed Kury needed a man—fast—and was taking what he could find, even if it meant putting a captain in the Second's place. Commodore Kuryin could do it. Teal thought quickly. "I know someone for you—Commander Yabroff." She was Sub-second on the Zharaghan ship *Balanze*, and she was a compatriot of Kuryin's, hopefully lure enough to get him off his scent.

"Yeah, I know the linda. She's a peahead and she don't speak English. Mine's an American ship. An' I . . . well, you know *me* . . ." *No*, Teal thought, *I don't*. "A woman's fine on a crew, keeps a ship happy, but when you get up there in the decision making, where the pressure is, you need someone who can take it. You know what I mean?"

"No," Teal confessed aloud.

"Makes no difference," Kury said. "I'm not looking for a Second, I found one."

"There's Commander Yamauchi—"

"Captain Stewert."

"I don't want it, sir."

"I'm not asking you," he said with finality. "You get your

hungover self on board by fifteen hundred. We leave for Loki at eighteen hundred."

"Loki. I have no battle with Gerens," Teal said darkly. What little Teal knew of Gereny led him to suspect they were much like Royalists in their unity. Gereny was composed of fifteen worlds, yet they were all the Geren nation, all descendants of one world. The original inhabitants of the other fourteen were no more, if there had been anyone there before the coming of the Gerens. Teal had little sympathy for the Lokins, Earth's imperialistic ally, engaged in a territorial war with Gereny, the Third Power of the known galaxy. He was certain he did not want to be aboard a spyship in Geren space.

"I know you don't," Kury answered derisively. "You'd rather blast the ones who put that dog collar on you."

It was true, but it was not the whole story. Kury would not guess that—he was not James McCreedy. Teal's thoughts lighted momentarily on the admiral. How long could he hide from Jim? Or had he already figured it out?

"I've seen your kind before, captain. An unnatural calm that comes from living through hell. Base Sixus."

Teal's file said he had been stationed at Base Sixus at the time of the massacre. That was to explain where he'd gotten the death collar. He *had* been at Base Sixus—but he'd been there long after the massacre when it wasn't called Base Sixus anymore. He was there after it had become Uelson Castor Base—which included a prison called Otranadoe.

"I wouldn't take you along if we were going to Uelson space," Kury said. "There's nothing worse on my kind of ship than a man with a personal war against the enemy."

Kury's kind of ship was a spyship. It was not a large vessel, nor was it the time for Teal's purpose. The personal war was indeed present. Perhaps Kury was right. But Teal did not want to fight Gerens.

Galaxy was a thirty-person spyship. She was old, almost twenty years, and Teal wondered why technology had not progressed to antiquate it in twenty years' time. He thought the Earthmen would rapidly renovate their fleet after the war, but it had not come about because of internal strife in UEF upper echelons. New ideas were wrapped in red tape and laid methodically aside. Chicago Base was the only place that underwent much change—under McCreedy's strict administration. It was a young base, McCreedy having little respect for the wisdom of years. It was called a "base of children in charge of a brat." Jim had gotten to his position by unashamedly being obnoxious. He had to know that as soon as a safe puppet position was found to slot him into, he would lose his base and his power and his board position.

Teal walked the corridor of the ship *Galaxy* (alias *New General Catalogue OOO*, as called by the crew, *NGC* for short), his dog at his heels. Dogs were against regulations, but Kury was notorious for bending rules. "Bring your bitch," he'd said. If Kury could keep his pet aardvark . . .

The crewmembers were all Kury's people—drinking partners, poker players, and lovers. His seventeen-year-old adopted son was Sub-second, Commander John Fox—Johnny. He was an orphan from Base Sixus, one of the few survivors—as Ray pretended to be. Although the boy had been only five years old at the time, Teal was afraid he would want to talk about a place Teal had only seen from inside a torture chamber. To his relief, Johnny was a silent, haunted young man who talked as little as Ray did. When he did speak, it was to a purpose: "Captain Stewert, radio five."

Teal thanked Johnny and answered the call, knowing who it would be.

"Ray."

"Admiral."

"What's this about your getting pushed onto *NGC?*"

"I wasn't pushed."

"That ain't the way I hear it," Jim said. "I can't see you on Kury's ship, Ray."

"Don't worry about it."

"I'm not worried about any it, I'm worried about you, Ray."

"Don't."

"Do you want to go?"

"I'll go," he said firmly.

There was silence on the other end. *What is he thinking?*

"All right, captain," he said at last and switched off.

Teal slammed his hand down on the switch. He noticed every time McCreedy called him by his given first name, whirri wings fluttered inside. All three times in the space of one minute. He was suddenly grateful for the aggressive Kury. He had to get away. He had to run away again. Run farther.

Galaxy/NGC was a small ship. She was to fly in caravan with an alien allied ship commanded by a Lokin squadron marshal.

The Lokin vessel was smaller than her Earth counterpart,

carried only five crewmembers, and was swift—as the *Tesah* had been—which led to speculation that the Lokins were responsible for the unknown ship in Armageddon I. The marshal laughed at such speculation. "Do you think if we had a ship like that, we would still have Gerens smirking at us from across the border zone?" she said with a bitter edge.

The Lokin ship had *Tesah*'s size and speed but not the power. And it was true that if the Lokins had possessed such a ship, they would not have sent it to defend Earth. Rather they would fire it against their mortal enemies, the Gerens, with whom they'd had border conflicts ever since both had had spaceships.

Captain Stewert was met with hostile suspicion by his shipmates aboard *NGC*. They constantly reminded him in subtle and unsubtle ways that this arrangement was temporary—only until their regular Second was out of the hospital. The crew was a close-knit group; they drank together, joked together, broke rules together, and this strait-laced desk captain they had as a new Second was unwelcome and mistrusted. They were afraid he would report their rule-bending, despite his obvious disregard of rules in bringing his dog. Kury was not fond of him either—he served his purpose of giving *NGC* a full crew, and, therefore, enabled them to fly. That accomplished, his new Second was swept out of the way—where Teal was very content to remain.

In his time to himself, he paused to think and rehash old questions that followed like raging Furies wherever he ran. Paramount was a question that haunted him every day since Armageddon: Whoever betrayed *Tesah* to the Uelsons *did not tell them where Tesah was from!* Why? *How?* How could the traitor have entered into a deal to sabotage the ship yet not tell where the ship originated? A fact the Uelsons wanted to know very desperately—perhaps more desperately than the Earthlings. Did the traitor make a deal at all, then? He had to. Then why didn't he tell them *Tesah* was an Aranian ship? How could he *not* tell? Vanguard—it was Vanguard—could not possibly withhold that information; the Uelsons would have it from him. Conflict. Paradox. None of it made sense.

Kury made a visit to his Second's cabin, not all that sober. He had no one else to drink with; they were all on duty or had already been drunk under the table. Kury still had command of his senses but not of his tongue. Johnny must have been in charge of the ship.

Kury lumbered in, giant frame tottering. He sat down

heavily. His creased face was flushed and had a roguish expression. "Drink, captain?"

"No thank you, sir." Teal had risen at his entrance and remained standing stiffly. His dog, Peritas, came over to have her ears scratched. He would not relax his cold air to tend to his pet. It was hard to be aloof while petting a dog.

"No drink," Kury said. "They also say you don't smoke, don't gamble, don't lay women—don't lay men for that matter. You don't even chew gum—thank God, if there's anything I hate. Anyway, you don't have any vices."

"I wasn't aware I was being talked about."

Kury pushed back a strand of brown hair. "We've already gone through everyone else. You're the new man on board. We've been speculating," Kury said, slurring over the word speculating, tongue suddenly too big for his mouth. "We figure you're really a robot from another planet made to pass as an Earthman, but they made you too good. They forgot the bugs that make people human."

Teal said nothing.

"Don't you ever smile?" Kury said, helping himself to a drink from Ray's Slave.

"No, sir."

"That explains why I never saw it." Kury was sounding very drunk, but Ray sensed that his intellect was still very sharp. "Ben thinks you're after my ship. He hates your guts. Ya know, Ben and Juan—the guy you replaced—were very close. It happens on long assignments. People get attached to each other. Take Ben and Juan—they're straight as they come, don't misunderstand—but they're closer than a married couple. Some married couples do come out of it—not always considering what sex they are. Ben and Juan are straight, but take some like Commodore Ambie," Kury said. His face showed disgust. "But then why am I telling you all this? You ought to know how it happens."

Teal took a few steps away from his dog, hoping the animal would not pick up his anxiety. "There's suspicion in your voice, sir. Why?"

"I think Ben has something—more than just missing our bedridden spic—"

"You've had too much to drink, sir."

The statement was a foolish move by an unwary doe, and the lithra sprang. "I've been waiting for you to say that. I know how much I'm affected and I still have my wits about me."

He did. What was coming out was the shrewdness and seriousness of the spyship commander, usually covered by an easygoing nature. And Ray had stupidly revealed that he was getting close to something.

"All right," said Ray. "I'm a Uelson political prisoner escaped from Otranadoe, chased by the UII and hiding out in the United Earth Fleet—how's that?" Lightness came hard.

Kury shook his sweaty head. "You weren't at Otranadoe."

"No?"

"For one thing, *no* one gets out of *that* place, and for another, they brand you in all Uelson prisons—you don't have a brand." Kury countered his banter.

Teal remembered painful attempts to get the markings imprinted in his skin. There was no way of permanently altering him, short of killing him. As long as he was not mortally damaged, everything regenerated without scar.

"That's another thing," Kury said, thinking out loud. "You haven't got a mark on your body—not a scar, a birthmark, or blemish. Did somebody make you?"

"You've read my medical file?" Ray said, concerned. The less people who saw that forgery the safer. "Isn't that confidential?"

"I'm your commander, mannie. Drink, captain?"

"No thank you, sir."

Kury scowled, and all his smile lines scowled with him. A light brown strand of hair fell across his forehead. "I already asked you that."

"Yes, sir."

"Now I've had too much to drink," he said, got another drink, and left.

III.

February 19, 2184 A.D. (Friday)

The Lokin base was on a small nothing world—no mountains, no trees, no oceans, no craters. "Smooth as a fucking billiard ball," Kury grumbled. What it had was a strategic location on the Lokin/Geren border zone.

The hangars, and most everything, were underground. There was no landing pad, since the entire planet was a natural landing pad of flat ground disturbed only by patches of yellow-brown grass. The wind came in brisk and unimpeded. The Lokins were used to it, but Kury was not. "Don't let 'em kid you—they'll tell you their base is underground—truth is, it blew away."

There was the control tower and a pavilion above ground which Lokins lounged in and used like a rec, apparently disliking the underground rooms more than the wind. There was also a prison above ground. "If the Gerens want to bomb this place, let 'em bomb that," Kury explained. It was a large forbidding building from which screams could be heard on occasion. Johnny Fox, Kury's son, knew all about the prison.

"It's a torture chamber. There's a man named Metrarch—you'll meet him—he tortures POWs for the hell of it. He tried to kill me first time I was here," he explained simply.

"Why you?" Teal asked.

Johnny shrugged with an almost sullen air. "I guess I reacted to him when I first saw him. He was covered with blood—he loves blood—and he loves strong reactions. I guess he thought I'd be fun."

Metrarch was worse than anyone described him, tall, waxy-faced, with a permanent leer over which crawled a shaggy caterpillar of a mustache and matching caterpillars over each sinister eye. It was a skin-crawling revulsion he inspired with a face that was a reflection of his soul.

105

Opposite of Metrarch was his superior, and commander of the Lokin attack force, General John Falco. He had the more typical Lokin fragility of appearance and a milky complexion like a china figurine, slender, honey-haired, with pale blue eyes in which Teal saw with painful clarity familiar desolation. Like all Lokins who live forever (as they were called) he looked young—twenty-four perhaps—when he was closer to eighty Earth years. The leering Metrarch was well over two hundred.

Falco was a carrier of a disease without a cure which they called menthiis, and no one could touch him. Menthiis was transmitted through water—blood, urine, sweat, tears. The moisture of his breath was to be feared, and he maintained a ten-foot distance when he had to move among others, and he wore a white mask over his face. He carried white gloves so that what he touched did not pick up his sweat. The Lokins were very careful, and no one on base had caught it from him. It was feared and terrible; it eroded the urinary tract, and the victim hemorrhaged, bleeding to death in great pain within three months. But Falco himself was not affected—just very isolated. Normally, a menthiis carrier would not have been permitted to live. But Falco was an important person's son, which had won him life to manhood. From then he had made himself an invaluable leader, winning continued life for himself. Teal drew the parallel and wondered if Falco, too, doubted whether it was worth it. He found himself asking, Given a choice between Red Madness and menthiis carrier . . . He never answered it. He wondered what Falco would say, he who could touch no one.

"Oh, he's touched a couple times," Johnny amended. "They won't tell you 'cause they think it's sick. A couple drugged Geren boys from there"—he pointed to the prison. "Metrarch, bless his soul," he said wryly, "finds a pretty one and fixes him up for Falco. Truth is Falco thinks it's sick too, but he's nuts crazy lonesome so he has his night with one and shoots him in the morning before the menthiis can hit him. I guess he's done that about five times."

"He's only touched five times in his whole life?" Teal said, trying not to sound empathic.

"I guess it's pretty hard to shoot them in the morning. I mean," his eyes stared at his feet, "it's one thing blasting down a spaceship that's blasting at you, it's another spending the night with someone and . . . well . . . forget it." The boy looked up to the sky as if distracted.

How different he was from his foster father, Kury. Kury, he was certain, would see no reason for hesitation in shooting "just a faggot." The closest he came to sympathy was, "You know me, I can't stand a queer, but that's one mannie I gotta feel sorry for."

Someone explained Johnny's difference. "There's this blond Adonis Johnny's age, you see." He winked. "They're . . ." he crossed two fingers and didn't finish, not needing to.

"I see," Teal said.

"Yeah. Name's Orestes."

Orestes. How common a name was that? Two visitors, one named Orestes. Who was the other?

I shouldn't be here, Teal told himself. He was in danger and he was compromising his own principles. Despite his sympathy for the handsome, tragic Falco, he could not shake the feeling that he was wrong. Loki was wrong. *What am I doing helping the aggressor?* Teal was not actually helping, for he was a spare part aboard *NGC,* but to be associated with was to condone. *I might as well be helping the Caucans.* On Arana the Caucans took the land, but they couldn't take the sea. Where could the Gerens go when pushed from their planets by the Lokins? Into space? It had been done before—in legend—the building of artificial worlds. If the Royalists could return to the sea, the Gerens could escape into space. But it wouldn't come to that. The Royalists would not lose their land, and Gereny would not give up her planets despite John Falco's military strategy. And Teal sensed Falco was aware of that fact.

Falco had a great respect for his foe—and a great love for his chief adversary in war, the Geren general Jaephah Merek. "It's a love affair," Teal was told. "He's madly in love with him and out to kill him."

Jaephah Merek flew a red solo ship called *Rita,* and whenever it was sighted, Falco was off in his one-man Voyager, on the prowl after him.

Jaephah Merek owned his life. Falco said so. There were two versions of the story. Falco's was that Merek let him get away once. The Lokins said Falco's own brilliance got him out of the impossible situation. Whichever story was real, Teal could see that Merek indeed owned his life—matching skill with Merek was the only thing that made life bearable for John Falco.

"The Gerens could have us if they wanted—Earth, Uelso, all. You don't know," Falco had said. "You don't know."

Ray Stewart kept to himself, avoiding the gruesome Metrarch, and brooded over the fact that his conscience told him to support the Gerens. He stayed in his cabin much of the time.

He was stretched out on his bunk, semi-sleeping. His alertness must have failed him, because he didn't hear the approach, only felt the boy's hands on his neck, slipped under the death collar. He bolted up, and Johnny drew back. Before he could yell at the boy and demand an explanation, Johnny was doing just that. "You're a liar. You weren't at Sixus, and you didn't get that collar at Sixus." The brown eyes had the same tormented look as his own or Falco's, eyes that saw his parents go in the massacre at Sixus. "Sixus was razed twelve years ago. That collar only has about a year on it. Like you got it around Armageddon. . . . But you were on an Alpha Centaurian ship then." With the last sentence a sarcastic tone had crept in. Johnny sat quietly on the edge of his bed, waiting for Teal to answer the charges. He was a handsome youth with olive skin and large, sad brown eyes. One of his natural parents must have been of Spanish descent—his mother, to judge from the name Fox.

Teal had assumed the attitude of a cornered wounded beast. "What do you want?"

Johnny folded his hands. "Do you know a girl named Natina?"

Teal lost tongue and composure. All his time at Otranadoe had not given away what this boy got in a few moments. Johnny continued simply, "Me and Orestes were on your planet a while before Armageddon. Did Holly tell you about us? We're the only Earth people who ever landed there. It was Orestes who guessed you people sent that ship. He made me promise not to tell anyone. I was the one who guessed who you were, though."

Teal shook his head, feeling more and more cornered; eyes rolled as if searching for a way out. All he could choke out was a plea: "*Don't* tell—"

"I won't. Orestes made me promise."

Teal sensed there was something very binding in that. Who was Orestes? Teal knew what he was to Johnny; he was certain now.

"How do you know Natina?"

"Orestes and I were on Arana before Armageddon. We had ship trouble—a Uelson blasted us—and Natina guided us there. She told us to sublight over the radio while we were flying blind. You people have a superlight radio—we didn't tell anyone that either. We met Natina there. I guess she can see the future. She knew who we were. She told Orestes—" He stopped and debated telling. "This is secret."

Teal nodded dumbly.

"Secret for secret, I guess," he decided. "Orestes can bend light at will. His mother can too. She taught him; she's a witch. They learned it on the planet Caldon. There's a bunch of old women they call the Witches of Caldon, and they can do things with light. It's psychokinesis of a sort, I guess. Natina told him he'd need that power. He could only refract his own image at the time, but she told him to learn to do things like airplanes—"

"Armageddon I," Teal said. "The images of the ships moved—"

"That was Orestes. Natina warned him."

"She's dead," he said.

It was Johnny's turn to be stunned. "How?"

"Your people killed her," he said, taking it out on the boy—simply because he was there, and he was the only one he could allow himself to be open with.

"She was the solo pod that came down in the Pacific, wasn't she?"

Teal nodded.

"Oh God."

"The Sea told her she'd die in the Sea," Teal said. "I don't know why she couldn't tell it was an alien sea . . . or that we'd be betrayed. . . . Maybe she didn't want to."

"She couldn't see everything," Johnny said.

Teal shook his head. "No, she couldn't."

"I'll have to tell Orestes." He was talking to himself as much as to Teal. "He didn't know she was . . ." He looked at Teal. "Orestes will be fleet admiral one day," he said with some pride, candid to the point of being childlike. "He figured out who your saboteur dealt with—you probably have too."

"No, I haven't!" Teal said and put both hands on Johnny's shoulders. "Who?"

"Uelson Castor Base."

"No, it's not the Uelsons—"

"Not the Uelsons," Johnny overrode his objection. "Uelson Castor Base."

Teal now listened.

"Uelson Castor Base is the closest point of Uelso to

Earth—it's a big attack base. The Uelsons who work there have a nice business going. If Arana should fall to the Uelsons, or if Earth should fall, Uelson Castor Base won't be needed anymore as an attack base. They lose their major business, and there'll be a lot of unhappy Uelsons on Castor Base. It's in their best interest to keep the war going, but never to allow a victory."

Teal chewed on a nail in unconscious imitation of Jim McCreedy. It would be easy for Vanguard to have dealt with Castor; it was close, the scavengers that had picked him up went to Castor, and Vanguard could have escaped the hands of the other Uelsons since his benefactors would reach him first. It made sense. And it explained why the Uelsons did not know where *Tesah* was from. Castor did, and was not telling.

"It's all economics," Johnny said. "Kury always said love of money is the root of all evil."

"Kury said that?"

"Not exactly—he said capitalism is."

Peritas had trotted up, given Johnny a sniff-over, decided she liked him, and was demanding an ear scratch. "Orestes had a dog named Peritas," Johnny said. "It died. Alexander the Great's dog was Peritas. You have to meet Orestes; I think that's who he fancies he is sometimes—Alexander."

McCreedy had named the dog.

"Your friend is right; it's Castor Base," Teal said. "It has to be. Everything fits. I was looking at the whole and ignoring the parts. He's right."

"You *have* to meet him. Orestes says when he's fleet admiral, Arana won't have to be afraid of Earth anymore."

When, not *if.* That was faith, and it was new to Teal Ray. "What's he going to do about *this* situation when he takes over?" Teal said, more as a remark than a question. He didn't expect an answer.

"You mean Loki-Gereny?" Johnny said. "He was against the alliance with Loki to begin with. His father received the ambassadors from Loki, and Orestes said it was wrong—it was imperialism—and his father agreed but supported the alliance anyway."

Orestes was obviously the son of someone notable. "Who is his father?"

"High Commissioner Agamemnon Peralta."

"The man who owns half the galaxy?" Teal said.

"How many Agamemnon Peraltas do you know?" Johnny returned.

The son would have to become no less than fleet admiral to best his father.

"Orestes wouldn't have advised the alliance because it's un-provoked aggression against Gereny for imperialistic gain. General Falco is a man of honor too, but he didn't have too much to say in it either. He told Orestes that Earth would be repaid for her loyalty—and we were. They saved us in Armageddon I. . . . We're in debt to *everyone* because of that war."

"Not really." Teal shook his head. "No one helped you for charity's sake. It was all self-defense. No one does anything that isn't gaining something for himself in some way. Like Earth's alliance with Loki is an excuse to attack Gereny. You have no real justification for that."

"I know," Johnny said. "And they scare me—the Gerens do. I don't like staring down their torpedo tubes. Sometimes I get the feeling we're fighting a dragon with pop guns. You know, we know nothing about Gereny. One of these days someone will take one step too far and the dragon will stomp on us. . . ."

NGC had an encounter with *Rita* and was nearly destroyed. When Kury was thrown to the deck by a shock wave, Teal was suddenly giving orders. Kury rose to his feet. "I ain't out yet, Second." In the time it took Kury to get back on his feet, Teal had gotten *NGC* out of immediate danger, and Kury glared at this captain who never commanded more than a desk.

NGC was grounded for repairs for a long stretch, and Teal was only too happy about it.

Then *Rita* stopped being sighted, and rumors spread that Merek was caught up in political snarls that might down *Rita* for good. Falco was despondent, and he ravaged the border zone in a series of raids, trying to force an appearance of the red ship. Each time he returned in a vicious temper and re-tired to his tent, which he kept at the edge of the base away from everyone and in the open air. He would sit and fret and plan even bolder campaigns, letting the Gerens know that they could not do without Merek.

At last, the long-awaited news came: the red ship was back in battle. *Rita* led a force that made Loki defender now, in-stead of attacker.

It was obvious John Falco was pleased with his game of interstellar chess as he launched his counterattack, and Metrarch was pleased to bring bad news.

"The Geren general is urinating blood. He may not be in action much longer."

Falco bolted upright.

"The general shows all the symptoms of tertiary menthiis."

Falco stood stunned, and Metrarch went on in an oily voice, "The irony is only too perfect—for your archenemy to go in a way that can never touch you, sir. Space chatter has it that he was going to be 'retired' shortly, but it is just too perfect that he go like this, don't you think?"

"Get the Voyager ready for flight."

"You are entering the battle, sir?"

"Yes."

"There is something else, sir."

"What is it?" Falco snapped impatiently, eyes glaring fiercely above the white mask.

"The men thought they'd . . . surprise you."

"Get the Voyager."

Metrarch leered and left to obey.

John Falco boarded his Voyager ship and took flight. Then, onto his monitor came Metrarch's "something else." Falco wasn't surprised—he was mortified.

It was the image of the scarlet ship *Rita* captive between two Lokin battleships, being led back as victor's prize.

General Falco's ship sped to meet the formation. He approached and signaled the other ships away from the prisoner vessel. They obeyed and the Voyager swept by, discharging all her weapons, and Jaephah Merek and *Rita* were destroyed.

As its ruins splintered and drifted in space, the Voyager made another pass by the demolished vessel, and jettisoned antimatter. An explosion ripped Merek's death site in a hazardous salute that could've killed Falco. (Was that the idea. . . ?)

John Falco then brought his Voyager to a standstill and let it drift.

Everyone on base witnessed General Merek's death from the control center, and they were all out to meet the Voyager when she left her death vigil and landed.

The only one who could speak to the distraught general was Metrarch.

"You should have let him land, sir. They're so beautiful when they bleed." Metrarch leered.

"You want blood, Metrarch? You can piss blood!" Falco rasped and spit in his eyes.

The leering man lost his grin and grew frightened. "Get me water! Get me a doctor! Don't . . . don't let me get infected!" He was condemned to die, bleeding. He grasped Falco's shoulder. "General—"

"I can't help you." Falco shook him off.

The general then turned to the Earthmen, blue eyes blazing and voice shrill. "On behalf of the Lokin government, I thank you for your service. You aren't needed anymore—now get the hell out of here."

The Earthmen backed off, both from Falco and from Metrarch, who was hysterical, begging for help from people who ran away, for Metrarch was now as deadly as Falco. He acted like a rabid animal, mad, dangerous, and dying.

Teal Ray watched as the crazed man tried to grab a frightened young soldier, and everyone looked on—horrified yet fascinated—doing nothing.

Teal took a Lokin soldier's weapon—it was a handgun—stepped forward, and shot Metrarch.

The rest stared in silent horror. It wasn't that he had killed him—someone had to—it was how: cold, calm, as though he had poured a glass of water, not shot a man. No matter that it had to be done, and that any one of them would've liked to have killed Metrarch at one time or another. One just didn't gun a man down as this man Ray Stewert did. There had to be some emotion. He was too cold-blooded.

Turbulent current swept beneath calm surface, and Ray prayed to any god not to let the Red Madness take him here. He was staring off at the wide expanse of sky when someone's gasp made him snap back and look to dead Metrarch.

Before he could scream, "Peritas, no!" the dog had stepped in blood and was sniffing the body, whining. Instantly, lest he hesitate, he fired again, and Peritas' yelp tore through him as the weapon through his pet.

Horror compounded at the unblinking murder of his own dog, the crew stared and backed off as if he were as diseased as the corpses.

Falco looked at him and saw something in the black eyes that the others had missed. He nodded. He looked at the weapon in Ray's hand. "Don't put that to your head. *You* still have something to live for." He took the gun from Ray, careful not to touch him, and went to his tent.

"Cold-blooded it was," went the murmurs as the spyship readied to depart.

"With no more passion than flushing the goddam head."

"Creepy, really creepy. I'll be glad when we get him off this ship."

"He's not an Earthman."

"Are you guessing or stating?" Kury asked.

"Stating. I'm guessing that he isn't even human."

Kury stared at the wall. "He didn't even blink. His own dog."

Wretching. Burning inside. Blood turned fire. Red darting across white wrists like snakes' tongues. Reill. Red Madness.

Staggering to the medicine chest for the little red pills. Binding wrists with cloth to hide the veins turned fiery red beneath the skin. Don't look at them. . . .

Eyes on fire, brain in flames. Wanting to scream, but he couldn't let anyone find him like this. . . .

"Where the hell is my first officer?" Kury growled.

"Far away, I hope," someone said.

"Damn, I need someone who'll pull his own weight. I don't need a triggerman."

He found Ray in his cabin, lying on the bed, pale, semi-conscious, drenched in sweat. Kury picked up the bottle of little red painkillers from the table next to him. He turned back to Ray and picked up a limp arm and saw the bound wrists.

"Slash them?" Kury said.

It was a plausible explanation. "Yes."

"Deep?"

"No."

Kury looked at the bottle in his hand. "Fuck it, Stewert, you took enough reddots to down an army!"

He was going to call a doctor. He had to say something to stop him. "I threw them up," Teal said feebly. "I'll live."

"What'd you do? Chicken out?"

"Yes."

"Do you want a doctor?"

"No."

"Anything? Drink of water?"

"No!" he said too emphatically. It was reflex. Water and Red Madness.

"Okay, babe, okay," Kury said, sitting at his bedside.

"Why do you have such a big bottle of reddots in your room? I didn't know they came that big."

"Kill myself," Teal said. Kury thought he'd just tried to. Let him think that.

"Six pills would've done it."

No, I just took six. "I don't know," he spoke weakly.

"You'll be all right?"

"Yes, sir."

Kury got up to go then turned and said, "I'm so glad you turned out human, mannie."

Teal shut his eyes. The crisis had passed and now he was just tired. Otranadoe couldn't compare with that kind of pain—and maybe that was what had gotten him through the prison; he knew worse. But if anyone ever found out . . . No one must know.

He returned to Earth more distant and aloof than he'd left, his "suicide attempt" unreported. He was now even afraid to run. Why hadn't he expected to meet his own plagued kind in space? Running the way he ran.

IV.

July 1, 2184 A.D. (Friday)

Teal arrived on Earth on the first anniversary of his infiltration into UEF. The crew of *NGC* found a different UEF than they had left six months ago, and it was under the command of Fleet Admiral James McCreedy. He had been busy overhauling the system with typical McCreedy swiftness and boldness.

Curiosity as to how it ever happened dogged Teal and overcame his better judgment to avoid McCreedy. The fleet admiral was in a cheerful, informal mood when Ray saw him.

"Ray, damn, long time. Sit down." He ushered him in. His office on Luna Base was as disaster-stricken and disorganized as the one in Chicago, only it was bigger, with more junk strewn about. The furniture was more expensive, but already it stank of cigarette and narcotic smoke. McCreedy was thinner and in need of twenty-four hours of sleep. Bloodshot eyes were propped open with pills that kept him in action, though his whole being shouted at him to stop. He overturned a chair and a pile of stuff fell to the floor. He righted it for Ray, then sat himself on his desk. "How do you like spyships?"

Ray shook his head. "No."

"I offered to get you out of it."

"I've got to take my own part without being some kind of admiral's leech." He searched Jim's face to see if he'd accepted the explanation. There was no indication either way.

"I heard you shot a man, Ray. A Lokin officer." He gnawed on his knuckles.

"Yes, sir."

"Don't sir me, goddammit. You aren't under report." He took his fist from his mouth and pounded the desk beside him for emphasis. His knuckles were bleeding.

116

"Why bring it up, then?"

"I wanted a personal reaction."

Teal stiffened his shoulders in agitation. "Sir, I have been damned by the entire crew of *NGC* because I didn't give a personal reaction."

McCreedy got up and lit a cigarette at the Slave. "That's what I heard. I don't believe it."

"The crew was there. They saw it," Teal said. A knot of pain in his shoulder told him to relax.

"They *didn't* see it," Jim amended. "I heard you had to shoot your dog."

"Yeah."

"I'll get you another dog."

"I don't want another dog."

"Okay."

Finding himself in an uncomfortable position, Ray fired back with a question. "What happened to Johnson?"

Jim cackled and flipped the lapel of his jacket to reveal a button proclaiming JOHNSON '84. "He's running for president of the United States!"

Teal straightened in his chair. "And you're endorsing him?"

"I am. They can *have* him. Anything to keep that bastard out of my fleet. He has a chance, too. He's being called Defender of Freedom or some such schtick like that. He saved Earth against all odds, etc. The Americans will believe anything they want to, and they want a hero now. Meanwhile, I'm going to make my fleet so powerful Johnson will choke on his campaign speech."

"How did it get to be *your* fleet?" Teal asked.

"*That*," McCreedy said, and took a long drag on his cigarette for a dramatic pause, enjoying this story immensely, "was the biggest mistake in UEF history. It's a bigger blunder than the Canda affair or the Sixus settlement. You see"—he tapped ashes into the Slave, which sucked them neatly away—"Johnson and the board had *one*—and only one—belief in common, and that was that Jimmy McCreedy was an archbastard who just *had* to go. So they put all their heads together (and almost had a full brain among them), and tried to figure out *how* to fix Jimmy's little red spaceship. Now, you can't demote a war hero, so they had to promote me to get me out of where I was—which was board member and base administrator; you can't get much higher than that. So they created this office of vice admiral of the fleet while they were doing some power reorganization. Fleet admiral gained almost autonomous power with inadequate checks and balances, but do you know what the job of vice admiral entails?"

Teal shook his head.

"Nothing," Jim said. "Absolutely nothing. It's a job tailor-made for Jim McCreedy. And vice admiral can hold no other position at the same time. Doublefine, eh? What happened is obvious. Johnson got sick of his deteriorating fleet and wanted a job with more prestige, and he resigned to go on the campaign trail. Once out of the fleet, he was rid of me and couldn't care less whether I stepped up to the top. The swearing-in was like a funeral. You have no idea how many people I've fired. And assassination attempts like you wouldn't believe. The only time I'm unguarded is when I go to church. I figure if I get killed there, God must want it. So far it looks like He still wants me kicking."

"Yours is the god of the cross, isn't that right?" Ray said, sounding far away.

Struck by the strangeness, Jim came to his side. "Yeah . . . yes, He is."

"Where is the sun?"

Sun or son? Jim could not tell, and assumed the latter.

Lack of sun had made Teal alabaster-white. Fine features and slender build gave an impression that he would break if handled roughly. Jim put a hand on his shoulder. "Ray, are you all right?"

At his touch Ray snapped back into here and now. A thought began to form and was shattered as the door slid open and Kury stormed in.

"McCreedy, you tell me what this means!" He was in all-out rage as he had never been. He paced the floor in great strides, expending energy that locked in would lead to murder.

The fleet admiral started at his entrance, but had obviously been expecting him and knew what he was referring to. "It wasn't my decision, Kury. It was the board's."

"Well, what the hell are you going to do about it?" Kury bellowed and flung up long strong arms and towered a foot over the fleet admiral. Ray had become air.

"Nothing," Jim said firmly. Kury blanked a moment in disbelief, and McCreedy spoke. "I do not approve the decision and I said so. What more would you have me do?"

"Hell, Jim, you can do better than that!" Kury said, loud

and mocking. "I've seen you bitch when you want something. And you always make damn well sure you get it. Now you listen—"

"*Sit down!*" McCreedy topped his volume.

"*Don't* play fleet admiral with *me*—you're McCreedy, I'm Kury—" he shouted.

"*I'm not pulling rank on you, but I will if you don't shut your fucking mouth and sit your fucking ass down!*" Jim thundered. He added in an undertone, quietly, "Sit down."

Kury obeyed but made it clear he wasn't cowed. He lifted a chair and dumped everything off it. Violently righting it, he sat and stewed. Jim stamped out his cigarette and looked very calm. "Here's how it is. You are asking me to cross the board—as a special favor to you. I give no special favors—"

Kury tried to cut in but McCreedy cut him off. "Shut up, I'm not done yet. If you are now thinking I owe you this because of friendship or some such reason, forget it. If this ruins our friendship, Kury, then I don't really give a fuck. Doublefine, eh?"

Kury made several attempts to reply and fell into exasperated silence. McCreedy added in a less harsh voice, "I can only advise you, and I haven't much to offer. The only solution I can see is to prove yourself the better man. Do that and I *will* cross the board, since it ceases to be a favor and becomes the only right course of action. That's the only way you'll get your ship back."

Kury stalked out ready to kill.

"What's this?" Teal asked. "They took his ship?"

McCreedy nodded and lit up a narcotic cigarette. "They took his ship."

Teal was amazed. Kury had commanded it since it had been built. If the crew wouldn't accept a new Second they would mutiny under a new commander. "Who did they give it to?"

"Commodore Decker," Jim said. "The board's darling. He's brilliant on paper. Graduated highest in the academy—ever. Blasts the roof off computer drills—but he's never had a command."

"And they gave him *NGC*."

"They did. He's never been in battle. All he ever commanded was a desk. That's like giving *you* a man-o'-war."

Not quite, Teal thought in slight relief. *He doesn't know.* "And where does that leave Kury?" he asked.

"Like a beached whale. The board hates him. They did

what they tried to do to me, only with more success this time—kicked him upstairs."

"There'll be howling in the old fleet tonight," Teal murmured, thinking of the crew.

"There already is," said McCreedy. "There already is."

Kury didn't know what to say when Decker pulled a surprise inspection of *NGC* and found beer in the cryophysics freezer, vodka on tap in the commodore's quarters, and pretzels in the torpedo tubes. At the latter, Decker blew up. "Do you realize, sir, what a hazard you have here? What would happen if a sudden need for the torpedoes should arise in an emergency situation?"

"We shoot a lot of pretzels into oblivion."

"Be serious, commodore! This is a bloody grave offense."

"I am serious, commodore. We've done it. The torpedoes work fine with pretzels. We just have to clean up the crumbs after the battle so we don't get ants."

"Ants on a spaceship!"

"They escaped from the lab."

"And you haven't corrected that negligence?!"

"It's almost taken care of—we let the aardvark out."

If the pretzels and the ants didn't do it, the aardvark did. Decker started filling out a formal report on Kury, compiling a list of fifty-six offenses.

"This is a bloody disgrace, Boris Kuryin."

"Call me Boris and you may bloody well have a bloody *face!*"

Fifty-seven offenses.

Kury took Ray out to a bar on Luna and bitched in his beer. "Listen, Stewert, I could arrange to have that fucker disappear without a trace except that everyone would know who did it. I could frame him, but all he'd have to do is put one hand on the regulation book and one over his heart and swear, and they'd believe him. I even shook his closet to see if any bones rattled. Pure as the driven. I'd even bet he was virgin. Say, you don't suppose he's queer, do you?"

"I don't think so," Captain Stewert said.

"No?" Kury said.

"He doesn't strike me that way."

"Now look, you never know. They can seem straight as a light beam in nowhere—not all of 'em have limp wrists and swish."

"I know."

"Some of the guys you'd least expect—queer as a three-eyed jack. . . . Ya know, he even made me get rid of my aardvark."

"Did he?"

"Yeah, well, the motherfucker was getting mean anyway. Took a swipe at me with those big claws, ya know? Those big—"

"I know."

"Yeah, well . . . glad Decker wasn't around when I had the musinot."

Teal put down his coffee cup. "You had a musinot?"

"Yeah." Kury's eyes were bright and watery. He laughed a little. "You know . . . you know, we had to leave behind several kegs of supplies when that thing got big. Talk about mean pets."

Teal could tell his having to get rid of the aardvark hurt Kury as much as Teal hurt when he had to shoot his dog.

" . . . they thought when I adopted my Johnny that he was another weird pet. Showed them. He's a good kid . . . he'll be in the war games tomorrow."

War games! "Kury!"

"Humph?"

"Pilot a Voyager in the war games." His voice was commanding.

"What for?"

"Do it," said Teal. "Trust me."

"Sure, what the hell."

Johnny's reason for being in the war games became clear. Orestes was in them, and they no sooner saw each other then they were in each other's arms, exchanging a rib-crushing hug and talking at once, each finishing the other's thought. "Young Adonis" had been a slight—the boy was a godling. Fair face flushed with excitement was dominated by blue eyes arresting all they lighted on, bright and clear. Fire-gold mane crowned a youth built like an idealized Greek athlete. Johnny introduced Teal, and young Orestes was awed. From the questions he asked—which were endless—Teal could see that intelligence matched his looks, and Teal wondered *where* Johnny had found this child. Orestes couldn't wait to see *Tesah*'s captain fly in the war games. "What Voyager are you?"

"I'm scheduled for thirteen."

"Thirteen," Orestes nodded.

Teal repeated with emphasis, "I'm scheduled for thirteen."

A smile of understanding lit Orestes' face. Johnny missed it. No doubt Orestes would tell him later.

A squad of fifteen Voyagers would meet another squad while *NGC* competed in separate trial with a ship of her own class. The Voyagers would not meet *NGC* at all, according to schedule.

Ray Stewert would pilot Voyager 13 and Kury Voyager 10. But as the pilots boarded individual Voyagers, Teal stopped Kury.

"Switch ships with me. Take thirteen."

"I'm scheduled for ten."

"Take thirteen," Ray said.

"Superstitious?"

No, Ten is my number. "Yeah."

Kury shrugged. "Okay, mannie."

"Oh, and Kury," Teal said. "Don't inform ground control."

It wasn't until the Voyager fleet was in space and going through mock battle that any of Ray's actions made sense.

Voyager 10 very quickly got itself "destroyed," then veered off and flew over on an intercept course with *NGC*, which had successfully completed its maneuvers to perfection and was returning home.

Decker wasn't prepared, and the Voyager landed a dummy bomb on *NGC*'s bow.

"GC, this is not on schedule—please instruct," Decker radioed the controller. He pronounced it "shedule."

"*NGC*, a Uelson man-o'-war has landed two force-five shots on your hull—don't ask *me* what to do," the controller's voice said, playing along with Ray's game.

"This isn't in the shedule," Decker's voice fairly whined.

"The Uelsons don't have a shedule," the controller said. "You'll just have to reshedule your shedule."

Voyager 10 played the man-o'-war and buzzed *NGC*. Decker finally caught on and began evasive maneuvers.

Decker's maneuvers read off of a history tape.

Voyager 10 mimicked an attack made on Admiral Johnson's warship back in Armageddon I, and Decker used the move Johnson had used to escape. But Ray knew the stratagem too. He anticipated Decker's move and fired at his predicted path. The shot hit home. After a number of similar shots the ground controller signaled *NGC*.

"*NGC*, you have been destroyed twice so far—get off your ass, Decker."

The textbook-bound Decker was bewildered. Why weren't these maneuvers working? They'd worked before. That was it. Voyager 10 had seen the same tapes. He had to do something that hadn't been done before. He began his own evasive maneuvers.

And Voyager 10 began its own attacks.

Voyager was one of the most maneuverable ships in the Fleet, but not more so than spyships like *NGC*. But no one had ever seen a Voyager move the way Voyager 10 did.

Decker froze. The little ship landed shot after dummy shot on the *NGC* and was never hit once.

When it was all over, the red-faced Decker found his ship "destroyed" eighteen times over.

Kury found himself being slapped on the back. "Mean flying, Kury."

The board began to have second thoughts about giving a ship to a man who lost it eighteen times in mock battle—unscheduled or no.

"But I was perfect in the war games," Decker argued, his face red beneath his beard. "The last encounter was not authorized. It was misuse of a Voyager. It was not part of the war games at all. It was a violation of regulations."

But eighteen times was eighteen times.

Decker filed formal protest against Voyager 10's actions.

"Commodore, what if that had been a real Uelson Voyager with real torpedoes? Would his shots not *count* because he wasn't scheduled?" McCreedy challenged the fuming man in his office.

So when probation period was up, Decker's assignment was not made permanent. And Kury was restored to his ship.

"Stewert, I am forever in your debt. What can I do for you? Name it," Kury said, swinging his great paw around Ray's shoulders.

"Don't ever tell anyone that we switched ships."

"But Stewert—"

"Ever."

"Okay, mannie," Kury said, then, "Hey, could you possibly do me another big favor?"

Teal waited.

"Could you take out one of those dummy ships against *NGC* with *me* in command?" he asked. "I mean, Decker botched up royally, but I'm not sure I could do any better. I mean, that was one hell of a flying job, Ray—it was incredible. . . . I haven't *seen* . . . not since Armageddon—"

"I can't, Kury," said Ray.

"Why?"

"Because *you* did the flying, Kury; I was in Voyager thirteen, remember?"

V.

August 28, 2189 A.D. (Saturday)

Days bled into years and Teal waited, jumping at shadows, all of them moving like Vanguard. All smells were Uelson. And the hidden double star of Diakyon was so far off. The death collar grew tighter every year, and Teal prayed that if there were a god of revenge for the fair-weather clouds to mount into a thunderhead that was to be Armageddon II before his time was done.

He lived in quiet obscurity, waiting, planning, and dreaming, watching the Earthmen age around him, himself unchanged since leaving Arana except to turn from dark to milky white. Thoughts of home were avoided; it brought Red Madness. He allowed himself a dream of a heroic homecoming, his father forgiving him. Teal had heard there was a way of transferring the pain of a Reill crisis from one person to another; a person could take the pain away onto himself. It was another part of the natural design—it was meant for the father to take it from the son. Teal had never heard of it happening (there were few instances of Reill in history, and fewer who lived past the time of trial as he had), but this was the only end to it. Reill was caused by the father rejecting a Bay son, so it followed that if the father loved the son enough to take the Reill, he might undo the damage. But Teal could not credit it ever happening. No one could ever stand to take Reill upon himself—it was inconceivable. And again, if the father loved his son enough to do such a superhuman feat, the son would not have gotten the Red Madness to begin with.

Teal walked from his office, out of the compound and into fading daylight. It was a warm August evening, and he carried his suit jacket over his arm. At home he would have worn nothing, but the Earthlings—so much like their kin, the

Aranian Northerners—were concerned with covering their bodies. Teal saw many people here who were sexually frustrated, deviant or perverted. At home, in the Royalist country, Teal was the only sexually unbalanced person he knew. He had had to seek companionship in a foreign land. But he had been hurt too many times to try again, and six years of celibacy had been preferable to two minutes of laughter. He was not ready to let any of these aliens close to him—James McCreedy included, though he could not figure out what the young admiral wanted from him.

Teal summoned a car and waited. Suddenly senses sparked, and a long, black, muscular arm closed around his neck. Bay instinct took over Teal's conscious impulses. His breeding and the strength of an inhabitant of a heavier world surfaced, and he left his dazed attacker on the ground.

Unarmed, in UEF uniform, head spinning, the man spoke. "Hey, mannie, peace, okay?"

Teal had bared white teeth in an animal snarl. Senses cleared, and he attempted to regain some semblance of an Earthling, closely watching his assailant, a lean, wiry black man clearing even Kury's height.

"Nothing meant. All in fun, honest to God. Jim didn't say you could fight," he said from the ground, almost laughing.

Ray glared at him hard. "You're a friend of McCreedy's?"

The bald black head nodded. "Yeah." He got to his feet slowly, and rose. . . . and rose. The Goliath-sized man pursed his lips and wagged his head. "You don't look like a fighter, mannie. No offense, but you don't look like you got it in you."

Jim came down the walk, laughing. "That looked pretty damn funny. What did you think you were doing?" He punched the stranger in his firm stomach.

"You didn't say he could fight." He shrugged broad shoulders.

"That doesn't mean you have to attack him," Jim said. It was the first time Ray had ever seen him out of uniform. He leaned against the black human pillar and presented him to a still-wary Ray. "This schmoe is Richard Barrett. We make excuses for *his* kind," he needled and ducked a cuff that looked as if it might take his head off. "He's in the merchant division—we can't all be perfect—and he loves to wrestle, which I'm sure you have already noticed. He already knows who you are."

He talks about me, Ray thought. *What does he say?*

"Where did you learn to fight like that?" Richard Barrett put a hand to his shining, hairless head.

Teal quickly improvised, "You grow up looking like I do and you learn awfully fast."

Barrett laughed. Ray looked to Jim; he didn't believe it at all.

The car pulled up, and all three got in. Teal switched from robot to manual. "Where are you headed?"

"My place," McCreedy said and keyed his address in the robot control.

"What on Earth are you doing here?" Teal finally thought to ask Jim.

"You mean what am I doing on Earth?" Jim half smiled. "I have given myself a nice long leave—"

"With a little arm-twisting from his doctor," the black man clarified.

"Don't listen to this pirate."

The men taunted each other, and Teal's mind drifted off in thought. *My face should be glass for all he can see of me.* He could keep his barrier intact before everyone but Jim. How could this man know where he'd been . . . *unless he'd been there?*

I am not a dark wall to him, Teal thought. *But neither am I glass. I am a mirror!*

McCreedy's home was an ancient two-story house that wanted to die. The lawn was overgrown, the robot mower having broken down in his absence. "I was afraid of that," he grumbled. They stepped out of the car, and the ground swallowed it up in the underground garage. "Now watch the door forget me," Jim said and put his hand on the metal key panel.

"That's impossible," said Ray.

"It gets stuck sometimes," he explained. The door opened a crack, then stopped, motors whirring. "Come on, babe, you can do it." McCreedy kicked it and it slid open. "This house is in real great shape, like its owner. What do you want to drink?"

"Don't get his coffee," Barrett warned.

McCreedy grinned. "Yeah, I wouldn't advise that either—it's the kind that doesn't need a cup."

"Doesn't need a cup!" Richard said, as if McCreedy had made a gross understatement. "It crawls out, does a tap dance on the table, spins a yo-yo, and sings the *Star Spangled Banner!*"

"No coffee of mine ever sang the *Star Spangled Banner.*"

"*Oh Canada,* then."

"My mother used to sing that," Jim said.

"I thought your Ma was the alien half."

"She was. She had a nice voice. I remember."

Mama, Mama. Mama, Teal thought. He talked about her, but Teal could not remember ever hearing him mention his father. *Why no Papa? Because Papa beat the shit out of you, you poor bastard,* he thought, referring to himself as well.

Jim fixed drinks and had milk himself. "Ulcer," he explained. "I have to drink milk. I hate milk."

Jim was talking trivia for the first time. He was making social noise. Teal sat on the couch, one leg under him, scowling. *What the hell are you doing?* he wanted to yell out loud.

" . . . see a Uelson? They have skin like bald guinea pigs." He was aware of the conversation.

"How do you know what bald guinea pigs look like?" Barrett said.

"I shaved one when I was little. Mama nearly fainted. I was a rotten kid. Still am."

Richard walked around the house with big strides. "Hey, Jimmy, since you're the big man and hauling in this fine, fantastic salary, why don't you do something with this dump—like raze it?"

"Because I'm not hauling in a fine, fantastic salary—I gave myself a fifty-percent pay cut. Which is still a pretty sum, but that's what it costs to live on Luna."

"You gave yourself a pay cut?" Barrett mouthed the words, unable to speak.

"I don't need it. Nobody needs that kind of money. You wouldn't understand, you pirate. The *fleet* needs everything it can get. Most popular decision I ever made. Didn't lessen the screaming when I did the same to the board."

"I hear you're also catching hell for dismissing the board's token Jew."

"Yeah, well, this token Catholic/token Canuck caught said token Jew up to his Star of David in graft. That isn't what they're pissed about; they helped kick him out. It's because I didn't *replace* him with a Jew. Not only that, really. He's Russian. Well, the Jews got mad 'cause he wasn't a Jew. The Americans got mad 'cause now there are as many Russians on the board as there are Americans. The *Russians* are mad because he thinks of the best interests of Earth as a whole, which ain't always the best for Russia, but it's exactly why I chose him."

"Naw, Jimmy, you blew it." Richard wagged his head.

"Why?"

Full lips pressed together in a line and he shook his head. "You should have chosen a nigger."

Teal laughed, and Jim looked twice to see where the sound was coming from.

"What are you, Ray?" Jim asked.

"You a WASP?" Barrett guessed.

"Mongrel American," Teal said.

"What mostly?" Jim asked. "By descent."

"Czechoslovakian."

"Oh."

When Barrett left, he took the car and sent it back by robot control. Teal sat alone in the living room, waiting for its return. The room was very lived-in and livable, despite disorder and slight disrepair, yet his senses danced to nerves singing in his brain. *Storm at Sea. What am I overlooking?*

He could hear Jim moving in the small kitchen, which served as an alternative to the Slave's meals ("Slaves always break egg yolks," he'd heard).

Plaster walls were like home, only they were monochrome eggshell and pictures hung on them instead of being painted into the wall. Teal rose and crossed the well-walked carpet within the walls that had seen many lives.

They'd stopped talking when Barrett left. Teal held back faded curtains to see out of the window. The car hadn't come back yet. The stars had come up, but Teal couldn't see Procyon. He looked back at Jim, who'd cleaned up his kitchen—as zoo-y as any room of McCreedy's—and was taking a triple dose of ulcer pills.

It was late. Jim sighed and started up the stairs for bed. Teal wondered where that left him. He didn't know if he was supposed to follow. He froze at the foot of the stairs.

No.

Storm at Sea raging full fury.

"Good night, Jimmy," he said after him.

McCreedy spun on the stairs to face him and looked down at him. Looked through him. And recognized what he saw.

Teal took two steps backward, a third prevented by the wall he'd backed up against.

"Now that you've let me drag you all the way out here, it's

a hell of a time to get cold feet. And I'll tell you something else, it's not *fair*, Ray."

The door was unlocked. He could run out. He could walk.

He tripped once climbing the stairs.

Teal heard birdsongs in a lightening sky when finally he woke, heavy-lidded, in a hot, stuffy room that stank of sex and an Earthman. Sparrows chirping and insect buzz, traffic and morning sounds seemed far away. Most of everything, he noticed he wasn't alone. There'd been no running off or ordering away. Worry followed close on relief—it was Jim's house, maybe it was up to Teal to go away. This was Earth, maybe they had customs he was unaware of. Feeling as upset as he was terrified, he realized bitterly that no one had *ever* told him the first thing about sex. He'd always learned by stepping in fires. Maybe Jim would awake expecting him gone—see him at the office sometime and salute—the end. He should have kept to his vow—not on Earth.

A robin sang just outside the window. Jim half-woke, groaned something, and fell asleep again, nose to Teal's neck and bristly chin ground into his shoulder. They were not signs to leave. A sleep-flung arm held him down. Teal guessed he'd stay. And listened to the robin.

In the morning that was really afternoon, Jim rose and stumbled through the ruins of his room and brought some coffee in. Teal sat up and slipped into a robe found for him in the chaos and pulled it around himself. He got up and sat in a chair. The furniture was an odd agglomeration of periods from the past two centuries, skipping over every period of glass and metal and plastic. All was wood and upholstery, from overstuffed, comfortable, twenty-first-century armchair to almost modern wooden end table. Nothing looked newer than two generations old. Ray got the impression that Jim never bought anything. The carpet was a heavily trodden, large weave of several faded colors. Once gaudy, it was now subdued.

He accepted the cup of coffee put in his hands. Dwelling on the night and his trusting not to be destroyed, the relief of the safe and sound after so much danger filled him and made him shiver.

"Hey," Jim said, sitting on the arm of his chair. "That coffee's okay to drink; I didn't make it. It's the stuff from the Slave."

"Oh."

Teal's hand found the silver pendant around Jim's neck. He'd never taken it off. "This too is a symbol of God of the cross," Teal said and held it in his hand. "I never saw this symbol."

"You've never seen the Madonna and Child?"

"I don't mean I never *saw* it. I mean I see things, a rosette, circle . . . no . . . it's nothing. Never mind."

"My priest gave this to me before he died. He was only a hundred and one. Died young because he made a goddam hero out of himself," Jim said. "What religion are you, Ray?"

"I don't have one."

"Do you believe in God?"

"He died."

A slanted shaft of light from a high sun shone in the window.

"Ray, are you really Lokin?"

"No, Why?"

"Anyone who wakes with no shadow whatsoever is either different or fifteen years old."

"I'm different."

"I'm sorry. I didn't mean to say that," Jim said, feeling even more clumsy than he had at night. He touched the hard death collar, hesitated, then spoke. "You didn't get that at the Sixus massacre. How long has it been?"

Teal would neither answer nor lie.

"Ray, Sixus was a good sixteen years ago. I *know* those things take about ten. How long is it?"

Teal wanted to talk to him. And say what? *Since Armageddon?* Then what would happen when Jim said, "But you weren't in Armageddon." But he deserved better than silence—that was for Uelsons. "Don't make me say anything, Jimmy."

"Should I just wait for you to die?"

Beyond sorrow, Teal could see his mind working, juggling pieces and remembering when he first heard of Ray Stewart, almost certain he was not an Earthman. From an unknown planet. *Tesah* was from an unknown planet. Two unknowns appearing within a year of each other. If he figured it out Teal couldn't know, for he did not ask for confirmation. If he didn't know, he was not troubling him further, but he definitely knew Teal was hiding something of great importance. The Uelsons didn't collar someone unless they wanted something of him. He said no more about it. *That*, Teal recognized as it was granted for the first time, *is trust.*

Ray returned with Jim to Luna Base. Teal disliked the moon but kept it to himself. Jim clearly shared his view and did not bother to hide it.

"There's something very depressing about sitting on a barren rock, home shining blue in the sky, within sight and unreachable, going through phases like a goddam moon. And you look out at the landscape and it's unreal."

It was a stark environment. The approach was foreboding. Luna Base was a giant dome, jutting out as suddenly as an unworn cliff, surrounded by smaller satellite domes, like a creature with many appendages.

Daylight was for fourteen and a half days, during which Teal never saw the sun, for the screens were raised for protection and to reduce wear on the dome. Fourteen and a half days of darkness were flooded with artificial daylight.

"I wish I didn't have to bring you to this godforsaken place. I put it to the council of nations' representatives to move the command of UEF back to Earth, and the same debate came up as when it was established—where on Earth are you going to put it? No way that many people are going to agree on anything."

Time passed on Luna. Teal heard rumor of a primitive superlight ship from Arana. When he heard no more about it, he wanted to ask McCreedy but didn't dare show interest. It was not a matter of trust. If Teal told him, Jim would be duty-bound to inform UEF while at the same time bound to Ray not to. He would not put Jim in that situation, not when he had an increasingly heavy load on his mind. McCreedy was beating the fleet into fighting order. The merchant fleet profited, receiving castoff old battleships revamped for hauling cargo, while the military division was a new and unrecognizable entity from the one that had fought Armageddon I. Teal lay awake many nights while Jim was tossing and fretting over some new international clash or failed test flight. Other times it had been Ray's fault, though he was unaware of it.

"You know, a couple of the women on base have a crush on you, Ray," Jim said.

"Me?" Teal was genuinely surprised.

"Some of the men too," he said. Jim fancied Ray could have anyone he cared to eye back, which made him marvel and thank God he was the one. Thank God while his priest told him it was a sin. One of many restless nights had been after a thrashing out of the subject with a priest, to no resolution. Another had been when Richard Barrett died. Barrett was one of the rare people who could make Ray laugh. He had Slinger's disease, a rare, terminal condition of the brain of unknown origin, only discovered in the stellar age. "How long have you know he had that?" Ray demanded.

"Several years now," Jim said.

"You introduced me to a dying man!" Ray cried. "I lose too many to walk into another on purpose!"

For Ray, life was mostly quiet and as close as possible to being good. Red Madness was still with him. His duty also remained, unforgotten. And revenge. He'd almost given up hope of ever resolving those troubles—till he heard the first hints of coming war. He was sitting with Jim, finishing off his cigarette as had become his conscious habit to do. His own lungs would regenerate. Jim's could not. This time Jim wouldn't give it up.

"What's wrong, Jimmy?"

"I . . ." Jim stared at the ceiling. "I hope I haven't heard Gabriel's trumpet."

"What is it?"

" 'Peace' messengers from the Uelsons. They want to negotiate. I verbally spit in their faces."

"Good," said Ray.

"It's a prelude to war," Jim said. "It's exactly like the first time, like a kind of Uelson ritual. First they try to 'negotiate' some outrageous terms, then they come back with warships. I see Armageddon II, and I hope it won't be *the* Armageddon. I can see them returning with a fleet of ships—ships just like the alien ship in Armageddon I."

"They won't," said Teal. He spoke with assurance. "They won't." He had to give Jim that, even if it gave him away.

"I've done all I can," Jim said. "Now, I'm just helpless, waiting."

All Teal could do was wait. But McCreedy had the power of command. "Take command of a warship," Ray said. "The *Kiev*."

"She's a Russian-based ship," Jim said.

"Can't you speak Russian?"

"No."

"The *Hamilton* then."

Jim regarded him like an over zealous child. "I'm fleet admiral; I can't go dashing off where I please."

"Step down. You said you can't do any more here. And if

there's a war, you can't sit here through it, and you'd rather be on a ship than here anyway—"

Jim smiled with an indulgent air. "You do it."

"What?"

"I'd give you the *Hamilton* if you asked."

Teal scowled, then saw he was serious. *He must know.* "I'm not a commander," Ray said. "Obviously."

"That says nothing. Some of the greatest leaders surrender in the bedroom. Back to Alexander the Great—never lost a battle, conquered the known world before he was thirty-three—but he didn't live out a year after his lover died."

"Did he kill himself?"

"No. He just got sick and died."

"His God was kind to him." Ray said. "Anyway, I'm not Alexander."

"Neither am I," Jim said. "A world, back then never to be forgotten. I look at my five stars and they aren't bright enough to shine two thousand years. They say he looked at the sky and wept when told there were more worlds among the stars because he hadn't yet conquered the one."

"He didn't win his world by sitting in a palace, did he?" Teal said slyly.

Jim laughed. "I'll think about it," he said, but his mind was already made up.

VI.

January 8, 2193 A.D. (Saturday)

UES Hamilton was a hundred-man, five-shell warship. The inner shell around the axis where the gravity was greatest contained the engines and automatic guidance systems. The second shell held secondary systems and could be shut down entirely in an emergency to conserve energy. The third shell was one-gee gravity and contained the manual controls and living quarters. Fourth shell was weapons, and fifth, defense and sensors.

Teal, once readjusted, was more comfortable in the heavier second shell, though he never revealed it, quietly serving in a noncommand position.

A change of jobs and scene did much for James McCreedy, who, for once in his life, had fingernails. As his replacement he had passed up all known potential candidates and left an unknown American as admiral of the fleet; then he hastily embarked on *Hamilton*, letting his successor deal with the angry multitude.

For almost four years *Hamilton* was a pirate hunter. It had been over ten years since Armageddon I, and since Ray had served on a battleship. He was thirty-six years old, still looking an ageless twenty-five. Ten years. Something tickled his neck like an insect. Ray absently brushed it away. It was blood. The death collar was doing its work, and time was getting short. McCreedy, he felt, must have noticed. He saw differences in Ray that Ray was not enough aware of to hide. Little ones—like the fact that the veins in his hands did not bulge when held below his heart and then collapse when held on a level with it, as Earthmen's did. The veins in his feet did not bulge when he stood. Ray's people were older than Jim's, and his circulatory system had adjusted entirely to the upright stance. He must also have noticed the ease with which Ray passed from shell to shell, through gravity and pressure changes with no ill effects—like a fish descending deep into the sea and surfacing. If Jim saw that, he must also see that Ray was dying.

As if on cue, a major diplomatic blunder touched off Armageddon II. Teal searched the face of his commander as *Hamilton* sped to the border zone, looking for a sign of foreknowledge, wondering if the well-timed blunder were a blunder at all. He would have to ask him when it was done. He'd have to let him know who he was. He couldn't die and leave him wondering.

A fleet gathered in well-drilled formation and met the Uelsons as they headed for the Diakyon system. Teal watched Jim on the conning platform when he first saw the fleet appear on the monitor screen. Not superships. His worst fear resolved, he plunged into battle assured and exalted. Teal could only watch. The time had come to act again after the long wait, and he was standing by, watching the battle that he considered his.

The command platform went dark before Teal's eyes, though the lights hadn't dipped in intensity. He felt a moment of dizziness, then shook his head clear. Choking. . . .

Twelve hours into the battle, *Hamilton* withdrew to breathe a moment. A Uelson scavenger poked within range, but was not worth wasting weapons on. They were unarmed. Then the shocked sensor monitor of *Hamilton* reported, "The scavenger has fired some kind of ray or beam at us—it passed right through the shields."

"Atom transport," Teal said.

"A bomb!" a young crewman gasped, but McCreedy shook his head. "Computer guard will take care of that." A bomb or nonregistered weapon could not finish reatomizing before the computer guard annihilated it. "The Uelsons know that. Where was it directed?"

"Center shell," the monitor answered.

"Ray," Jim began, but he was already gone by the time the monitor gave the location.

The center shell was the labyrinthine heart of the ship; the place to find a saboteur if one knew where to look.

"Vanguard."

Brown eyes looked up and smiled. "Captain." The same Vanguard, older, fatter. He was nodding, smiling. His hand twitched, and Teal dodged the needle dagger—a primitive weapon as deadly as the beam gun Ray held, but just a piece of metal, not recognizable to the computer guard as a weapon.

In the time it took Teal to sidestep the needle, Vanguard had taken cover, and Teal was once again a hunter in the jungle—while Armageddon II raged about them. His quarry was a beast whose life was demanded by eight shades.

"Captain, you're what I call a waste of talent." Vanguard's light-toned voice came from around the life-support computer bank. Teal couldn't let him sit there; Vanguard had proved his ability at his work. Teal rushed around the corner, but Vanguard had fled. To where?

"Silent, Ray?" Vanguard's voice came from behind the directional controls. Although "Ray" was what the Earthmen called him, this was an Aranian using his Aranian feminine name as a taunt. Teal made his way over.

"Always silent. But we know beneath the controlled exterior there burns the passion of a woman. We know you've got yourself an admiral." He was using the royal plural to refer to himself, but Teal knew that was not what was angering him.

Right around the corner—kill the bastard—

No! Something said no. The hair on the back of Teal's neck stood up like a wolf's and instinct said no.

Teal sprang backward as a needle dagger shot down from the other direction—not where Vanguard was supposed to be. He could throw his voice.

Anger-inspired oversight made Ray more angry. Vanguard wouldn't be talking if it would give away his position. He was maneuvering Ray into line of fire while he himself was sitting still—*doing what to the ship's controls?*

Teal moved silently and as quickly as possible in the weighted environment, trying to confuse Vanguard as Vanguard had done him. He listened. Vanguard was moving.

"Of course, that's not your fault. The Uelsons overlook defects like that. And can take care of that necklace of yours as well."

The death collar. It was choking him. Vanguard must know he had ten years, and that those ten years were almost up. Vanguard had known he was alive—despite the fact that Teal had arranged his own "death" in his escape from Otranadoe. No one, not even his Uelson captors, knew he still lived. Vanguard did. He must have also known Teal would be on this ship. It had to mean Vanguard wanted this showdown as badly as Teal did. Teal at last knew how he had escaped from inescapable Otranadoe—he had had help from the same person who was responsible for him being taken there. Someone had left his cell door unlocked. For a tight-security prison that was unbelievably careless. But it had not been carelessness after all. All this too was contrived. Sickness was the realization that it was all a game, and Vanguard was having a well-planned laugh with his power exercise.

Teal's keen sense of hearing came back with concentration, and he located Vanguard. As he moved in with gun poised, doubt screamed at him, and he stopped. *Vanguard does not take chances.* He must know of Teal's heightened senses from all the tests run at Otranadoe. Teal realized there was something vital he did not know in this game. Being aboard a UEF ship, hunted by an old enemy with a beam gun, could not be the risk for Vanguard that it appeared to be. Vanguard was not a gambler but a careful calculator. It meant the Uelsons had perfected the atom transporter. UEF's was only 80 percent efficient and unsafe for human transport. Vanguard would not trust his life to an 80-percent-efficient machine.

"I understand you're—how do they put it—flying a desk now, captain. Don't they trust you with a ship? How many desks have you lost?"

He doesn't know where I'm hiding. He's trying to get me angry enough to show myself.

Suddenly, Vanguard jumped out into the open. "Come out, captain, and we'll fight man to . . . whatever it is you are."

Vanguard had his back to the lift door. He was in the open. *He must not be afraid of guns,* Teal thought, feeling the urge to shoot at his laughing eyes. Vanguard never took chances. Ray did and showed himself. But didn't fire. He dodged a dagger and it stuck in the deck by his heel. Vanguard waited for him to fire.

Teal had heard in theory of a device that mirrored rays back to their source but had never seen one or could even be sure that they actually existed. He guessed that one did. *If it doesn't and if Vanguard doesn't have it, he is taking a chance. He wants me to fire.*

The lift door behind Vanguard opened, and Admiral McCreedy held up his weapon.

"Jimmy, don't!" Ray screamed shrilly as Vanguard turned. Ray seized the needle at his heel and let it fly.

Too abruptly to know who killed him or even that he was

dying, Vanguard died. It didn't matter. The eight crewmembers of *Tesah* had never known who killed them either. Except Natina, and Teal guessed that somehow, in some way, Natina would see this too.

Teal's eyes met Jim's.

"Did he touch anything?" the admiral asked.

"I can fix it," Teal said.

Admiral McCreedy made his way back up to the command platform, and Teal stayed behind to undo Vanguard's work. A shot was landed on *Hamilton*, and what felt like a split second without gravity threw Ray off his feet. Winded and dazed, he gave his ribs a quick check before rising. One might have been cracked, but he had no time to care for it. He got to his feet and finished his work, and then ran out of the central shell toward the conning position. The way was blocked by the collapsed braces of a corridor that had caved in with the last shock. The machinery from the fourth shell showed through the gaps in the wrecked structure.

He began to take a longer route, but suddenly spun around to look at the collapsed corridor. That was the route the admiral would have taken. . . .

Teal ran to an intercom and signaled the command. "Admiral McCreedy!"

Another voice answered, "This is Commander Lawrence. The admiral is in the central shell—"

No, he's not! And if he hadn't yet reached the command platform he was somewhere between, as were the collapsed braces.

Teal ran down the corridor and made his way through the darkened wreckage. "Admiral?" he called out. It was dark. Some light came through from the next level up, but it was still hard to see. "Jimmy?"

Something moved in the darkness. Ray stumbled over the rubble to the admiral's side. That he was hurt very badly, Teal could see without a light.

"Captain," he said weakly.

"Sir."

"Hell, Ray, this is a hell of a way to go."

"You're not—you're all right, Jimmy—I'll get somebody down here," Ray said and started to rise.

"No! Stay. And that's from your admiral."

Teal knelt by him. "Yes, sir."

"I want you to take command of the ship, captain. You outrank everyone on board—"

"I haven't battle experience—"

"Goddammit, don't lie to me, Captain Ray, I'm dying."

"Yes, sir."

"You had a battle command, damn you anyway."

"I lost . . ." Teal began but couldn't finish. Tears.

Jim paused, then spoke in a gentler tone, "How do you say that—is it Teal?"

Teal blinked. "Yes. Teal."

"That's a girl's name."

"No. Ray's a girl's name."

Jim smiled through pain, then said, "Take command of the ship, and if they give you any trouble remind them that to disobey in war means the death penalty."

"I'll get a doctor."

"Never mind the doctor. It's too late," Jim said. "There's something I want you to have."

"Oh no—"

"Shut up," Jim said.

It was the tiny silver pendant of the Madonna and Child he wore around his neck. As he undid the clasp Teal noticed his hands were steady. The man was calm. He couldn't be dying. *People don't die like this. Not really. Not again.*

"I'm not Christian."

"I know," said Jim and put it around his neck. Teal was trembling violently. Jim took his hand and squeezed it. "Go take care of my ship," he said. His eyes were bright.

Jim closed his eyes and died.

The command personnel were stunned when Ray ordered Commander Lawrence to step down, and even more stunned when he threatened to carry out the penalty right there.

Teal was a commander. He was born to be king and was a leader despite himself. He had watched and waited enough, and he wanted to go home.

A Uelson destroyer dogged *Hamilton*, which veered off out of battle and headed for the Diakyon system at near light speed. Two more followed and didn't return.

Then *Hamilton* left the solar system to return to battle, but not before Teal had caught a glimpse of his blue home like a bright star on the monitor.

When *Hamilton* rejoined the battle, Teal could sense Uelson panic across the vacuum of space, until at last they fled back to Uelson Castor Base.

Ray was signaled by the UEF attack commander. He

crossed to the radio with spinning head. Admiral Regan's image was on the radio screen, and, beside him, a black-and-white Uelson of apparent high rank. Beady eyes narrowed and blotched face moved in recognition. "Teal Ray!"

Where are you from. What is your name. Six months had drilled that voice into his mind beyond forgetting. The Uelson had moved up from his role as torturer.

The crewmembers around him were staring. *Go to hell, all of you,* turned in Teal's jumbled brain. Regan was speaking. "Prepare to board survivors."

Teal coughed and spat blood. "Sir, I will not be responsible for what happens to any Uelson on this ship!" he answered in a shrill voice. *Did he want them to remain survivors? Can't they keep this ship still . . . ?* The Uelson was blubbering—no, don't make him board *Hamilton*—in the name of *decency. . . .* Regan was saying something, but Teal shut it off and walked away . . . or forgot to shut it off . . . Regan's voice was screaming at him over the radio, but Teal couldn't hear him. He felt dizzy . . . tasted blood. . . . "Captain!" He vaguely heard a frightened voice . . .

. . . pitched forward and would have fallen if his Second had not caught him.

PART THREE:
Sovereign

I.

"Why didn't you let me die?" Teal ran his fingers over the diamond-shaped holes in the collar where spikes had been. He focused on a spot on the ceiling. From his cot it looked like a bug, but not even a bug could get through the tight security which guarded him, half protected, half prisoner. His eyes unfocused.

Kury stood over his cot in sick bay and thundered, "I nearly lost my brass getting that dog collar off you, you goddam motherfucker. I had to make a deal with the Uelson commander; see that you appreciate that."

Teal smiled faintly. "Good ol' Kury."

Kury crossed his arms over his huge chest with satisfaction. "The deal was either he gets off the collar or a certain Ukrainian tears him apart."

"Which is why you nearly lost your brass." Teal rested his head on his arm.

"Speaking of which, you're in a hell of a lot of trouble, captain." Kury kicked the foot of his cot.

"I couldn't help noticing the MPs at the door," Teal said in reply. He glanced about the private room. Not even a bug of the live variety could creep in or out unnoticed. He fancied he could see through the mirror, and the windows looked suspiciously like a monitor mockup. "Am I in trouble?"

"Let's put it this way: how would you like your goose— rare, medium, or well done? They don't know whether to decorate you and make you an admiral or shoot you at sunrise," Kury said. He sat on the edge of the bed and leaned in conspiratorily. "Tell me, did you really pilot *that* ship? Back in Armageddon I?"

"What do you think?" Teal dodged.

"Ain't no thinking about it, mannie." Kury rose. "The doctors say you ain't from Earth, Loki, Gereny, Zharaga—"

Teal stopped him. "Kury?"

"Yeah?"

"I know."

Kury laughed and nodded. "Yeah, guess you would." He sat on Teal's cot again. "You know that guy you killed on the *Hamilton* was an Aranian."

"Really?" said Teal. The Earthmen overlooked the same thing the Uelsons had—that there might be two species of men on Arana. They thought they knew that Ray wasn't Aranian. He just wasn't Northern Aranian.

"My kid's been to Arana. The Aranians don't know whose side they're on—"

"When do they bury Jimmy?" Teal cut him off.

"Jim? Oh . . . I don't know."

"Will they let me go to his funeral? Am I under arrest?"

"Stewert, I don't know what they're going to do with you. . . . Hey, Stewert?"

"Yeah, Kury."

"Uh . . . are you human?"

"Yes. Yes, I'm human."

Teal shut his eyes and held Jim's pendant in his hand. Calm bright eyes one moment—the next he was gone. Teal trembled at the memory. Suddenly alone. Alone again.

Don't leave me, Jimmy. I'm so alone. So lonely. Don't . . . don't die. A child again back at Dianter watching the one he loved most die. *Everything I touch. Mother. Akelan. Lia. . . . Jimmy, Jimmy, Jimmy.*

Time passed. The sick-bay room was replaced by a room on Luna Base no better than a prison cell. He paced, panther-like, waiting for the powers that be to decide his fate. This Earth-type Otranadoe was painless and almost comfortable, but there was no freedom and no company save the stern MPs. And *they* were frightened.

November 2193 A.D.

After months of imprisonment, apologies, and indefinite promises, Teal hardly expected radical action from the board. But Jim, being the daring man he was, had left a daring man in his place; and when the fleet admiral got a free hand, action was swift and decisive.

Teal was put in command of the newest and largest ship in

the fleet. She was a 250-person warship. Her name was *Sovereign.*

They said taking command of a ship was marrying her. Teal touched the bulkhead and thought to it as a ship and as a wife, *I won't lose you this time.*

He was warned in advance about his ship's Second, proud, man-hating Nora Jemenez, who, Teal sensed on meeting, felt cheated out of the captaincy because of her sex. From what Teal had seen of UEF administration, especially under James McCreedy, she was doubtlessly justified in her feeling. In UEF Nora was surrounded by men like Kury, who had told Ray, "Show that Guatemalan bitch who's boss. Don't let any linda pull anything on you." Teal made no reply but kept to himself the explosions he envisioned if ever Kury and Nora should be stationed on the same ship. Teal learned by way of gossip that Kury had once made an advance at Nora in his usual bold self-assured style—and had landed four meters down the corridor. So went the story. But more than men, Nora hated weak women—or weakness in women. She would be good for discipline, Teal decided. And he didn't have to deal with her much, the Second being acting commander while the captain was off duty.

It was Sub-second he had to associate with, not only on duty but off, sharing a cabin with him; no one had the privilege of a private cabin, for it was little more than a sleeping place. Meeting this man was an unpleasant surprise. He was an attractive, easygoing American of thirty, with auburn hair and a pleasant smile—named Lieutenant Commander Richard Barret.

"You don't look like a Richard Barrett," was all Teal could say to him.

Friendly brown eyes masked slight offense.

He thinks I hate him.

He *didn't* look like a Richard Barrett. Richard Barrett was tall, beanpole, black with shiny pate and goofy smile. Richard Barrett was dead.

"You look like a Terrel," he said. Whatever Barret's feelings, "Terrel" stuck, and most of the crew did not know his real name. In time, Richard found himself introducing himself by his new name.

When drills began, Teal realized just how good his crew and his ship were. And it was all entrusted to him—even though they didn't know who he was.

Jim McCreedy *had* left a daring man behind. Teal could

have wished for less daring—just Jim. Some god, whichever one was really there, had decided it was not to be, so he lived on alone. He sulked in a rec on Chicago Base between training sessions, his mind a few blocks south and a few months back in time with a short, dog-toothed, cantankerous, imperfect Catholic.

A voice scattered his reverie. "Your coffee can't be *that* interesting. What do you have in there, a submarine?"

Returned to the present, Teal came face to face with young Orestes Peralta grown up. Twenty-five and as stunningly handsome as he had been beautiful as a child, he seated himself across from Ray. He had reacquired his silent, devoted shadow Johnny Fox, who had grown into a man while Teal wasn't looking, his slight figure filled out sturdy and masculine. He retained his quiet reserve and haunted almond eyes.

Orestes wore a black captain's uniform. Johnny was now a full commander. Teal congratulated them on the promotions.

"Thank you." Orestes beamed. "They finally caught you, you faker. They gave you *Sovereign*. Are you collecting superships? I'd have given it to you if I were Admiral Cory."

Teal accepted it silently with a smile. He valued Orestes' faith.

"They gave me a ship," Orestes continued.

"Did they?" Teal asked, realizing how wrapped in himself he had been—as always.

"A new ship, a green crew and a brand-new captain. And a brand-new Second." He slung his arm around Johnny's shoulders.

"You deserve it," Teal said.

"I know," he said, openly as he did to only the most trusted people with whom false modesty would be an insult. "Tell me what you did in Armageddon II," Orestes demanded like a boy asking for a story. He gathered up all the salt and pepper shakers in the rec and set them on the tabletop. "The pepper's them and salt's us. Now, what happened?"

Teal demonstrated as best he could a three-dimensional battle on a two-dimensional surface; Orestes gazed, fascinated.

"Tell me about your ship, *Sovereign*," Orestes said afterward.

"I beat my crew," Teal answered.

"Really?"

"To hear them wail you'd think so."

"Good. They trust you enough to let you hear them. Otherwise they'd do it behind your back. Be glad you hear them."

"I hate to be a drill master," Teal said. "If they're not good I turn my Second loose on them." He winked.

"Who's he?"

"She. Nora Jemenez."

Johnny whistled. "I know her," he spoke. "She's mean."

Teal shrugged. "Misunderstood. The only reason she doesn't have a ship of her own is that she was born the wrong sex. I don't blame her for hating me. But she *is* mean on those drills. We had our first casualty—a broken leg. A suffragette was climbing down one of the monkey tubes, and she fell two shells. I'm surprised she didn't break her skull."

Orestes sucked air between his teeth.

"Luckily it was the outer two shells and the gravity wasn't so great. Nora called her a stumble-footed halfwit." He stamped out his cigarette. He'd have to break that habit—there was no reason for it anymore. He hadn't noticed that it had become a habit until he was allowed to quit. "I told Nora to shove it up her monkey tube."

Orestes giggled, and Johnny choked on his coffee.

"That was one surprised Second," he said. "I had the monkey tubes fixed up so that if you want to break some bones you really have to have your heart set on it."

Orestes nodded. "You can bet your superiors have noticed that—you're looking out for your crew. You know you're being watched."

"I guessed as much."

"What about your ship?" Orestes asked. "What does she do?"

Teal smiled at his barrage of questions so typically Orestes-like. "She blows up into four pieces."

"You're kidding."

"No. She has three independent life-support systems, one in three out of four quads, so if one quad gets wrecked it can be jettisoned. Or if three are gone you have one for a lifeboat."

"What about the fourth quad without life support?"

"Those are the engines. If they get critical—God forbid—they can be jettisoned, but the life support in there depends on one of the other three quads. Now I've talked long enough, Orestes. You tell me about your ship."

"Her name's *Gemini*. It's funny that your ship is four parts—mine's half a ship."

Teal waited for clarification.

"She's half of a double ship. After it was built, it seemed silly to have two ships docked—that's what it amounted to—so she was split into *Gemini* and *Pollux*."

"Why not *Castor* and *Pollux*?"

"Because 'Castor' is a bad word." Orestes grinned. "My ship's not as pretty as *Sovereign*. I've seen pictures of her. She's beautiful. And I've heard so much. You had different designers, Brandeis and Calvin. Best of the best."

"Calvin?" Teal echoed. It couldn't be.

"Yes, Paul Calvin. He's an absolute genius—"

"Pauli Calvin?" Teal repeated, paling. It had to be a different man. A coincidence, two people with the same name, like Richard Barrett. "What does he look like?"

"Ugly," said Johnny. "Green-eyed monster."

"He's . . . well, not good-looking," Orestes began.

"Admit it, he's grotesque," Johnny insisted.

"Okay, he's ugly," Orestes conceded. "Redhead. Butch cut. Freckles. Green eyes. Pudgy—"

"Fat."

"Fat. Shaking his hand it feels like a marshmallow—"

"A large dead fish."

"A large dead—"

Teal felt blood drain from his face, then suddenly rush back into his cheeks.

"Are you all right?" Orestes said. "What did I say? Calvin?"

Teal had no one else to confide in, and so he told them. "He designed *Tesah*. How did he get here!"

Orestes shook his head. "I thought he was one of us. That's what we were led to believe, anyway."

Like me, Teal thought sardonically. He remembered the rumor of a superlight ship from Arana, the one he had wanted to ask Jim about. That must have been Calvin coming to Earth. UEF had seen fit, for some reason, to hush it up, and smuggle Calvin into Earth's population. *Why didn't he tell me?* It had to mean Arana still wanted her secrecy. Aranian Calvin couldn't claim any knowledge of Teal Ray. Calvin was perhaps playing a defector's role—that would explain UEF's hiding him. So Arana must still want *Tesah's* origin secret.

He was fortunate that he hadn't accidentally run into Calvin. He was certain he would have spit on him without thinking, for no other reason than he was still jealous.

Now he knew. Again he was in command of a Calvin ship.

"He's been working on the atom transporter," Orestes said. "It's up to ninety-five percent efficiency now."

"The Uelsons have it perfect," Teal said.

"How do you know?"

"I know."

"Ninety-five percent is getting there. Better than eighty percent."

"Still unsafe for human transport. One out of twenty times your garbage dies."

"Huh?"

"We've been testing the atom transport with garbage," Teal explained. It led to some new phrases. Any test—of anything—that was a failure was announced: *Sovereign*, your garbage died. A success was: *Sovereign*, your garbage is here. "Calvin will get it to one hundred percent."

"I thought you hated him."

"I do. That doesn't mean I don't have faith in his swollen brain," Teal countered. "Holly chose his children well."

Once training was over, real flights began immediately, first as a messenger, then an emergency vessel, a police ship, and a pirate hunter.

Teal began to suspect cross motives when *Sovereign* received unusual orders. She was to proceed to the Diakyon solar system. *They want me to betray my origin.* The watchers were still with him, reporting every move and reaction to UEF. He knew who a few of them were and took special care around them. These new orders came while three of them were on the conning platform with him.

Approaching Arana, Teal felt the beginning of anger at the affront of this trap. These crafty Earthmen with their tricks were as bad as Uelsons and their Otranadoe. Both still probed for forbidden information. He hid his irritation. Arana would be just another planet to him as far as anyone could see.

Homesickness hit like a gun blast in his abdomen as *Sovereign* swung into wide orbit around the water world. Arana moved away from conjunction with her two suns. It was Mild Hot Season. At home it was autumn. He needn't see it to know. His home still ruled him, far away but never detached. Home would govern his life always, wherever he went. Born a Bay Royalist, he was a part of Arana, part of her seas, her rotations and revolutions. Just another planet; the spies were watching.

"Damn, it's pretty," the monitor said appreciatively.

Teal nodded. "Yeah."

Another UEF s   was in close orbit. and a radio scream-out was taking place between its commander and Holly White.

Teal felt faint for a moment hearing his voice, and an impulse to grab a shuttle down and throw his arms around Holly and cry flashed across his nerves. A more sober thought reminded him that an Earth shuttle would never land on Arana should he ever forget himself like that.

The radio voices were shouting war. On *Sovereign*'s arrival both began demanding aid. Holly insisted *Sovereign* haul off this invader and have him locked away, and demanded an apology from UEF for the interplanetary aggression. His face on the screen gave no hint of recognition in an act so flawless Teal felt wounded. The spaceship commander claimed to have been investigating possible Uelson spyship traces in the area when the Aranians attacked his ship. Not equipped to take on a planet himself, he was yelling for war and wanted *Sovereign* to fire back. Teal could see through his act. This was a test—at Arana's expense. Fury followed discovery.

The sly Earthmen would be watching to see how he handled this. What he wanted to do was settle it, give in to Arana because there was no other logical choice. He had expressed that opinion to McCreedy at one time—not without arousing his suspicion. That would not be a wise choice of action now.

So he left. He ordered *Sovereign* out of orbit with a callous signal back for them to fight their own battle and a warning that *Sovereign* would make the victor look like the loser.

Nora watched the crisis pass with quick observant eyes. She was not one of the plotters; she was a jealous commander watching for his mistake. But she conceded. "That's diplomacy."

"Is it?" he asked.

"I'd have gone in blasting," she said.

I won, Teal breathed. *So there, Admiral Cory. Not quite McCreedy. You have his daring but not his eyes.* He retreated to his cabin and downed three reddots. They helped the constant pain, leaving him numb.

"You can't hold your liquor worth beans, but you're sky-high on reddots and you don't show it at all," Terrel said as Teal lay open-eyed on the bunk.

He gave a start. "What are you talking about?"

"I've seen you choking the reddots down," Terrel said. "I just never knew what they were before."

"So report me. You want the ship, Sub-second? Doublefine, eh?" He bit his tongue. He'd even picked up the man's accent—all he had left of him.

Terrel sat on the edge of Teal's bunk. "I didn't mean it that way," he said. "Those are painkillers, captain."

Teal stared coldly.

"If you're in that much pain, I want to help," he said, lamely but sincere. He wasn't a watcher.

Teal wrapped his arms around himself and turned away toward the wall. "There's nothing wrong with me."

Terrel sighed. "Yes, sir."

II.

September 2, 2194 A.D. (Wednesday)

Teal, seeing the need for disguise gone, reverted to some of his Aranian ways. He wore a Royalist widower's hairdo and dropped his imitation Earthwalk in favor of his own smooth motions.

His crew changed also—many of his crewmembers were by now not of the original 250. He had rapidly weeded out those he could not function with. Once, in a surge of transfer requests, Terrel had added his own and was shocked when the captain came close to *begging* him to stay. He stayed; his only reason for wanting out was the notion that he was not wanted. Far from clearing up the misunderstanding, the incident left him more puzzled than before. He had learned a tremendous respect, even love, for his commander, but he did not pretend to understand him in the least.

The same presence and power that enabled Teal to command had a disturbing consequence. Remembering how he had received with disbelief Jim's comment that some men and women on Luna were taken with him, Teal now saw it for himself and found himself forced to, yet not able to, say no. Teal had never been approached by a woman he did not desire and was at a loss. Putting himself in her place, a denial would crush him; so he accepted. He was uncomfortable with the solution. Hearing Caucan laughter still, he felt as if he was in some kind of performance rather than making love. She must not laugh. He was all too successful and gained an unwanted reputation as a captivating lover—and for not talking. A woman didn't fear him answering an inquiry, "How was she?"

Relieved and deeply shaken at the same time, Teal asked Terrel, "How do you say no?" An Earthman should know how to cope with Earthwomen, he guessed.

154

A number of smart answers came to mind. Such problems. A laugh tickled Terrel's mouth, but the eyes he met said don't. "You're serious," he said.

"Yes, goddammit, I'm serious," he cried.

Terrel couldn't help. He couldn't even see the problem.

It came apart in Cleveland. It was a hot September afternoon following three days of cold and rain. *Sovereign* was preparing to meet *Gemini* in war games. Cleveland was to be *Sovereign*'s object of defense while Oretes' ship protected Luna.

Teal gazed out over the gray waters of Lake Erie as a Voyager came in for landing. Choppy waves hurled themselves against the man-imposed structure of the spaceport on the lake. It happened in Cleveland where an old enemy resurfaced to capitalize on trouble that didn't yet seem severe. Dressed in UEF uniform, Calvin pretended not to notice Teal's existence, and Teal did the same. Calvin made no sign except for a passing mumble that no one noticed, because Calvin always mumbled to himself. This time he happened to be near Teal, within mumbling distance. "I wonder what this sounds like in space chatter. The skysnoopers must be reporting some *pritty* interesting things. I'd be ashamed to go home—if they'd even claim you." He walked away, mumbling.

And Teal Ray ran.

He had been standing, gazing out the window with Terrel, when he suddenly bolted out the door without a word or sign.

It was eight hours later and drawing near twilight in Cleveland when *Sovereign*'s Sub-second received a phone call.

"Terrel."

"Captain, where are you?"

"Columbus."

"How did you get there?"

"I ran."

Terrel couldn't speak.

"Listen, Terrel, I'm ready to drop; will you come get me?"

Teal told him he was in a hotel under the name Ray Stewert. "And bring some cash. I forgot to. It shouldn't be much; it's a horrible place. There isn't even a video on this phone. The door'll be unlocked and I'll probably be asleep when you get here."

"Yeah, okay. I'll be there as soon as I can."

Terrel entered the room very quietly and shut the door behind him. Teal lay curled on the bed, looking very wilted and wrung out.

"Terrel?" he said without opening his eyes.

"Yes, sir."

Teal rolled onto his back and looked up at him. "I'm glad it didn't rain," he said.

Terrel sat down on the bedside. "You ran the whole way?"

"Full speed. Earthlings can't do that, can they?"

Terrel shook his head.

"Neither can I. I have blisters all over my feet," he said. "I could swim that distance, but I should've never run."

"How far is that?"

Teal shrugged. "About a hundred and forty miles as the Kantak flies."

"Kantaks can't fly straight."

"Yeah, well, I got lost."

"Why did you do it?"

"I'll tell you someday," he said. "Since there's no one else to talk to . . . not anymore."

"Are you all right?"

"In a little bit," said Teal. "What's there to do in this town, anyway?" As soon as he spoke his mind went back ten years to Jim McCreedy saying the same about Chicago, and his gaze was far away, lost in memory.

"Captain?" Terrel's voice brought him back to Columbus, Ohio.

"I'm okay," he said. "Isn't this a lousy room? At least it doesn't cost much—you're paying. Otherwise I'd have to hang an earring on the door and start a business to earn my keep."

Terrel smiled. "Do you want anything? Anything to eat? I could get something to drink and you and I can get smashed."

"Let's you and I get smashed."

And they did.

"Where are you from?" Teal heard the question—and himself asking it.

Terrel looked up from his drink; brown eyes had an alcohol shine. "Around here. Illinois."

"Chicago?"

"Bloomington."

"Family there?"

"Mom and Dad."

"Brothers and sisters?"

"Older brother in Chicago, little sister at school in Michigan."

"Bet you have a dog, too."

Terrel chuckled. "Yeah. Family dog—named Phideaux."

"And the house is white stone with green shutters and a picket fence and a garden with a brook running through it."

Terrel eyed him a moment and said, "No brook and the shutters are orange. . . . You've really got me pegged bourgeoisie, don't you."

"Uh huh."

"And we have our own car," Terrel added in almost defiance. "And my mother plays organ for the church choir. . . . What does an outsider looking in think? I can't tell if you're putting me down or not."

"No . . . it's just so . . . *normal.*"

Terrel laughed and poured a drink for both of them.

"What's it like being normal?"

Terrel was shocked and put down his drink. "I guess . . . I guess it's pretty good. I can't complain. Maybe I'm a little bored—or why would I have joined UEF?"

Teal mumbled in the pillow he lay on, "Wish I had a mother and father . . . brother and sister . . . and a dog. . . ."

Terrel moved to sit by him, took the drink from his hand before he went to sleep and spilled it. "Yeah, well, I wish I was a war hero." He leaned back on his elbows. "I guess I'll probably retire after a successful, unremarkable career with a couple of stories I can tell. Build a house somewhere in a little unhurried place—like some of those Zharaghan planets. Someplace where the sun shines a lot with lots of green things. . . ."

Terrel thought Teal was asleep and stopped talking, but Teal mumbled in reply, "Sounds normal . . . take me along when you go. . . ."

It had grown late, and Terrel shared the bed with him. "Don't worry, I'm straight," he quipped.

"I'm not, but I'm too drunk for it to make any difference," said Teal.

Terrel laughed and poured another drink.

In the morning they returned to Cleveland and took a shuttle up to *Sovereign* to prepare for the next day's war games.

They ran through a few drills and exchanged taunts with *Gemini*. A voice from *Gemini* sneered over the radio, "We'll beat you with one ship tied behind our back," referring to their twin ship *Pollux*.

To which a *Sovereign* spaceman retorted, "Aw, your garbage died."

When the war games came, Teal knew for a fact that Orestes had grown up: in the computer score, *Gemini* won a close victory. His pride was boyish, and he even apologized to Teal for beating him.

"It doesn't matter," Teal said. "At least we came out with a live crew."

"I noticed that in your battle patterns," Orestes said over a cup of coffee. "If you had risked a little more, you could have had us and our base—but you chose to protect your crew, even in mock battle."

"We were to respond as in an actual battle," Teal said.

"The crew is expendable in war—they are to give their lives if necessary for their planet," Orestes said.

"I lost one crew," said Teal.

"I have lost men," said Orestes.

"I lost a crew," said Teal.

"Not this time."

"And never again."

Before leaving Earth, Teal visited the UEF cemetery in Illinois, resting place of UEF men and women who had died in action. There were large monuments for early casualties and pioneers of interstellar exploration. The majority of the graves dotting the green hillside with white marble were crewmen killed in Armageddons I and II. The UEF Memorial Park was restful and green. A robin hopped across the wet grass, stopped, cocked its head. It abandoned its hunt and took flight at Teal's approach.

Teal knelt at Jim's grave and placed a red rose on it. It was the closest he could find to a mourning flower. He touched his fingers to the damp stone. A light drizzle, a mist in the air isolated him. He was glad of the absence of onlookers. He laid his hand on the grassy mound.

I love you, Jim.

I know.

Why? Oh why?

That's war. Corridors collapse.

We might never have touched.

Whose fault was that?

I was frightened.

So was I.

Did I hurt you when I wouldn't tell you who I was?

Very much.

I'm sorry, Jim.

I know.

Did you love me?

Very much.

He rose. Eyes fixed on the stone walk, he was hardly aware that he was cold and wet and moving without direction.

"Captain."

Teal looked up from the walk. "Terrel."

"I'm sorry to bother you . . . We have new orders."

Teal nodded and returned his gaze to the walk. A jay screamed at them from a tree. Teal looked to see Terrel brush something more substantial than mist from his cheek. He grasped his Sub-second's sleeve. "What's that for?" Teal said.

"What?"

"Why are you crying?"

"Someone has to."

The thought occurred to Teal that he had been waiting and watching a short way off. "You aren't going to last long around me if you don't stop being so empathic."

"It's starting to rain," Terrel said, and fell in step with him as they continued down the walk.

While investigating the new report of pirates *Sovereign* received a distress call via messenger ship from a mining colony reporting Uelson raiders.

Teal found the miners in near panic, though there was no sign of Uelson ships. Looking at his awesome vessel on the monitor screen as he descended in a shuttle, Teal saw why none had lingered to match them.

The foreman was a giant, twice Teal's weight and a foot taller, but he ranted like a spoiled and terrified child. All of the miners were brawny. Teal did not know women could be so bulky and muscular—even Royalist men never got so big. But the imposing miners were all afraid of the little weasel-like Uelsons—*with reason,* Teal thought in pained recollection. He touched the shell of the death collar, spikes replaced with silver diamond-shaped filling for the holes.

After reassuring the miners as best he could, he reboarded his shuttle to *Sovereign*, not at all reassured himself and very puzzled. He would scout the area for Uelson pirates. He did not expect to find them. At superlight speed they would be millions on millions of miles away before he set foot on *Sovereign* again—and he had no warning of how long that would be.

Just as the small ship approached the shuttle deck, a beam apparently from nowhere centered on the craft, then ceased as abruptly as it appeared. Terrel was alarmed and immediately roused the sleeping Nora and tried to trace the mysterious beam, which must have been an atom transport beam, because the shuttle that *Sovereign* received was empty.

Teal opened his eyes. He couldn't remember what had happened or where he had been. Looking up from the floor, he saw white.

He got up and saw his cell—all white, all smooth, no variation in color or texture. A small cube of a cell. He was naked. There was no sound. To the touch it was neither warm nor cold. The light source couldn't be pinned down, for it reflected equally from the white surfaces, but Teal guessed it was in the ceiling, as must be the air vent, carefully concealed, if there were an air vent.

Unable to figure out where he was, he tried to remember where he'd been. He slowly remembered coming up from the planet surface and the strange vague feeling of the atom transport breaking his body apart and then putting him back together. But whatever had hit him afterward, drug or gas, had been too quick to be recognized. And now he was here. It all seemed like seconds ago but his inward clock said days.

He felt all the bounds of his cell within his reach but found no variation in the smooth surface. He struck its unyielding whiteness. He called out, but the walls swallowed the sound, making his loud voice sound very small and very alone.

Alone.

Teal paced the cell. *Like a zoo animal,* he thought.

Zoo? Was he being observed?

He called out again. "Can you hear me?"

He suddenly shut his mouth. Don't talk. Don't say *anything*.

He had become aware of the faint odor of an antiseptic—

almost imperceptible even to his jungle-heightened senses, but he recognized it; and with a sinking feeling too desperate for even panic, he realized where he was.

Otranadoe.

III.

Alone.
Neither hot nor cold.
Nothing.
Heart beat.
Breathe in, breathe out.
Inhale and heart beats faster.
Exhale and heart beats slower.
Nothing.
Almost overwhelming urge to cry, but don't give them that. *You've been over the whole cube a thousand times— 1,023 times—there's no speaker, no monitor; they can't see . . . don't give a little or you've given all.*

He curled up in a corner, thin arms around his knees. They must feed him while he slept. No sensation but breathing and heart beating; see whiteness, self; touch hard smooth walls, self. Lower left eyelid twitched.

He put his head down on his knees, locked into self. And shut down as if wounded—like in the mountains after Dianter. A hibernation, all slowed, no conscious sensation—there was nothing to sense.

Memories flowed into blank mind. Race memories. Stewert line memories were confused; like looking at a double exposure, as if the memories of two lines were jumbled together. Two lines. *Am I so severed from the Stewert line that I can't remember it at all? Nothing but my own raving imagination of two lines. . . .*

His mother's and father's marriage. Teal saw her through his eyes . . . and him through her eyes. . . . But she was a Lowlander; he shouldn't have her memory. This was also raving.

Nomad dancer. Heat. That was his own memory. That was real. Life. . . .

Time? What time? Cold Season Spring. Over twenty-nine Beth-enea had turned since his birth. The Night Sun was at opposition. But what Earth time? Days and years of Earth had grown vague and muddled in the nothingness. Inside he knew what home was like, what time, what season.

He could see the Night Sun in the sky directly overhead. Was it the sky of Arana as it was at the moment? Or was it his remembrance of one Star Year ago? He had not been alive one Star Year ago, but he remembered. The stars he saw now were different than the memory, for the planet Arana had shifted position following its rosette-shaped path around the Sun. The sky was a living image, not a vision of the past. But whose eyes was he seeing through? They were not his father's—his father was out of reach, and his grandfather was dead.

I am going mad, he thought.

Whose eyes looked up at Arana's night sky to show him the stars, the time? His mother's parents? The bloodline was not strong enough. His mother, Raya, was a Lowland woman of no breeding. He could get no visions or memories from them. Who showed him the sky?

Arana hung balanced between the blazing suns on her distorted elliptical orbit, poised at the moment of opposition marking the passage of another Beth-enea. The Time Between the Cold. Another petal on the rosette had been traced across the solar system. A rosette, Royalist holy symbol. And a purple mourning flower.

Teal started, almost waking from his dormancy. Purple mourning flower was Brekk. Red was Stewert. Why a purple mourning flower? Why did he see purple when he was a Stewert?

Did my father lose the crown to Ven Brekk? Is my father alive? What does this mean? Who is showing me this? Whose eyes?

He shook the vision from his head. It had crept into his empty mind. Purple mourning flower on his mother's grave.

Nothing.

Nothing.

There will come one who has seen the face of hell and he will make way for him who has seen the face of God who will be the father of the new race, the Trieath, through whom we shall be reborn by the blood of the one who wears hell in his eyes.

He remembered the prophecy. *I saw hell, Akelan, and you saw God. Why did you die? By whose power was this prophecy broken—leaving me here—in hell?*

By the blood. *Would you have killed me had you lived, Akelan?*

Blood. Fire. Don't think.

Nothing.

Find him! The Earthlings again feared waking to Uelson superships.

"He won't talk," Nora said. "All we gotta worry about is their killing him. *We* ain't in danger—*he* is."

"I don't know if he can take it," Terrel said quietly.

"Hell, he already did time in Otranadoe—almost a year. He won't crack now."

"He's not the same person he was." Terrel tugged on an auburn strand of hair, a habit he'd picked up when he started smoking, when Teal disappeared.

"How the hell would you know?" Nora's mocking voice reproved. "You didn't know him then."

"He's changed even since I've known him." He seemed so . . . breakable.

"What I don't understand," Nora said, pacing at a fast clip, "is why they didn't grab him back sooner. We've had him eleven goddam years—where the hell have they been looking? Up their asses?" She sat; stood; then sat and lit a cigarette with Terrel's, which went unsmoked; he just flicked the ashes.

"They didn't know," Terrel said. "Till Armageddon II they thought he was dead."

Nora's almond eyes fixed sharply on him. "How did you know that?"

"He told me."

Nora propped her chin in her elbow and sucked on the long fingernail of her little finger. A small gold ring from her girlfriend flashed by her lips. "They didn't know," she mused. "Hell, neither did we."

"Now they've got him and they know we've had him but don't know he's told us nothing. They must think he's told us because we made him captain; and Nora, they're gonna—"

"We gotta get that fucker back," she declared, grinding out her unsmoked cigarette. The Slave sucked it away with mechanical indifference.

"Where is he?"

"We know where he is."

"Not Otranadoe again—they wouldn't risk it. If he could

get out once—besides, Castor Base is the closest base to Earth—they wouldn't put him there."

"Stop thinking like a goddam Earthman. These are pi-dogs," she ranted.

They reported to Fleet Admiral Cory himself. *Sovereign* was not given a new commander. Nora was charged with finding the alien and getting him away from the Uelsons, even if she had to kill him. A number of other ships were also given the same assignment, but Nora was determined to find him first and bring him back alive. She was a tyrannical commander, but she was endured because she was most severe on herself. She seemed never to sleep, and many a night she would ignore a groan from beneath a shiny blond tangle on the pillow, "Nora, come to *bed*." Her blue-black hair lost its shine, and she cut it all off to get it out of her way. Spanish eyes lost mysterious appeal with bags and bloodshot gaze. The whole ship had changed character. *Sovereign* was looking for her captain. Day after day after week after month . . . ten months.

"If he's not dead, I'm afraid to find him," Terrel confessed.

Nora looked awful.

"And everyone thought you hated him." He shook his head sadly.

She tossed her head disdainfully as if to say, Of course I do. "I *have* to find him or people will think I gave up so I could keep the command," she explained.

"Yeah, I'd grown attached to him too," he read through her facade.

Softly slanted eyes met his. "Screw you."

July 2195 A.D.

Sovereign returned to Earth, but with no indication of having given up. Nora went into conference with Admiral Cory. When she came aboard and called for leaving orbit, it was with a new attitude of determination and triumph. "I knew Cory'd be game. No one else would've. No one else."

"Captain Jemenez, where are we going, sir?"

"Castor Base," she announced loudly. "It's our Base Sixus, you know."

"Captain!" Terrel's brown eyes widened. "Are we attacking Castor Base?"

More than twenty years before, 24,000 men, women, and children had been slaughtered on the peaceful, unarmed settlement of Base Sixus, now Uelson Castor Base.

"We're going to Sixus," she said, calling it by the Earth name. "We're not attacking anyone. We're just expelling intruders from our base. Terrel, I'm gonna want some battle drills before we get there."

Gemini joined *Sovereign* in transit.

"What the hell!" Nora blazed. "This is mine! That motherfucker Peralta is moving in on my kill!"

"John Fox is Second on that ship," Terrel said. "He's one of the Sixus survivors. His parents died there."

"That's all I need. Some revenge-crazed orphan and a rich glory-thief."

Peralta hailed *Sovereign* by light radio. "*Gemini* to assist. I await your orders."

Nora grinned a Cheshire grin, "Well, I'll be damned. I got two ships now." She had a small squadron by the time she reached Sixus.

The base was not the Sixus of Johnny's childhood. It was Uelson Castor Base, with low alien buildings. Nora's orders were simple: destroy all the ships and control buildings, but don't fire anywhere near Otranadoe prison. Undaunted by the number of ships at Castor Base, Nora felt she could take them all on singlehanded.

A little rusty-colored weasel-like creature was the one that told them where Teal Ray was, whining and whimpering so much that the translator could hardly make out his speech. The sniveling beast was an officer of importance. He spilled all he knew, convinced that Earth had its equivalent to Otranadoe to extract information and that it was where he'd be bound if he didn't tell. His terror infected Terrel; the creature did not get that fear from anything he'd seen of Earth, so it must be from what he knew of his own torture chamber—where Teal was.

When much of Sixus was once again rubble, Nora put a weapon in Terrel's hand and gave him a shove. "He's in Otranadoe. Get him."

She almost sounded as if she meant kill him, but Terrel knew the rougher her voice the more tender the thoughts it disguised.

He took the russet man-creature with him and was rougher

than he knew he could be, threatening the Uelson with all the horrors he saw in the prison if he did not direct him correctly. He ordered the translator, "Tell him if he's wrong, I'll . . ." he described the worst thing he could call to mind. "And . . . I don't know, make up something else too, and listen: I mean it."

"I know you do," the translator said. "So does he."

Terrel found his captain catatonic, but a few days back on *Sovereign* brought Teal back to normal. Apparently he had not suffered long-lasting effects, and he seemed to recover as fast emotionally as he did physically.

"It was just . . . nothing," Teal said. "Didn't have to eat or drink. Slept a lot—in fact, constantly. It was just complete solitary confinement." Just what Teal dreaded most after Reill.

He was soon in command again, unchanged from his ordeal—except at night. Terrel didn't notice it at first, but during a night of insomnia, hovering between consciousness and sleep, he felt, or dreamed, a touch as if . . . making sure he was real. It made him wonder, but what would he say? "Teal, I had this dream. . . ." Ray would deny it with level calm. So Terrel made it a point to stay awake one night. He heard uneven breathing, heard Teal stir. He hardly heard or felt him, just sensed Teal peering over at him, verifying his existence. He stayed there some moments, then returned to his own bunk, but not to sleep. The breathing was awake. Terrel climbed down and sat on his bed. He looked into wide, terrified Otranadoe eyes.

After a nightmare of nothingness, Teal had wakened to an inundation of sensations; colors flooded wide eyes; he heard breathing, rustling, a voice; felt textures, bed, walls, pillow, clothes, another person. Another person. Not alone.

"Hey, why didn't you say anything?" Terrel scolded gently.

"Don't leave me."

"Why would I—"

"Don't leave me."

"I won't."

"Don't leave me."

Finally Terrel realized that he wasn't to be answered in words. "Move over." He shoved him to one side of the bed and crawled in. Teal fell asleep with the sound of his Subsecond's heartbeat thundering in his ear, his hands locked around Terrel's arm like bird's feet on a branch in sleep.

Nora was almost glad to have him back. But having been captain so long, she could not tolerate stepping down. She didn't have to. Admiral Cory gave her a ship, along with a personal commendation. So Nora was ushered out with a drinking party. Teal granted her girlfriend a transfer, and Nora thanked him in her own fashion—"Aw, shit."

"Give me a hug and a kiss, fucking dyke," Teal said.

She did, and whispered in his ear, "Hey, faggot, hang on to that one." She motioned at Terrel with her head. "He's a good man."

"But I don't have him."

"Like hell."

Terrel cornered Teal after the party. "Can I ask you what's probably a real dumb question?"

"What, is my mother a virgin?"

"I'm serious."

"Go ahead."

"Did . . . did you talk?"

Teal shook his head. His black hair brushed the edge of the death collar. "At Otranadoe? No."

"I'm sorry, but you just don't look like you could take it."

I can. Maybe because I've known worse. Nothing man could devise could be worse than the Reill that Nature had inflicted on him. And while torture stopped, the Reill remained. He'd give everything to the one who could take that away—and the only one who could wished him dead. Yet someone's eyes had shown him the Aranian sky. . . .

IV.

Over a year passed before Terrel thought Teal was actually recovered, before he could be left alone without fear, before he stopped screaming in his sleep. They had begun sleeping together after he had come back, and Terrel wondered how he could be so sane and stable when on duty yet completely fall apart at night. He never betrayed him to the ship's doctors, who had already tested him thoroughly without finding anything amiss.

At last he seemed to be improving. Terrel was at first relieved, then alarmed at his change. For no reason that he could see, Teal was actually happy. Teal could not explain it either, but did not bother—or dare—to question it. He smiled and black eyes smiled as well—for the first time. He took fewer and fewer painkillers, forgetting them altogether at times. He learned how to do something just for the sake of merriment—how to have fun, a word he had never really understood before. He allowed Orestes Peralta to drag him to his "little island" for a swim.

"You have a little island?"

"He has a very large island," Johnny Fox answered. "With a very large castle on it that he calls a cabin."

Orestes' "little island" in the Aegean was even larger than Teal's home at Skye, where his father reigned as king of the Royalist nation—if he were still alive; if Ven Brekk had not claimed the crown. He could not forget the image of a purple mourning flower.

Teal rediscovered sun and sea. He was pale ivory next to gold Orestes and olive-skinned Johnny. He smelled salt, chlorophyll, and pebbled, rocky wetness of the beach. Sunlight glinted flecks of brightness off the dark ocean, which looked like the ocean of any other planet—a universal Sea into

169

which he could dive and find himself instantly home. Fourteen years telescoped into a day; he cut through the water like a dolphin never parted from the sea, and, in a way, he never had been.

Orestes tried to keep up with him, as overmatched and daring as a four-year-old challenging his father to a foot race.

"Could you swim to Athens from here?" Johnny asked Teal, amazed by his speed.

"Yes," said Teal.

"*Don't* swim near Athens," Orestes warned. "You'll dissolve." His water-darkened hair was turning blond again under the sun's drying warmth. Teal fastened his eyes on the fiery disk of the sun and held them there so long that his Earth companions feared he'd blind himself. "What do you see up there?" Orestes asked. "You'd swear you'd never seen a sun before. You had two to look at—what's so special about ours?"

"Didn't these people worship the sun?" Teal asked.

"Yeah, I guess they did in ancient Greece. Apollo."

"Did he have the sun as a holy symbol?"

Orestes shook his head, and water droplets traced down his shoulders. "Not the sun. I seem to remember laurel boughs being one of his sacred objects. Bow and arrow, lyre. People think I should know this stuff because I'm Orestes. He was associated with a wolf sometimes . . . no, that's wrong. He wasn't really sun god—everyone says he was, but I don't think so. Helios was the sun."

"Did he have a holy symbol, the Sun?"

"I don't know. I don't think so. They had a different concept of the sun. It was a fiery chariot. Helios drove it across the sky, then he took a night boat to Ethiopia and started over."

"Oh." *I thought I'd found the Sun. What have I found?*

He returned to *Sovereign*, dark-skinned and cheerful.

"Captain, can I ask why you're acting like this?" Terrel asked as Teal sailed into his cabin.

"Why not?"

"But *why?*"

"For the hell of it," he said in a new, bantering voice, gesturing with a carefree flip of his hand.

"I can't believe how you've changed—'for the hell of it' never used to mean anything to you."

"You disapprove."

"Captain, it frightens me," he said with genuine fear in his voice.

"Terrel, I'm happier than I've ever been."

"Any reason?"

"No," said Teal.

"That's what scares me. It's always calm before a storm. Sick old people rally just before they die. Right now you're *crazy*—that's fine—but where is it leading? . . . I hid your reddots—you didn't even notice."

Teal frowned. "You're too serious, Sub-second. It isn't like *you*."

September 27, 2197 A.D. (Thursday)

Terrel grew accustomed to Teal's laugh, merry and bright instead of, as formerly, bitter. He had a glow to his face, a red highlight to his cheek. "Like a pregnant woman," some-one cracked. Teal would have made a beautiful woman, Ter-rel observed, and it was rumored he wasn't just consenting to the ladies.

He would look long into a mirror and murmur, "I wonder if my mother looked like this."

Didn't he know? Terrel wondered.

Teal was turning in as Terrel was rising. It was morning on the inner deck and night was coming to the outer deck as the ship maintained simulated Earth cycle of night and day. Teal kept no cycle, no standard hours. He often worked twenty-four hours a day. His waking hours ranged from seventeen to thirty-six at a stretch.

"Captain, why aren't you dropping dead?" Terrel asked, rubbing sleep from his eyes and trying to wake up fully.

"Do you want me to?"

"No, I mean with your schedule—lack of one, really. How do you do it? When I was first assigned on board I gave you three months to kill yourself off. Haven't you ever heard of a circadian rhythm?"

"Not until I came to Earth," said Teal.

"You're from a multistar system," Terrel concluded.

Another slip. The Uelsons could not have wrenched that out of him.

"I should have seen that earlier," said Terrel. "I don't know why no one else has."

Teal hadn't thought that his biological clock could give anything away. "How did I let that slip?" Teal said aloud, but directed at himself.

"You're less guarded than you were. Why do so many people think you're still straight man? You're . . . *fey*. You've been changed for over a year," Terrel said, putting on his uniform jacket and checking himself in the mirror.

"Not so long," Teal said.

"It was around Christmas and New Year's."

"Only months."

"Almost a year. Nine months," Terrel said and went to the door.

"That's not that long."

"Long enough to make a person," he said, walking out of the cabin.

Then Teal knew.

He was forty years old. Almost one Star Year. One cycle.

One cycle.

Exactly one Star Year ago he had been in his mother's womb. For the past nine months he had been reliving the first sensations of his life, within his mother. For the last nine months he'd been happier than he'd ever been. One Star Year ago he'd been happier than he'd ever been, cradled in a safe warm place—and loved. His memory of that time was vague feelings—contentment, peace; perhaps the "feyness" was from his young mother who carried him. All those forty-year-old feelings were recurring now, one Star Year later.

And approaching was the day that marked one Star Year from his birth.

Long enough to make a person—time was almost up.

He could sense the time approaching, Arana nearing opposition, change of the Beth-enea.

The day of his birth had been Cold Season winter. Teal could remember the feelings that flooded from his mother before his actual birth—fear, cold, terror—alone. Pain. Desperation. Terror of a frail young girl alone in the wilderness in the dead of Cold Season winter. Then from his mother no fear, no pain . . . no life.

And there came the emotions from the other one. Loss. Emptiness, loneliness, sorrow—and hate.

Next he remembered feelings of his own. Reill. Red Madness.

All almost a Star Year ago.

At this moment he was feeling the peace and happiness of one Star Year ago—and soon would come the moment one Star Year from his birth and the feeling it would bring with it. And the Reill. This time he could not live through it.

Teal sank to his knees where he was. *Oh God, if you are there, please God help me. Help me. Someone help me.*

He closed his eyes.

A rosette.

A circle.

A fish.

A cross.

The Sun.

He opened his eyes. *Is anyone there? Help me.*

He rose. *I am going to die,* he thought, strangely calm. *In less than a month I will die.*

He could have calculated exactly how long, but he didn't want to. All he knew was that it was just short of a month, having gone nine months so far. He didn't wish to know exactly, because he wasn't going to die then—he would kill himself first.

Royalist women carried their children ten months. Less than a month to live. Still calm—calmness of forty years ago.

He thought of his home and his father, whom he would never see again. His fourteen years in space to end in suicide, mission incomplete.

Teal didn't take command at all that day but sat alone in thought. It grew late, 2,000 hours, and the calmness of the last nine months fled to be replaced by shock and apprehension.

And it dawned on Teal what the feeling meant. It was too soon—Royalists carried their children ten months.

No one had told him he was premature—and that was why his mother had been alone in the cold when the time came.

Sudden. Too sudden. He saw simultaneous sunrise and sunset.

Like ignited oil surging from his heart engulfing him in fire from within, Red Madness leaped into active fury. Red licked his neck and stabbed every nerve in a violent convulsion of pain.

"Oh God, don't let me die like this!"

A rosette

A circle

A fish

A cross

The Sun

Take me but not like this, God, not like this someone, someone help me. . . .

He found the knife in his hand, turned inward to his heart, which felt as if it were pumping molten metal, not blood. White hands with red-veined wrists clenched the blade, wavering, unable to hold it straight. He shut his pain-dimmed eyes tight and readied to stop the traitor, incendiary heart. But he faltered at what his closed eyes saw.

A cross

The Sun

A circle

A rosette

The door opened and the blade was wrested from his hands. He turned away, suppressing an animal cry, fighting back tears; can't have tears, water burns. A hand grasped his own and bared inflamed wrist.

"Jesus, Ray!"

"Kill me, kill me, don't let me die like this. . . ."

"Dear God—"

"Kill me, please, please," he cried, and through tears saw a white mourning flower, though his eyes were shut.

The clock said 2000. What Teal's numbed mind grasped as time stopped dead was the passage of twenty-four hours. Drained, exhausted, he felt as if he were the ashes left after the fire. And he hadn't been the one to endure the full crisis, now passed.

Terrel looked dead. Teal touched his neck, not sure if he were alive or not. Quivering hand found his pulse. The unconscious Terrel's body was wet with sweat but his skin was cool to the touch. There was dried blood on the bed on which they lay, and Terrel's hand was crusted with blood from a deep gash. Teal couldn't remember it being inflicted. The blade was in the middle of the floor. Teal touched the brown-red wound. That had been the least of it.

Terrel woke to a hot trickle on his stinging hand. He thought it was blood, but it was tears.

"That burns," he said weakly, withdrawing his hand.

Teal was alarmed. "Still? Isn't it passed?" Water burning meant Red Madness.

"Salt on an open wound," Terrel said. Aranian Royalist tears were even saltier than Earth tears. Teal sighed audibly and dropped his head back down on the bed. "It's over," said Terrel. The dull throb in his hand was a blessing in comparison to the previous day. "It's over."

Teal's face was wet, salt-streaked from tears like ocean brine.

"It's over, isn't it?" Terrel asked, now unsure.

The black eyes returned a look of sorrow and adoration.

"Isn't it over?" Terrel repeated.

"For this time."

"It's still there?"

Teal answered with tears.

"But . . . how do you . . . get *cured*, or . . . is it a sickness? What is it?"

"I don't know."

"I don't understand what I did."

Teal couldn't understand *how* or *why* he did what he did. Then it was true; someone could take Reill on to himself. . . .

Teal suddenly bolted up, "Who's running the ship?"

"Luz."

"Twenty-four hours? She's supposed to turn in at twelve hundred."

"You called in at twelve-hundred—don't you remember?"

"No." He remembered panicking, thinking Terrel would die. He had never known what to do in his crises, and was still more lost trying to care for someone else—especially when he was the cause of it. *It should have been me.* He couldn't remember thinking of the ship at all. "I don't remember."

"You must."

"I've got to get back on duty."

"After that?" Terrel was exhausted and incredulous.

"I have to," he said. "Get up. I'll change the bed."

The bed was taken care of by the Slave, clean sheets replacing bloody ones. Terrel's hand took more time and tears. Terrel was in pain as the wound was cleaned. "You'd think after yesterday this would be nothing, but it still hurts like hell."

"I can give you a reddot."

"How many are you taking?"

Teal was silent.

"Teal."

"Eight."

Terrel tried to swallow, mouth dry and sour. "I thought it was over."

"Sleep as long as you want and then have someone in sick bay look at that hand before you report for duty, understand?"

"Are you all right, captain?" Terrel caught his arm with his good hand.

"I never was."

V.

After two days of semideliberate avoidance, Teal had to face Terrel's inevitable question. "What happened?"

Terrel was sitting up in bed, hand healing cleanly after the ship's doctor had fused the chipped bone back together where the knife had struck it in "that careless accident." His loyalty and sacrifices both amazed Teal and placed him under obligation to deny him nothing, especially not the answer to this particular question.

Teal sighed heavily and sat also. "Where do I start?"

"At the beginning?" Terrel suggested.

"I was born," Teal answered, not meaning to sound as short as he did.

"You don't want to tell me," Terrel concluded, resting his hurt hand in his lap. "You don't have to if you don't want to."

"I do. I am," said Teal. "I'm not being sarcastic. I was born. My mother died because of it . . . I can remember that. It's funny, Earthlings can't remember that far back. I can remember before I was born, before I was conceived even. I have the memories of my ancestors. It really begins back there, with my ancestors—I'm not hedging, Terrel, really. It's directed evolution. This is all caught up in my people's trying to control Nature. Basically our plan is sound, but it has had some unlooked for side effects, and *that's* what happened—a side effect.

"The Royalists have found a way of controlling—well, speeding up—evolution. Maybe 'adaption' is a better word than 'evolution.' Well, anyway—"

"Who are the Royalists?" Terrel interrupted.

"I'm sorry— this is stuff I *know*, I've never tried to explain it," Teal said. "My people are called the Royalists—because we have a king. We're a *species* of people. I'm a Royalist, as opposed to a Northerner. You know about Northerners—you call them Aranians."

177

"You're from Arana?" Terrel was more surprised at his telling him than by *what* Teal was telling him.

"Yes. I'm of the second species of human life on Arana—the one you Earth people don't know about. Arana has one species of human, they'll tell you, and one of semi-intelligent beast. I'm a semi-intelligent beast," he said with a sarcastic lilt.

Terrel cut him off, "Teal, I'm not supposed to hear this."

"I trust you," said Teal.

"*I* don't trust me. If I get carted off and questioned because someone thinks I know something, it will take a lot less than an Otranadoe to make me talk. Don't trust me."

"I'll never let that happen to you," Teal said. "You've done enough for me—you've already taken the worst that could happen. I don't know how you did. The Reill is worse than anything anyone could do."

Terrel nodded. "Like having hell explode inside you. But what *is* it?"

"A mistake," said Teal. "It's the result of a sort of selective breeding—not really, but sort of. I'm sorry, I'm not making myself clear." He thought a moment, then started again. "I come from a long line of only sons—sixty-six of them."

"You're the only son of an only son of an—?"

"Yeah. With each successive generation of an only son, the line grows more powerful, more adaptable, allowing for change. Actual change becomes noticeable after the thirty-third generation of only sons. After the thirty-third generation they're called Bay Royalists."

"Bay?"

"*Bay* means . . . *new*, new as in 'different from one in the past,'" said Teal, having trouble with word-for-word translations. "It takes thirty-three generations to achieve Bay Royalist. Then after thirty-three *more* generations, another big change occurs. This pivotal generation is pretty unstable. That's why it's called 'crisis generation.' It's the sixty-sixth only son in the line, which is to say the thirty-third-generation Bay Royalist. That's what I am."

"You mean this is what you get for trying to direct evolution?" Terrel said.

"No. It's not supposed to happen. It wouldn't have, if everything had gone right. With every generation the line improves, but also with each generation the links of the chain grow more dependent on each other—and when it breaks, it breaks. My mother died at my birth—and my father . . . rejected me. That's what went wrong. I was cut off from the chain. It's more than a physical link. It's not like an Earthman or a non-Bay; if your parents didn't want you they could've given you up for adoption and you'd be none the worse for it. It's not like that for me. I am linked to my line mentally, emotionally, spiritually, and in other ways that I don't have Earth words for. The link is there. And when it's cut . . . it's like I've had a pyramid kicked out from under me. And since our evolution is more than physical, I'm a walking disaster, a monstrous deformity that shouldn't be allowed to breed and perpetuate deformity—"

"You're not—" Terrel started to defend him.

"I *am*. And there's a natural defense built in to keep my kind from living and continuing a defective line. They call it Red Madness—it destroys the defective link. I was cut off—I was defective. I guess it's less of a *disease* than a *deficiency*. I was deprived of my father, and these are the symptoms."

"What about your mother?"

"I can live without my mother, as an Earthman can. The link is through the male, except in very rare cases of a female Bay Royalist, but that's something else. A Bay can do without his mother, but not his father. In my race the seed of change is in the male. What this is leading to is a New Race—after four hundred generations we will reach this new evolutionary stage. After four hundred generations of only sons, the fourhundredth is the New Race. The father of the New Race needs three hundred and ninety-nine generations of breeding behind him. The woman exists now. The man, not for thousands of years. Our women don't have to breed as we do. My wife tried to explain that to me a long time ago. . . ."

"You have a wife, Teal?"

"Had. She's dead. So is my line."

"I'm sorry," said Terrel.

"Twenty-five years ago. I should be over it by now," he said, trying to believe it. "That's about it. . . . You probably don't understand any more than when I started."

Terrel tried to summarize. "You're a disconnected link in an evolutionary chain?"

"I guess you could put it that way."

"Why *only* sons? I mean, what's wrong with two or three children?"

"Because . . . if a Bay's mother had another child, the Bay would feel it, go through labor with her. If it was a Bay's father who sired a child, the Bay would go through it too, with whoever the woman was. If it were both parents, he'd get it from both directions. And suddenly he would have this other mind like his own. It sucks everything that makes you a Bay out of you. Instead of having just a long line behind you, you also have this immature thing, not adding but taking, and because it's your same generation the pull is greatest. You lose your memory; and mind and matter go hand in hand. Even if it's your mother's child he would be linked to your father through *you*. He's in her womb, where you began, he's linked to you, as you are to your father's line. It's a dissipation of energy. Am I making any sense at all?"

Terrel was thinking. He spoke, "If your father had another child you wouldn't be Bay anymore?"

"That's right."

"And only Bays can have this . . . Red Madness?"

"Yes."

"Would that cure you, then—I mean if your father had another child?"

"I don't know." Teal had never considered it. "I think it would kill me."

"Why?"

"I just think that if my father had another child, I'd die. No reason. I just think I would. . . . I don't think he'll ever remarry, though. He was too attached to my mother to ever look at another woman. That's why he hates me so much. I killed her."

"Good lord, it's more his fault than yours. *You* didn't get her pregnant. You didn't have any say in the matter."

"You tell him," Teal said. "I know you're trying to help me . . . but . . . just forget me; it's hopeless. I don't want to drag you down with me."

"Teal, is this ever going to happen again?"

"I have it always, the Red Madness. I've had a—I call it a crisis—a couple of times. Something like this one I'll get again in another forty point six years," he answered dully. "I imagine."

"How can you tell?"

"What happened now was . . . I was a Star Year old. I was born. I felt my mother die. I felt my father's hate; and then Red Madness. . . . That was all one Star Year ago— that's forty point six years. If you don't recognize the number, it's the time it takes for the two suns of the Diakyon system to orbit each other. Do you remember your comments about circadian rhythm? I'm not on a daily rhythm, I'm on a

Star Year rhythm. I was reliving my birth . . . and it almost killed both of us."

He didn't look forty, Terrel thought. He looked closer to a delicate twenty-five. "What happens now?"

"I don't know. I shouldn't be alive. I should've died in childhood. I don't know how or why I haven't. I wouldn't have lived through this if it hadn't been for you."

"If your father took you back, would that solve everything—or anything?"

Teal looked at him with watery black eyes. "That's a lifetime dream of mine."

Teal had dreamed innumerable ways he would come home. But all his dreams ended the same.

Thoughts forced on his home, Teal fretted about the state of Arana. Base Sixus had been recovered and rebuilt by the Earthmen—due directly to himself but with no effort on his part. That ended the menace of Castor Base ever snarling at Arana, and repaid the dogs who had dealt with Vanguard. It also meant that Arana was no longer between the two great Powers, but was within Earth territory. He was tempted to call the situation good enough and go home. But then *Sovereign* would be called to stop a raid, and he knew the Uelsons were as great a threat as ever. And Arana was more helpless than ever: Calvin was on Earth; Natina, the prophetic Water Nun, the eyes of Arana, was dead. Perhaps another of the Daughters of the Sea was watching now. Holly would be beginning to age slightly, as the Earthmen did, with a trace of gray around his temples. His father would be unchanged. And Tras—Tras' hate-filled, ruddy face would be wrinkled, crowned by dark hair peppered gray which would toss as he pounded his fists and screamed for war. Or had the Caucans won already, and the entire Royalist nation been destroyed or forced to live like dolphins in the sea?

Terrel dominated his thoughts. He had taken on himself that which was worse than death. Teal doubted even Jim could have done it. He had not thought it possible for anyone.

Terrel held his captain in awe and respect and in total faith. Faith carried guilt, since Teal felt himself unworthy of any kind of faith. With all the stories circulating, he still had a spotless name in Terrel's eyes—because Terrel didn't believe anything about him that he hadn't heard from Teal himself. And Teal couldn't tell him, guilt building and compounding. Terrel, fearing for him, asked what was wrong. But Teal couldn't bring himself to confess that Terrel had misplaced his trust. At home, honor was everything. What wouldn't bother an Earthman drove Teal to hold a knife again.

April 9, 2198 A.D. (Tuesday)

Terrel was furious. He didn't know if he was more upset with that fat-lipped spaceman for talking dirty, or with himself for giving him a fat lip. He was an ugly man saying ugly things about the captain. Malevolent green eyes gleamed dully in puffy sockets, and his whole fleshy being oozed hatred. Terrel told him to shove it up his rudder.

The man turned as red as his butch hair and sneered, "Are you defending your captain or yourself by association, captain's roommate?"

Unable to walk away, Terrel turned on him, dark brows lowered and drawn together. "Mind your own business—or haven't you got. any business to mind? What's the matter, spaceman, can't get a lay?" The man inspired hate. Still, Terrel surprised himself.

"Why, can't you? How come you never sleep around, Teal Ray's jackal?" He went on to theorize in more and more vulgar terms, till Terrel, who thought he'd heard everything, was shocked.

That's when he got the fat lip. Terrel felt he should have never even recognized the man's remarks, let alone dignify them with a defense or degrade himself with a fight. He wondered if he should even bother the captain with it. He went reluctantly to tell him.

It was the next morning that he woke and found Teal on the floor with the knife in his hand and blood all around. When Terrel had told him he'd stood up for him, Teal resolved to kill himself rather than admit that he really didn't deserve defending. His reputation stank to Arana, as a red-headed, green-eyed monster had reminded him. He could not live. He ended up confessing anyway, then trying to kill himself.

Am I really dead and in hell? If I cannot die, I must be dead. Did I die with my mother? If this is hell, what is he do-

ing here? He looked up at Terrel, sitting by him in sick bay. Teal couldn't talk because of his slashed throat. Apparently nothing was dearer than life to these Earthmen, not even honor. Despite his murdered name, Terrel had seen fit to keep him alive. Terrel scolded him with the cliché, "Where there's life, there's hope." That might be, Teal considered, but he was too tired and too scared to try anymore. All his life he had attempted to make himself someone to be proud of, and instead had sunk himself deeper in disrepute. He would live and try again, because Terrel asked it.

Once recovered—to the amazement of the doctors—Teal presented a stable, rational calm for the psychiatrist, and the incident was recorded as just one of those things that happen in space.

The doctor told him, "You're very lucky. An Earthman wouldn't have made it. You cut all the way through your jugular vein. I wish I could take credit for your spectacular recovery, but it was nothing we did. Your regenerative faculties are nothing short of miraculous."

Teal resolved to do a quicker, more thorough job next time. If there was a next time. He had little doubt but that there would be. By now, he was not an optimist.

August 16, 2198 A.D.

Teal received a special written commendation from Fleet Admiral Cory for rescuing a Lokin vessel in trouble. It had just been something he'd done because he had to. For things like that, Earth made men into heroes. He read and reread the letter.

"Does it mean a lot to you, what he thinks?" Terrel asked.

"Yes."

"Why?"

"I don't know. A psychologist would probably say he's a father figure. But that's Earth psychology. Maybe he is."

"What would you do if your father wrote something like that to you?"

"Faint, cry, swing from the chandelier by my heels."

"We don't have a chandelier."

"That's all right—my father will never write me like this."

"Teal."

"It would be better for you if you still hated me."

Terrel winced. "I didn't hate you."

"You didn't like me."

"*You* didn't like *me*."

"Richard, don't die. Please don't die."

He started. "Why do you say that? Do you know something I don't?"

"They always die. Please, don't you go, too. Don't leave me."

He knew Teal was half-raving out things he had to say. "You know I'll try my best not to."

VI.

May 2202 A.D.

Anna Molina confronted Teal Ray, angrily. Teal couldn't understand why she was upset with him. He felt strongly about her, as he'd felt about no one since his wife or the Nomad girl by the fire. She made him feel alive.

Teal hadn't known what to make of Anna at first, when he found her purring in his bed while Terrel was on leave. He'd had to make a decision: he could walk out, or he could stay. He'd stayed and decided he liked Anna. Now she was angry; she was almost crying.

The popular verdict of the situation was that it had to happen sometime. People had been beginning to wonder if Teal were sterile or so different that he wasn't quite human. But he wasn't sterile and he wasn't of human stock, and Anna was pregnant.

She barged into his cabin, woke him up, spat her announcement at him, and ran out before he saw her tears. Like a flash of sun-caught copper when she tossed her hair angrily over her shoulder, she was there and gone. Teal was left bewildered and flying. Suddenly he pinpointed his feelings, what they meant. She made him feel alive—the life of an unborn daughter. He knew it was a daughter. Alive like the Nomad dancer made him feel alive. . . . An instant focusing of a picture he'd never known was blurred till he saw it clearly.

"Terrel!" he almost shouted. "I have a daughter!"

"I know," Terrel said drowsily, having wakened to Anna's loudly stated news. Two half-closed eyes peered from under sleep-mussed auburn hair. A shadow of stubble on a wakening Earthman's face had ceased to shock and now looked natural. He cleared his gravelly voice and propped himself up on an elbow. "I heard."

"I mean at home! I have a daughter I never knew about! I

had a feeling—I never knew what it meant before. It's a girl!" He laughed brightly. A feeling of life . . . it was really life. The Nomad dancer had borne him a girl. He sensed her presence clearly, now that he knew what he was looking for.

Terrel didn't know what to say. "Congratulations?"

"She's thirty-five years old," Teal said, voice light.

"You have a thirty-five-year-old daughter?" Terrel was awake now. He sat up and listened.

"I was hardly more than a kid. She danced by a fire. I never forgot her. Now I know why. . . . Terrel!"

Brown eyes blinked. "What? You found another daughter?"

Teal was ecstatic, laughing jubilantly. "No, no. *My line's not dead!* I have a line skip daughter!"

Terrel climbed off his bunk, dropping down to the floor, bare feet landing with a quiet, padding sound. They were soft, pale Earth feet that never touched anything rougher than the inside of a shoe. He faced Teal. "Am I supposed to know what you're talking about?"

Calmed enough to speak, Teal explained, "I told you my line is of only sons, but there is such a thing as a female Bay. A line ends with twins, with more than one child, or with a daughter *except* past thirty-third-generation Bay, which is the same as saying after sixty-six generations of only sons."

"What generation are you?"

"Thirty-third-generation Bay. A lot of changes come at this stage, which is what makes it crisis generation. Past this point, a daughter doesn't end the line—she sets it back. Eldest daughter of a thirty-third-generation Bay can continue the line. My oldest daughter's son—if my daughter has an only son—will be a first-generation Bay. The Stewert line isn't dead; my eldest daughter lives. I know she's there. I sense her now, always have; but she was so close to me I couldn't see her separately. I thought that life was part of me. It's hers. Natina always said you can't see what's closest to you. . . . My line's not dead!"

I believe in miracles again. I thought they died with Ak-elan. Miracles have been resurrected. Anything's possible now.

July 2202 A.D.

Help, Father, they're going to kill me.

Teal woke and sat up. *Who said that?* No one was there. No one had spoken. He lay back and put his mind in a blank state.

Father, help.

It was just a feeling. The words had been his own addition, a kind of translation of an abstract, wordless plea. . . .

Father, help!

"Good God, she's going to kill her!"

Terrel stirred in the bunk above. "What . . . kill who? . . . Teal, wake up, you're having nightmares again." he dropped tiredly down to Teal's bunk.

"No! No!" he was babbling and quivering. "Anna's going to have an abortion. I know it! My daughter's calling me for help! I—"

"Is she on board?" Terrel asked in a firm tone.

"I don't know! I don't know," he said hysterically. "I—"

Terrel hit the intercom and tracked Anna Molina down, while his stable-on-duty captain was falling apart completely and crawling up his back, mumbling, "Not like my son, not like my son, not my daughter too. . . ."

He found Anna seething, livid with rage at the court injunction he presented her with.

Teal had calmed . . . *like a dormant volcano*, Terrel thought.

Anna summoned a lawyer and a doctor, and raged at them when they took "this silly injunction" seriously. "My constitutional right—"

"This is an interstellar case," Teal interrupted coldly. "The United States Constitution rules a very small part of the universe."

"We have no treaty with you!" Anna turned her attack from the two traitors who were supposed to be helping her to the actual criminal.

"No one wants to provoke someone who builds ships like Armageddon I," Teal countered, calling up Earth fears in a massive bluff for his daughter's life. "You don't know us. All the more reason not to hurt the only two *hitherto* peaceful ambassadors you have." All the Earthlings were duly apprehensive. Except Anna.

"This is not an ambassador!" Anna cried, hand to her abdomen. "It's a fetus!"

"A fetus that told her father you meant to kill her." Teal bristled like a wolf. Terrel stayed close to his elbow, watching warily.

"It's not a her, it's an *it!*"

"She talks. She's frightened . . . she's trying to reach you. Don't hurt her."

"No fucking man can tell me what I can and can't do with my body."

"*You* came to *me.* What was I supposed to do? Say, 'Wait a minute, I have to go down to sick bay and get a prescription'? I'm not telling you what to do with your body. I'm telling you to take responsibility for what you've already done with it."

"You can't tell me what to do!" she screamed, and Teal blew up.

He shrieked and growled, but no one understood, since he had slipped into Royalist tongue. They understood mad, blind rage, however. Terrel would no more have touched him than he would a snarling badger, certain Teal would bite his hand if he tried to restrain him. Anna shrank back, fearing for her life. Teal screeched at her and at these Earthmen, ignoring Terrel, not including him as a target for his rage. "What gives you the right to take life from me? Do you think we are a pack of disconnected semi-intelligences as you are? That you can take life that is mine? that is my father's? that is my grandparents'? her sister's? You would take the life of all her descendants that would have been. Mass murderess! I will count them and take an equal number of Earth lives if you take our Royalist lives. Do you think we have them to throw away as you do? You are made to be criminals—the amount of damage you do can never be extracted in retribution. You have no linked chains to rip and ruin. Yet you think you can tear ours at your convenience—" He gasped for breath, realized that none of these aliens gawking at him with their dumb open mouths understood a word, and if they did they'd stare just as dumbly. He took another breath and recovered his calm. As Kury would say, it was time now to pull the ace.

"You kill a king's daughter. Answer to that." He latched on to Terrel's arm and let himself be led away. *If it weren't for this one Earthman,* he thought, *I'd join the Gerens.* He heard Anna screaming after him, "You can't make me have a baby. You can't make me."

He realized, after they were out of earshot, that he was digging his fingers into Terrel's arm hard enough to bruise him. He relaxed his grip. "I hope she doesn't do anything. . . ."

"Will she?" Terrel asked.

"I think . . . I hope she might listen now. . . . If she can just *hear* her I *know* she won't hurt her."

"Who gets custody?"

"I do," said Teal. "Anna doesn't want her."

"What are you going to do with a baby?"

Teal shrugged. "Same thing Kury did with Johnny, I guess. Raise her."

"But a daughter? An *infant* daughter?"

Teal shrugged.

When the child was born, Anna had changed her mind and decided to keep her. As her daughter grew within her, she began to receive the little signals, feelings and sensations, and by the time the child was born, she was no longer a stranger or an *it*. Teal contested it in court, and Anna won.

Anna's change of heart did not apply to Ray. Neither had Teal forgiven her, but he knew he needn't worry about his daughter's safety any longer.

He saw the baby only twice. She had some of Raya's features—Teal's features. Teal wondered why he looked so like his mother when his father's line was such a powerful one. Raya had no breeding, was just a Lowlander. Yet he'd inherited as much from her as from his father, as if she were a Bay from a powerful line like Kaela.

"I'm sorry you didn't get your daughter," Terrel said.

"Just as well," Teal sighed. "I'd be a lousy father. A girl needs her mother. I hate her—Anna. She'll be a good mother, though. . . . I will never love an Earthwoman again."

April 19, 2207 A.D.

Years of waiting, preparing, watching; fantasies of becoming some kind of avenging angel, a planetary hero; it all came to an end in anticlimax that sat dull in Teal's stomach, when news spread like the flare of a supernova: Uelso had invaded Gereny—and was destroyed by the invaded fifteen-planet nation. The report did not say "defeated." It said "destroyed."

No one had ever really known the power of the Gerens. From time immemorial Loki and Gereny had been at war; and now Loki, a minor power, saw what kind of Power she'd been throwing pebbles at, and wondered why she hadn't been annihilated long ago.

The answer was simple. Gereny was basically a peaceful nation.

"I *knew* I should have joined the Gerens." Teal rolled his eyes. "They did it without me. They had Armageddon III without me."

"Are you sorry?" Terrel asked in mild reproof.

"I feel a little foolish for wanting to take them on single-handed, but no, I'm not sorry. I don't like slaughter," he said. "Terrel . . . I can go home now . . . and I'm scared to death." *I've turned into an Earthman. I don't belong there. I can't go back. . . .*

"You don't want to go?" Terrel asked, coming to his side.

"Terrel, I want to die," Teal said in a small voice.

Terrel seized his shoulders and held him at arm's length. "Goddammit, I've had enough of that!" he thundered as Teal never knew he could, and shook him harshly. "After all we've been through! You keep telling me I own your life, so stop trying to take it from me! I didn't go through that for nothing. You die and part of me goes with you. So next time you get it in your head you want to die, you kill me first, understand? I'd like a little choice on how I go!"

Teal raised his hand to Terrel's face—not that there were tears until after he touched him. "Tears for an ocean on Canda."

Terrel blinked them back and continued quieter. "Teal, go home; you go see your father and . . . if it doesn't work out, come back, understand?"

Teal said nothing.

"Understand?"

Teal nodded. "Send the dead garbage back."

"Promise."

A promise to live. He hesitated, but he had to give Terrel what was his. "I promise."

The room was unrecognizable as Jim's old office. Teal had never seen it neat. The furniture was new, as was the carpet, with no cigarette burns in it. It was hardly the same room at all. Teal settled uneasily into a chair and stared across the desk at Admiral of the Fleet Cory.

"I want you to give me a Voyager and a promise that you won't follow me," Teal began.

Cory looked quizzical, sitting back in his chair, observing the catlike man curled in the chair across from him. Cory was a tall, handsome American in his sixties, well-groomed, very youthful, yet very mature. Where was the short, dog-toothed man half his age, in perpetual shambles, who would throw temper tantrums in council, who used to wear that tan uniform and five stars?

"You are leaving UEF service?" the Admiral responded.

"Yes."

Cory lifted his eyebrows, then nodded. "May I ask why?"

He would figure it out by himself anyway. "No more Uelsons."

"There are Gerens."

"I'm more afraid of *you* than of Gereny."

"Captain Ray, I'll spare you the board's rhetoric; we would like to establish peaceful relations with your people, whoever they are. That is why I am reluctant to let you go without another word, even though I'd like to give you what you want. Did you ever consider that for twenty-five years we've been afraid of *your* people?"

Twenty-five years. Had it really been that long?

"Then give me a nonaggression, noninterference pledge, and I'll give you my world's pledge." He had not been able to protect Arana from Uelso, but this the Gerens could not take from him—he could protect Arana from Earth. Twenty-five years would not go for nothing.

"Without knowing who we're pledging to?" Cory asked.

"If you don't muscle in on any world that doesn't muscle in on you first, you don't have to worry about breaking your pledge."

Cory laughed loudly—not at Teal. His plan was childlike in its simplicity and a grandly idealistic idea—if he could ever sell it to the board. "Then Earth has to end her imperialism for fear of treading on the tiger's toes?"

"If you have to do it out of fear. I thought honor was a nice idea."

Cory pursed his lips and smoothed back light brown hair. "In the time I've known you, you've never ceased to amaze me. I like the idea too, but let's be realistic; you're dealing with Earth. They'd only do it out of fear, and in time that would wear off, and they'd feel bold, and go their imperialistic way, daring you to take them on however powerful you are."

"Well, don't tell anyone, but we're bluffing."

At first Cory thought he was kidding. Then he was struck by wonder and felt the weight of trust settle heavily on him. "Why do you tell me that?"

"Because you have to know it's got to be by honor and not out of fear."

Cory sat brooding a long while, then said, "I'll see what I can pump out of the board. It'll be a few days, never mind that it took us five minutes."

Teal uncurled and rose.

"Oh, and, captain, you've got your Voyager."

Back in the cabin, Teal confided, "I'm getting scared again."

Terrel wanted to say something reassuring, but he could make no assurances about the world Arana.

"I'll be home in time for another war," Teal said dully.

"You time them?" Terrel said, half-joking.

"Yes."

"How do you time a war?" Terrel said, now serious.

"Almost forty years since the last one," said Teal. "Every forty years there's a war—and every forty years there'll be a war as long as there are two peoples on Arana."

"Um . . . do people get warlike every forty years like you get . . . you know . . ."

"No. It's not like that. Not the people. It's periastron. The Pup Star is approaching its closest to the Central Sun."

"Then it gets hot?"

"No. Not from the Pup Star anyway. We receive next to no heat and light from the Pup Star—how much heat does Pluto get from your Sun? Double the distance and dwarf the star and you have us. It's nothing for heat and light, but the dwarf star is a massive sun, and it's the *gravity* that affects us.

"At apastron Arana is a lot like Earth; it has a nearly round orbit. Periastron rolls around and our orbit gets very distorted; Arana is pulled in close to the Central Sun, then pulled way out into the cold. That's Hot and Cold Season. In the northern hemisphere at periastron, Hot Season and summer coincide, and Cold Season and winter coincide. So in the years near periastron, the northern hemisphere is literally a deadly place to live, and the Northerners move south. But the Royalists live in the South. And the Northerners don't just move in, they push us out."

"So there's a war."

"Every periastron."

"But don't Hot Season and summer ever coincide in the South also?"

"Yes, every forty years at apastron. But the Pup Star is far enough away that the Hot and Cold Seasons are much milder."

"So the South is the place to live."

"That's why we evolved there, I guess. The Royalists are the natives of Arana. The Northerners are the imports. The Northerners aren't adapted as we are to life in a double star system. They aren't used to the changes, the irregularity and extremes. My people see nothing wrong with the severe seasons except for the warring Northerners they bring. Physically we're adapted to the severe changes—our lives even depend on them. Our waterbucks wouldn't know when to mate; without them we'd freeze. Red fish eggs wouldn't hatch if the waters didn't rise up the beach to where they were laid forty years before. And without *them* we'd starve. We are children of our planet."

"I'm sorry you have to return to a war," Terrel said.

Teal shrugged. "If Gordon Tras is still alive I'll kill him before I go home. I'll see my daughter . . . and I'll find out who showed me the sky. It wasn't my daughter; I saw a purple flower. I saw Brekk cry at my mother's grave. I thought I was dreaming. . . . I must've been, mustn't I? I was at Otranadoe. Ven Brekk came to my island to cry for my mother . . . and put a purple mourning flower on her grave."

"Maybe he liked her," Terrel said.

"He hated her. Everyone told me he did. Brekks hate Stewerts. Anyway, you only give mourning flowers to your kin or as a representative of your whole line. The Brekk line would not mourn a Stewert wife. I must've been hallucinating badly in prison. I wonder where the vision came from. I thought someone was trying to tell me something."

Teal finished packing—not realizing how much he had to pack. There were some gifts, a flag from the crew, the treaty, and a number of things that he had just collected over the years. He looked over his belongings and took out a stuffed animal (was it an aardvark?). A young crewwoman had given it to him. "Keep this." He put it in Terrel's hands. "I can't take it."

Terrel was going to laugh, but Teal was grave. "Why?"

"It's purple."

Terrel wanted to say he was just prejudiced; there was nothing wrong with a purple aardvark. A black forelock fell across Teal's fret-lined brow. Purple?

Teal locked his hands around Terrel's arm and stood there, delaying. "Richard?"

"Yes."

"Can I ask you an unfair promise?"

If he could ask Teal to live, turnabout was fair play. "Yes."

"Don't get married."

"That *is* unfair."

"Not till I see you again anyway. 'Cause I have an awful feeling I'm going to be back. . . ."

PART FOUR:
The Sun

I.

Day 226 29 Beth-enea
Star Year 532 Third Epoch

Bright sun shining huge overhead, blinding glare on sand of desert turned inferno, flood waters of the harbor, air pressing thick, hot and close, weighing an outworlder down—Teal took it all in as he stepped out of his Voyager on his mother planet. The white Vakellan Fleet buildings gleamed under the sun's Hot Season brilliance. Many of the buildings were new.

A rush of cold, reviving air exhaled from the old central building as Teal opened the door. There was no welcoming—he'd only made his presence known five minutes earlier, announcing his intention to land, and telling them not to shoot. At this instant, few besides Holly White himself would know of his return. Teal ran up the stairs, ignoring the new lift, and down the hall to the admiral's door. He paused a moment, flushed, panting and dizzy. *It's the gravity, that's all.* He drew a breath and entered with slow, reserved poise.

Dignified entrance dissolved when Holly, on seeing him, instantly crushed Teal in a warm hug and scolded him, "*Why* didn't you come back?"

Teal spoke muffled into his chest. "You told me not to."

"I *what?*" Teal felt the rumbling voice reverberate in the resonant, barrel ribcage.

"Right before I left," Teal said in a childlike voice. "You told me not to return while the Uelsons were still a threat." He was beginning to feel like an old Earthman lost in the jungle in World War II and never told the war was over, an object of pity, not glory.

Holly smothered him in an embrace which he could have withstood before he left, but now he felt weak and short of breath in the oppressive, heavy world he'd become strange to. "Holly, I can't breathe."

Holly loosened his hold and smoothed his hair from his face. "I should have known. Oh child . . . you're home now. You look flushed. Are you all right?"

"It's the gravity," Teal said breathlessly. "I'm spoiled."

"They turn you into an Earthman?" Holly grinned and sat him down. "You have an accent, too." He laughed. "You've been keeping the Americans company. You sound funny with a midwestern accent."

"Do I?" Teal asked. "I was in Chicago a lot."

Holly nodded. He touched the death collar. "What's this? I thought I knew Earth styles. Is it American?"

"It's Uelson. It *was* a death collar. It doesn't have the spikes anymore, but I can't get it off."

"God, Teal. I didn't hear about that. I tried to keep track of you on the radio."

Teal blushed darker.

"I didn't hear anything for years, and I'd given you up for dead. Then suddenly I heard so much. I want you to tell me what happened. I heard your voice on the radio sometimes. I wanted to yell at you to bring your ass home."

He questioned him at length, trying to learn instantly the events of twenty-five years. When Teal brought out the treaty from his jacket pocket (slightly creased now) and gave it to his disbelieving commander, Holly stared at it and forgot to close his mouth. Then he looked at Teal with the same disbelieving wonder. Praise, pride, and utter amazement was all Teal wanted from Holly—and he received it. *This is how it's supposed to go. For once. For once.* Teal could have cried, but he was too busy being pleased with himself. He answered all Holly's questions gladly, until he asked, "How is Pauli? I heard he designed you another ship."

Teal studied his small, finely tapered hands. "I'm going to rearrange his face if I ever get a chance. Holly, what the hell was he doing there?"

"I'm sorry there was no way to tell you. We decided he would do us more good working on Earth with their facilities than he could here. So we arranged for him to 'escape' from us. Earth still doesn't know we're on their side. . . . You two never did get along."

He never mentioned what must have been the bulk of what he'd heard on the radio. Holly looked so much older than

Teal had expected, wrinkles around his eyes and furrows in a much-creased forehead.

The sun shone through the many windows of the room. The blue carpet was sun-faded despite sunproof dyes. The light reflected illusively off the dazzling sand of the desert around the base. A glint caught an approaching ship, and it flashed like a mirror.

"Has it changed here, Holly?" he asked. "I've heard nothing."

"I'm sorry, child," Holly said. "I was so busy asking questions. Let's see, it's been a long time. Phaetha has a different ruler, a queen. . . . Um. . . . A little island nation shot up out of nowhere into a first-rate merchant state in the past fifteen years or so. Called Luon—you've probably never heard of it; it was pretty insignificant when you left. You'll see their ships and planes everywhere, so don't be alarmed, they're harmless. Ah, let's see, Natina's island went up in a volcano—went down, rather. It sank. That was a good twenty years ago. We had black skies for the longest time. . . . Ah, your country's at war again."

"I knew it would be. Do you know who is king?"

"We never knew anything about your people, Teal."

"Is Tras still alive?"

"Yes, dammit. Cauca has developed into a frightening power. I'm afraid _we_ may be fighting her someday. . . . My sister died," Holly said.

"I'm sorry."

"Vensar was a hell of a woman. It was a heart condition. Anyway, my kid brother is leader of Vakellan now."

"You're making this country a regular family business," Teal said.

Holly laughed but then felt uneasy. Teal had never joked with him before. This was not the open, easily wounded child who had left. He'd learned to defend himself.

"Are you going to be staying with us?" Holly asked him after they'd talked the sun down.

"No." Teal rose. "I'm going to knock off Tras and go home." He walked to the window and gazed south over the sand and the harbor, forbidding and beautiful in twilight. "Keep the Voyager for me. I think I'll need it again."

Holly walked to him and embraced him, trying to release the sensitive child he'd known—if he hadn't died in space. "I'm sorry I ever sent you out there, child. I am so sorry."

Day 235 29 Beth-enea
Star Year 532 Third Epoch

The buildings of the Capitol City were ablaze, and the mobs in the streets, like sharks in a feeding frenzy, wanted blood. Whistles and shrieks of Royalists in cacophony with Caucan shouts, an anarchic and dissonant harmony forced between two peoples against a common hated enemy—Gordon Tras. His private army had either shed their uniforms to escape their ravaging, rebellious countrymen, or they'd been beaten, stoned, and torn apart at the hands of so many Maenads in a hate-drunk Dionysia. The man they had lauded as savior was a fake, a lying, greedy little man with a fiery tongue that inspired awe and love—turned full circle now to violent hatred.

This, Holly, is a volcano. And it will blacken the skies for years to come.

The people would storm the leader's mansion and howl like dogs at their treed and snarling victim. But Teal wanted revenge for himself, for hatred and as something to tell his father. He knew he must get the shrieking mob to follow him, or else surrender his revenge to them.

Teal ran, barefoot, down a darkened stone alley where there was no fire and no clawing masses. His feet touched night-damp grass, and he heard the snorting and crying of hoofed beasts stamping in their corral, panicked by the smell of smoke and the unnatural glow over the city. The leader of the herd showed itself, calmer, more powerful, searching for an escape for his herd, his hoofs sounding dully on the ground in a restless trot. That was the mount Teal wanted. Teal, dressed in black like the night, sprang over the fence and onto the chosen animal before the beasts saw him. The leader reared at the sudden weight on its back and the pressure of knees clamping against its sides. It bolted and bounded over the fence, lashing the air with its two uncut horns. The third horn, a long spike in the back of its heavy-jawed head, would have slashed Teal apart, but it was cut to a stump, like a handle for him to grasp. He took hold of the furious beast by the cut horn and pointed its head back to the burning inner town. The beast ran in the only direction it could go—where its master directed it. One hand keeping a grip on the horn, Teal shed his black garments, his skin again pale, ethereal white in the darkness, among brown and ruddy bodies in the street. He grabbed a firebrand for a torch, a flame for the moths to follow unquestioningly. He galloped into the midst of the crowd, on a smoke-frenzied beast, a ghostly, avenging angel bearing cleansing fire. Teal knew his own power now, knew how to hold and lead a mass, appearing as a bright light they would follow to heaven or hell.

He led the swarm, as mindless as the beast he rode, to the mansion of Gordon Tras. He knew what lemmings were now. Pawns of power, they rammed down the door, and Teal rode through, telling them to wait for him to bring down the Executioner.

Royalist and Caucan language felt odd to his lips, and his Earth accent added to his eerie, other-world aura. And the crowd obeyed him.

The beast was more frightened in the confines of the building, its hoofs loudly knocking on the wooden floor as it tried to gallop after its head, almost forgetting to stop for walls it met. Teal had intended to ride it up the winding stairs of the mansion, but it tripped on the first step, and Teal was thrown from its back.

The gray beast reared, singed by the firebrand, a red spot on the short gray coat, its head at its own command. Two running leaps and it crashed out a large window into the street.

Teal paused a moment, stunned, then snapped back into stark reality by the clumsy outcome of what had been building into an awesome dramatic conquest. He chased the image of Don Quixote from his mind. After all, no one was watching.

The fallen firebrand was licking at the old wood at the base of the stairs, and a dried-up three-legged table was quickly turning to ash. *Let it burn.* Teal seized a hunting pike from the wall and bounded up the stairs.

Closed, rounded doors had to be his target. Caution gone, Teal bounded into certain death and leapt at the doors. They flew open, and he sprang, landing light and sure on his feet in the center of the richly carpeted room, facing his enemies with his pike.

They looked at him calmly, bearded faces unafraid; some

sitting, some standing, sipping drinks in civilized fashion, windows closed against the din of baying, noisome animals.

Unnerved for a moment, Teal recognized the trap. These hopelessly cornered quarries, facing superior strength and numbers, had attempted their last desperate plan—to try to shame the animals into going away by presenting a coldly civilized front. Their calm, condescending—pitying—gazes infuriated him. There were seven elderly men. They looked as if they'd been interrupted in a civilized chat on the theory of existence by the invasion of a street urchin—a pitable and annoying nuisance.

They would not steal his moment. Teal pursued his honor-imposed directive with single-minded resolve. The face he wanted wasn't here. Teal growled at them sitting there in their stuffed three-legged chairs among richly woven wall hangings and holding their warmed drinks. "Where's Tras?"

Sheep. Dumb woolly sheep with the wolf in their midst. Soft men, like the soft carpet under his bare feet—himself softened from wearing hard soles for so long. He was distinctly aware of the effete softness around him.

A tall, fair-skinned blond spoke evenly, a sneer in his too sweet, almost eunuch's voice. "You came here to kill Gordon Tras?"

Cold black eyes met laughing pale blue. "Yes," Teal said in a strained, rasping voice.

The blond face flooded merry red and broke up into a wrinkled smile. "You came here to kill Tras?"

The others smiled in amusement and exchanged glances. Something was just too funny. Teal felt the weapon grow hot in his hands, his knuckles white from the pressure with which he clutched it. A faint smell of smoke from the fire on the stairs fanned seering senses while these men shared a little—or was it a big—joke. One sipped his drink, and Teal smashed the glass with a snakelike strike of the pike.

"You came to kill Tras?" the voice laughed this time, not in mirth, but sharpened and aimed to kill. He spoke mockingly: "Tras has been dead twenty years."

One of them had brought out a black-and-gray-and-pale-reddish mass of something and was offering it to the speaker. Teal braced himself for a weapon (one he could defend against, unlike the rippling vibrations of sound waves bringing unbearable laughter). Yet what he saw was not a weapon but a transformation.

The laughing man pulled the hairy mass over his head; his

tone dropped an octave; and he became a laughing, ruddy Gordon Tras. Like a snake crawling back into a dead, discarded skin, the viper became Teal's long-dead enemy.

Laughter boomed with a dead man's voice in an imitation perfect enough to make the hair at the base of Teal's neck stand on end, wolf's ruff pricked at a threat.

"So much for your glorious revenge," the voice hushed to a snake's hiss, in the type of dramatic contrast that Tras had manipulated so well. He gained momentum. "Twenty years to hunt down a dead man. You pathetic fool," Tras' voice mocked him. "Pathetic hero. Glorious fool." Caucan laughter.

Out in the streets people with torches rumbled and grew restless; fire glowed within the demon's mansion. Then the doors parted to a white angel backed by the fire in the building that had become furnace and funeral pyre. Unscathed, he emerged from the flames, bloody head of the Executioner on the end of a pike, waved like a banner as he'd once seen in an old Earth play. The people roared and the Royalist prince bore his flagpole, dripping sticky, vile red onto his pale hands, leading the mob to the city circle, where torches and firebrands were touched to the trophy, and the demon head burned. If one watched carefully, he could see melting plastic give way to blond hair for a fleeting instant before black-and-red obliteration.

Day 240 29 Beth-enea
Star Year 532 Third Epoch

They had erected a great wooden cross at Dianter. Coming around the cape, its silhouette on the horizon chilled and saddened him.

Teal had swum past his father's island. He wanted to lay a mourning flower at Dianter. How much longer, he chided himself, could he put off confronting his father? He was beginning to admit that it had not been the Uelsons nor even his strict adherence to Holly's words that had kept him twenty-five years in space. He could have gone home any time. *No.* He rejected the thought. His mind wouldn't accept it.

He wondered whose idea the cross had been. They wouldn't have erected a circle. For Royalists it should have been a rosette. He chastised himself—how could anyone throw together a wooden rosette? Coming ashore, he could see that it was definitely thrown together by a great mass of people who did not wish to tarry there long. They'd burned their dead and buried them, raised their cross in prayer to God—anyone's god—and left.

Teal felt he was the first life to touch this place since then. Charred skeletons of trees and a thick carpet of ash were all that was left of paradise. His soft footsteps crunched loudly on the blackness.

The scattered drums of the colonnade marked his path. The crater where Akelan's white bench had been was half filled with rubbish tossed in by the careless wind. Here was as good a place as anywhere for his small monument, since he could not remember where Akelan had died—not sure if he'd ever really known, except that it was at the base of a hill north of here. He laid the flower by a chunk of marble he guessed was part of the bench. He voiced no prayer.

Not feeling Jim's pendant around his neck, Teal was suddenly panicked at the thought of losing it. His hand fluttered to his neck. It was still there. He had just grown too used to it to feel it.

A bird poured out song, celebration of itself, from the top of a charcoal tree. Teal glanced up at it singing to life among the ashes. He then noticed that there was life, little shoots of green peeping here and there in the cinders. Phoenix plants, they were the first to come back. Dianter would grow back like any other burned place. It was just taking longer—something in the Caucan bombs, perhaps. . . .

Teal recrossed the rubble and gave himself to the rocking arms of the sea.

Only one place left to go before he would be forced to return to Skye. It was a little island between Dianter and Skye. He remembered it yellow, on a scorching day like this one near the turn of the Star Year. He didn't know why he was going there other than to procrastinate. He was a salmon that had to return to his birthplace—but one that chose the route with the falls and white water so that he might not make it.

He had to rest, he told himself. He was not used to swimming, holding his breath, or even breathing in this world.

He rose from the sea, hair dripping water that rolled down browning shoulders. He wore nothing but the indestructible Uelson death collar and his tiny pendant, even nakedness seeming strange after Earth customs. He stretched out on a sun-warmed rock to rest.

Dreaming? Faint strains of a rillia touched him. Madness calling with a siren voice. He heard it as clearly as his own brushing against the rock when he tilted his head to listen. He had thought it death or a divinity the first time. The replay of yesterday awed him. What would he find where he'd found Akelan? Would he meet his own madness? An image of a bomb-shattered wreck singing to the rillia urged him to flee. Run or follow? Run to where? He sought out the voice and the rillia.

He crept over the parched green-yellow grass, hearing the soft rush of his own footsteps. It was just over the rocks where he had met Akelan, where the music, clear as life, originated. And that was Akelan's voice.

The music stopped.

Teal dashed forward and sprang in a blind leap, sailing over the rocks and landing on his feet in the sand below. He whirled to face Akelan, standing on the rocks, rillia in hand, like Apollo with his lyre, golden in the light.

Numb and disbelieving, Teal froze, not daring to move lest the illusion resolve into nothingness, insubstantial as the wind.

Akelan set down the white instrument, and the strings sighed a small tone. He stepped down from the rock. "Teal."

Teal shook his head and took a step backward, but the specter touched his face, "Don't be afraid." Gentle gray eyes, and a sandy halo of soft unkempt hair, and the breathing, living form could not dim the memory of red and mud and bone and a tiny voice fading to silence. Close enough to feel his warmth and smell the scent of his body and see the shine of moisture on his lips, Teal sensed life, not illusion.

Teal sank before him, and Akelan grasped his shoulders, helping him up. "Teal, you know better than anyone that I'm not a god," he argued against Teal's unspoken thought. Misted gray eyes were pleading. All hell gazed back.

"You died," Teal cried, frightened by the warm, real grasp preventing his kneeling or running away.

"I'm a man. You know I am."

"You rose from the dead," Teal protested in a weak voice.

"I didn't die. Remember everything I told you—"

"I remember Dianter."

"Teal, it's just me!" Akelan caught Teal to him and held him close and tight. A human heart pulsed beneath flesh that was real, human and unghostly. "No ghost, no god, just me."

A tear ran down between them. "Tears for an ocean on Canda," Akelan scolded softly. "Those aren't needed. Come now, stop that. It's just me, don't you believe me?"

"You died. I saw." A look of terror was quickly merging with one of worship.

"I did not and you did not. Don't you remember the Mountain People finding us?"

"I woke up in one of their caves," he mumbled. "I guess they found me."

"They found me too. I was a long time healing—I was next to dead. My father helped care for me. I've been a worry for him always. I came back and you had gone."

Teal was hot and wanted to swim, sweating as if touched by the sun.

"No, Teal, you go home now," Akelan said.

Teal's eyes flew wide.

"Stop wasting time," Akelan said. "When I let you go, go straight home."

His mouth opened, searching for words, and he sputtered, "I . . . can't!"

"Did you ever consider that your father might be dying too? He could die tomorrow."

"Will he?" Teal cried in distress.

"I've seen him every day since we heard you had come back—when we heard of your revenge in Cauca. He asks me every day if I've seen you, and every day I say no, and every day he dies a little, and he wonders why you don't come back. I know he thinks you're trying to kill him. If you want revenge on him too, this is the way to do it."

Either Akelan let go or he broke away—nothing could have held him—and he ran for the sea and home.

II.

The sea was high enough to allow an approach to Skye from the cliff side, now mostly submerged. He climbed up on the rocks and paused once again, this time for an almost prophetic feeling that he should dry off. When the sun had made him dry and lethargic he started up the cliffs with no more excuses to be found. Until he saw the house.

The levels stepped up the cliff, firebrick walls reflecting the red tinge of the now setting sun. Fear like a slithering snake coiled around him inside, and he stopped again, too frightened to go on. The excuses appearing, the snake's tongue now on his wrists as Reill suddenly and without warning welled up out of inactive state.

In maddening pain, one thought prevailed, a loud war cry sounding over the din of battle: *If I die now my father will die never knowing, thinking it my choice.* He stumbled up the cliff, everything washed red before his eyes, pumping blood deafening to his ears. The thought of showing himself made him lose his footing and fall, cowering with an impulse to flee, not to be seen. He scrambled to his feet and up the cliffs. The last of his strength vaulted him over the railing to the terrace, where he collapsed, bleating softly, wanting to die quickly.

He saw his father, felt his presence first, then looked up in a red blur, not even able to beg for help. *I'm sorry, Father. I tried.* All becoming swimming redness. He was home and he could die.

I am dead. I have to be dead.

Lying on his back, Teal stirred without opening his eyes, fingers straying in sand which he picked up and let fall in a stream on his stomach, a tickling, faintly biting trickle.

Is there sand in hell?

Suddenly he sat up, opening his eyes and screaming to the world, *"Why am I still alive!"*

The echo died, and his slightly hoarse throat was the only clue that he had ever spoken. A trace of yellow sand clung to his stomach. Yellow sand and yellow rocks by sparkling ocean under half-clouded blue—this was not the island he had been on. This was not Skye at twilight. Hair on his back crawled up toward his neck, and he spun to face Akelan sitting behind him.

Akelan brushed some sand from Teal's hair and shoulders.

Too confused to ask a question, Teal remained silent, pushing a handful of sand in agitation, trying to think, feeling like an empty cathedral Jim had taken him to once—sensing that even God had abandoned it. Empty and deserted—like a big chunk taken away. A strange sensation he had never felt before he suddenly knew as the absence of something that had always been there. Absence of pain. Reill was gone.

He clutched at Akelan, who held him as if he were still five years old, still drowning. He calmed, and calmness frightened him, too new to be dealt with. The pressure from within was gone, and he was suddenly aware that the great pressure from without it had balanced. As if realizing for the first time that Akelan was not dead, he held onto him, afraid of losing him again.

"It's all right, Teal. Come walk with me," Akelan said and helped him to his feet.

Teal looked at him and started to sink again, knees giving way.

"Don't kneel! Come with me," Akelan said and took his arm.

"You were dead, Akelan. I saw you die!"

"Teal, it happened to me— I know what happened to me—"

"You were hardly in any condition to know what was happening—you were dead!" *As I must've been dead, and now live and he is here. . . .*

"Teal, when you were lying there with your throat spitting blood, you knew you weren't dead. When you rose you knew it wasn't from the dead, though someone looking at you might not have seen life—"

"How did you know I slit my throat?" Teal said, more and more convinced of divinity.

Akelan was silent, then said, "I will tell you something if you promise not to kneel again."

Teal nodded slowly.

"It's not so strange when you remember that you can feel when your child is going to be killed—"

"How did you know *that*—"

"Hush, wait. Or you can remember what happened to your ancestors one hundred years before you were born. My abilities are no more mystical—I only have more of them because I am a Trieath. I'm not a god, I'm a Trieath. What I wanted to tell you is that years ago and light-years distant I felt someone knew and loved dying. I saw through his eyes and felt blood leaving me, and I don't really know how to describe what I did—lent you life while you were unable to sustain it yourself."

"Then I would have died."

"Yes."

"And I thought I'd wrecked it." He smiled slightly. "A cross, a circle, a fish, a rosette. . . . Oh God, Oh God—"

"Hey—" Akelan stopped him.

"I only promised not to kneel," Teal retorted. "Is that how I made it through Armageddon? Otranadoe? . . . They said the devil was with me . . . funny, it was just the reverse. . . ."

"Teal, please."

"Did you help me all those times, through all those things when I thought it was me?"

"Sometimes, Teal."

"And . . . through . . . something red and very terrible . . . ?"

"I was there."

No one pilots a ship like that.

No one comes out of Otranadoe.

No one lives through Red Madness.

Not without the aid of someone greater. . . .

"How can I believe you're a man after that?"

"I am. What else can I say?"

"How . . . light-years . . . how could you *hear* me?"

"The two strongest lines of Arana have a loud voice."

"Two?" Teal was confused. "Stewert and who else? Yours?"

A flicker of indecision, then, "Later," said Akelan. "You will find that out soon enough."

"I think I'm going to break my promise."

"Don't you dare kneel, Teal Stewert."

"A rosette, a circle, a fish, a cross—why did I see all those if you aren't Him?"

"There's someone else, Teal . . . not me. I'm Akelan."

"I was here," said Teal, eyes gazing into the distance.

"When, Teal?"

"Here—when I . . . all was red and terrible . . . and I remember *here.* I was brought here. . . . Did you cure that too?"

Akelan answered, "No. You were here, but I didn't do anything."

"Then how—"

"Your father, Teal. He's the only one who could give it to you and the only who could take it from you. He brought you to me. I said I could do nothing, but that he had the power—if he was willing to."

"Where is he?" Teal cried. "Is he alive?"

"I couldn't tell you. Till it passes, we have to wait."

"But where *is* he?"

"I don't know, Teal. And there's nothing you or I could do if I did know where."

"But you helped *me!*"

"It's different. What I could have done would be temporary. I can take a crisis on myself: but I can't take *it* away. Only Kaela can do that. Now that he has, he must conquer it within himself, and no one can help him."

"Where is my father?"

"I don't know."

"When will I know?"

Akelan sighed, gently annoyed. "I don't know. If . . . if he dies you may never find him. If he lives God only knows how long it will be."

"So how long?" asked Teal.

"You're as stubborn as your father. Teal, would I ever lie to you?"

"No."

"I'm not God. Believe me?"

"I guess I have to."

Akelan changed his tone. "You haven't seen New Dianter." He tugged on his hand. "It's just as nice."

"You're trying to distract me."

"Of course I am. Would you rather sit and wait?" Akelan pulled him along. "Don't fight me. Come."

New Dianter—Bay Dianter, the Royalists called it—was as Akelan said, as beautiful as Old Dianter had been. What it lacked in gentle subtlety it made up for in drama. Set at the

foot of a mountain, it was backed by massiveness and lorded
over by the lofty summit; and all around wound the tree-
filled river gorge. It was harder to reach than Dianter and
protected from airplanes by the mountain called the
Guardian.

No attempt had been made to copy Old Dianter in any
way. The colonnade was replaced by a U-shaped building.
The central courtyard contained a mountain spring bubbling
year-round to refresh pilgrims after the hard journey there.
The building was firebrick instead of marble, and the
columns were wooden this time.

People Teal didn't know or remember came up to him in
welcome, calling him by name. There was no one who did
not know who he was. The attention disturbed him, and he
whispered to Akelan of his desire to be more alone. Akelan
took him to a secluded walkway under shade trees.

"It's almost as hard for a king's son and legend to be alone
as it is for a Trieath," said Akelan. "Did you know . . . no,
how could you . . . your father is king. Neither you nor Ven
Brekk can be king, though you're both a higher generation
than he is."

"Why?" Teal asked, relieved as he was puzzled.

"When you left there was going to be another fight over
that piece of gold"—he referred to the crown. "My father re-
claimed it just long enough to pass a law that says crisis generation may not hold the crown. Ven Brekk took it fairly
well. Thoma . . . I think it did something to Thoma."

"It's a good law," said Teal, feeling as unfit for sovereignty
as was Ven.

"My father abdicated again, and your father is still king,
unless . . ." He didn't finish. Unless Kaela had died, in
which case the next line would rule.

A whirri nearly blundered into the pair as they walked.
Teal watched it go, tumbling through the air with its ludi-
crously small wings flapping to keep its ungainly fat body
aloft. Stupid and useless, the whirris survived. Teal almost envied them. It bounced off a tree and bumbled into the forest
and out of sight.

A soft hissing voice spoke from the shadows, halting Teal
where he was, "Vilest offspring of the vile, brought forth in
shame, grown like a spreading infection." Sound rebounded
off the rocks, obscuring the exact origin. First Teal thought it
had to be Brekk; then the voice spat, "Brekk."

Over a stone wall along the walk slunk Teal's tormentor,

disguised by the skin he wore, a gray hide with a burned scar. "Brekk bastard. Proud polluted line sunk into the sewage of a more putrid quagmire, last excretion of the Stewert line."

Teal started for him, but Akelan's arm was as unyielding as the death collar.

"That was not called for," Akelan said sternly to the covered figure. "Did it take a long time to compose? It sounds practiced."

"I put a lot of thought into it," the voice said.

"Your time could have been better spent."

"My apologies, Trieath," the voice beneath the beast's skin spoke courteously. The hooded head turned to Teal. "I'll be simple, Ray"—he used the feminine to address Teal. "Your mama was a Brekk bastard."

Teal lunged, but was held back by Akelan.

"Let me go, 'Kelan!"

"Teal."

"He called my mother Brekk—" The offender sounded like Thoma Brekk, but Teal felt sure Thoma wouldn't use his own line name in insult.

"She was, Teal," Akelan said. "Raya was a Brekk."

Teal turned on him in anger but couldn't do anything to Akelan.

"She was also a bastard."

"She was born of respectable Lowland parents—" He halted. Shame of bastardy was an Earth concept. "Bastard" was not the taunt here, "Brekk" was.

Akelan stared down the defiant eyes, which were forced to drop groundward. "Two Beth-enea before Ven Brekk married his wife, he had a daughter by a Lowland woman. The daughter was Raya. Ven didn't want it known that the Brekk line had been set back with a daughter, so he had the woman married to a Lowlander who accepted daughter Raya as his own, not knowing what she was. Your mother was a line skip link—just like your daughter. The Brekk line did not die with Thoma and Igil. It's still alive and you're its heir, first-generation Bay by the Brekks—as well as thirty-third-generation Bay by Stewert. And I really don't know what that makes you. That's what I meant by 'two strongest lines.' . . . I meant to tell you, but not like this."

All was spinning and the mountain moved beneath him as if in a quake. He was Brekk. He was Stewert. Teal shook his head. "*No.*"

The creature on the wall bounded down, and the skin hood fell back. Teal knew who it was now anyway.

Thoma growled, pride mortally wounded, shame of his Brekk line that he'd held so high turned to hatred toward all. The only way he could strike back at the Brekk line that had caused him so much humiliation was to end it. He gripped a ceremonial knife.

"Thoma, I forbid this," Akelan said. "The Law and I."

"Where were you and the Law when this atrocity was committed against me?"

"No atrocity has been committed against you," Akelan said. "Nothing has changed regarding your situation. You blame another person because you aren't Bay and you aren't heir. You have not been wronged. You have the status of a Lowlander. There is no shame in that unless you choose to put it there."

"So easy for a Trieath to speak," Thoma said in a dangerous, wounded voice. Dark eyes glowering and heavy muscles tensed, he stood ready to strike at Ray.

Teal stood alert but undaunted. His breeding and the Trieath beside him assured his own safety. But he didn't want to fight Thoma.

Shrill Brekk whistle broke Thoma's readying attack. Ven Brekk appeared following his challenge whistle, breathing hard.

What Teal at first thought was a lucky arrival he saw was not chance at all. Igil stood, a quiet shadow behind his father, a terrified replica of Thoma. Thoma's accusing gaze fell first on his brother for betraying him, then on his father who had come to stop him.

"You can still show your face?" Thoma mocked. "Don't come near me. I'm about to do some cleansing of the line."

"Son." Ven was both commanding and begging. "There has been shame in our line. No more. Don't bring any more on us."

"On *us?* I've had mine! You mean on you. You get what you deserve."

Thoma had always walked all over his father, who bowed to his wishes. But Thoma had mistaken devotion and an attempt to compensate for harm as weakness. His father was not weak. He stepped forward.

"Come near me and I'll kill you," Thoma said solemnly. He glanced over his father's sweat-gleaming shoulder at his pleading identical self. "You too, my weaker, worser half.

Since you betrayed me to him, you hold him back or I'll take you too."

"I love you, Thoma," his brother whined, strange-sounding since he spoke with Thoma's voice. "I'm your brother. I don't want you to die."

"You have so little faith in me. Is that a brother? You think *that* is any match for me?" He thrust the ceremonial dagger toward Teal. Teal watched warily, still feeling slow and weak, and he knew well what power shame and revenge lent. And he felt a drain of strength—pain and strength had fled at once. He stayed close to Akelan. At his side he was invincible.

"He's a Bay," Igil said helplessly.

"He's a thirty-third weak link freak like *him*." The dagger pointed its hard, cruel finger at Ven. "*Crisis* generation isn't the word! You two weren't born—you were vomited!"

It was fast. Ven called challenge and Thoma met him. The knife, not lawful in challenge, came toward Ven and was turned back by a powerful hand. Thoma's eyes went wide as he stiffened a moment. His father caught him and whispered some parting word meant only for him, perhaps offering forgiveness or asking it, and Thoma died.

Ven met no one's eyes, lowered his son to the ground, and quietly left the way he'd come. Igil was at his brother's side, kissing his hands, Narcissus trying to bring his reflection to life.

Akelan pulled a horror-struck Teal away and back down the path.

Teal huddled close to him, shivering even in the heat. "What will happen to him? He's so alone."

"Igil? He'll become a person. It will hurt for a long time. But I can't help feeling it's for the best . . . though I regret Thoma's death very much. It needn't have been. Ven will have trouble."

"Why did he fight me? Ven. If I am his heir, why?" Teal cried, remembering the challenge in the Womb at Old Dianter.

"I don't know. He's a thirty-third-generation Bay like you. I don't even know why your mother was born—that's not an insult. I mean, when he had the power to prevent conception till he married, why didn't he? I don't know."

Teal looked blank.

"Teal," Akelan said, "you didn't know? Teal, thirty-third-generation Bay has the power to choose . . . if you want a child or not."

Teal's thoughts swam dizzily. He reached out and caught one. "Is that why I don't have so many Earth bastards?" He had been using his unknown ability unconsciously. Either that or the Earthwomen had been very careful.

"That's one of the changes at thirty-third generation. Teal, don't you know why it is that a line which makes it past thirty-third won't break?"

Teal shook his head. Realizing that that was an Earth gesture, he spoke. "No."

"From thirty-fourth generation on, a Bay has the ability to determine whether he'll have a son or daughter. He can choose to produce only male seed, and after he has an only son, he can choose to produce none at all. At thirty-third generation you have the second ability—to produce nothing. It's both or nothing. Before thirty-third Bay, having offspring is as chancy as for a Northerner."

"No one ever told me," Teal mumbled.

Purple mourning flower. Ven Brekk had shown him the sky . . . and had mourned his daughter Raya. "I'm a Brekk," he spoke forlornly.

"Brekk line saved your life, Teal," Akelan said. "While Stewert was rejected and feeling Red Madness, Brekk was a lesser-generation Bay, not crisis goneration and not so dependent on the last link—it forced you to live."

"This whole galaxy is converging on my shoulders!" Teal cried out suddenly. A pawn stuck in the middle when worlds clashed, child of a double star burning between them. "Everything . . . everything . . . happens to me. But you know, that doesn't make me feel the least bit significant or important . . . because . . . if I had never existed . . . this galaxy would not be much different. Someone else would have commanded *Tesah*. There would have been someone else to take *Sovereign*. And so what if my line—lines—live or die? You're the Trieath and there's no need for breeding anymore. How can that be? How can I be in the middle . . . and make no difference at all?"

"You've made a great difference to me. Is that something?"

Teal held onto his arm as they walked and didn't speak for a while. He broke the silence further on. "My father will kill me! Does he know I'm a Brekk?"

"He found out some time ago."

"Did Ven tell him?"

"I did," Akelan said. "When you ran. I was very hard on him . . . to the point of being cruel. It wasn't necessary. . . ."

"Why did Ven let his daughter marry a Stewert?"

"He just couldn't own up to having a daughter. But he wasn't actually trying to make the line appear unbroken. He married a woman whose seed twinned. That shows some regret."

"Did my mother know who she was?"

"Certainly. It is typical of feminine intrigue (Mother, forgive me) to try to reconcile enemies with a child. A female Bay is a rare thing, and Raya had no trouble attracting your father. But while she was playing with her own breeding scheme, crossing thirty-second Bay with a line skip link, she made a very, very tragic mistake—and I'm afraid to tell you this."

"What?"

"The reason why your mother was alone in the cold at the time of your birth."

"I was premature." *I found that out.*

"Only Northerners' babies are premature. You were on time. After thirty-third generation the gestation period shortens with every succeeding generation, till finally mine was fifty days shorter than a Lowlander's. You're thirty-third-generation Bay *and* line skip first-generation Bay. That makes you something else—I told you that I don't know what—but your time was twenty-six days shorter than the normal, and Raya never took into account that it might be different." Unspoken was the thought that it was her own fault she got caught alone. Kaela must have seen that too by now and could no longer maintain his rage at Teal as the cause of her death—not that his hatred had made sense before the discovery. And so the change upon Teal's return.

"Where's my father?"

"I told you I don't know. I don't."

"I can't find him! I look . . . and there's my daughter . . . and my Earth daughter . . . and I even know Ven and Igil . . . but I can't find my father. . . . I should see him first. . . . I can't feel his presence at all!"

III.

What seemed like forever was actually three days. Teal crept back into the house—strange that the fear had not gone with the pain as he had imagined it would. The house seemed deserted and empty, but Teal checked all the rooms.

Kaela was in his own room, lying still as death. Teal crept in and would have whined in distress. But the image of an Earth dog silenced him; he was ill at ease with the old animal habits. He timidly touched his father's shoulder; life ran through like an electric current—and, like electricity, would not let him draw away. Kaela's eyes opened black and piercing, and a powerful arm enfolded Teal. Kaela licked his cheek (again, an Earth image made Teal feel barbaric—infected with a new set of cultural standards). He turned Teal's head aside, growling at the death collar. "What is it?" The alien, ungiving collar upset him.

"It's a death collar," Teal mumbled, confused and frightened. "It doesn't come off."

Kaela bit it and snarled and only let off when he realized his terrified son thought that the hate sounds were directed at him.

Apologies and forgiveness were understood, and awkward words were dispensed with. Curled up next to him, hanging on his arm, Teal couldn't understand why he wasn't happy. It was like the end of a long long war when instead of feeling jubilation one was left drained and weary.

"I don't feel well."

"Are you ill?"

"No . . . I just . . . that's over, but I don't feel well."

"You don't need that to feel badly." "That" was Reill. Its name was never spoken between them.

"I know . . . no, I don't . . . I thought it would end all my problems." He was feeling let down. "But just one is gone. All the rest are there."

He felt better after a few weeks of ghosting his father as Igil had Thoma. Though the man was almost a stranger to him, he felt he had known him always. He knew he was part of Kaela and couldn't help but adore him. Being loved in return, he discovered, had to be one of the greatest things that could happen to him. Later he ventured out on his own and could appreciate his freedom from pain and impending death. But he was also restless. He felt guilt at his ingratitude for his change of fate, but he couldn't help wanting more. There had to be more. For one thing, he wanted to marry.

"When are you going to marry, Akelan?" he asked as the two sat under the shade of a mountain tree at Bay Dianter.

"You have a daughter, Ariadne—" Akelan's face glowed red.

Akelan had taken Teal to see his daughter, Ariadne—only ten years Teal's junior. She was a dark-skinned, copper-haired enchantress like her mother, and she knew Teal for her father at once. She was taller than he was—Akelan's height. Her facial features were his, though the large expressive eyes were brown and clear of pain.

"You're going to marry my daughter!" Teal cried.

"Do you object?"

"I . . . I don't know. You're too old!"

"*What?*"

He was thinking like an Earthman again. "You're going to marry my daughter . . . why?"

"She's different from any of the others. A Bay woman is a rare—and beautiful—thing. She doesn't worship me—as *some* people do. I want a wife, not a worshiper. She never lets me forget I'm a man. I mean that in all ways—"

"Watch it; you're talking about my daughter—" Earth again.

"You asked."

"They say Ariadne is a lot like me."

"She is. Maybe that's even part of it. All I know is that she's the one."

Teal leaned back against the tree, watched some whirris bumble by. He looked down at the gorge where the river wound its way from mountains to the sea. The Sea. He thought of Natina and of prophets and prophecies. "You can marry my daughter," he said at last.

"Well, thanks," Akelan said, making it clear he didn't need permission.

"The prophecy said you would, so I guess I'd better let you."

Akelan was puzzled. "You mean the one that goes: 'There will come one who has seen the face of hell . . .'?"

"That one. 'The Trieath through whom we will be reborn by the blood of the one who wears hell in his eyes.' I thought that meant you were going to kill me. But I guess it could mean you're going to marry my daughter."

"So you'll let me marry her so that I don't take the other interpretation and kill you," Akelan joked.

"Uh huh."

Akelan laughed but it had a cry in it—Teal was serious.

Teal thought of his daughter and of marriage. Broken link mended and set back on course, his thoughts turned to a more normal obsession. He was fifty years old and wanted to marry. He asked Ariadne's mother to marry him. She smiled, was flattered—as flattered and bewildered as when she'd found he'd given her child—his line's heir. She kissed him, paced a light dancing step. She said no.

November 30, 2207 A.D. (Wednesday)

"Dear God, Teal, I've been worried sick about you." Terrel hugged him. "You'd swear I was your mother." He pulled back and looked at Teal, unchanged by time except that his eyes seemed gentler and brighter. "Did it work out? Tell me!"

Looking into brown eyes, Teal could finally be happy about it. "It's gone—he called me son—"

Terrel's smile was elated, the kind of reaction Teal thought he himself should have experienced.

He told him of Akelan, still firmly convinced that he'd risen from the dead. "But what convinced me that he wasn't God was that he wanted to marry my daughter. I couldn't believe God was marrying my daughter. Where is God then? Gods all over the galaxy die and rise again. Rising from the dead seems to be common to almost all of them."

"It tends to lead to the idea that there is only one God with lots of names," Terrel said.

"Or," Teal countered, "It points to the primary reason that

religion exists—mortals fear death and wish for immortality. The will to survive is universal—it's only logical that the gods men create should fulfill their wish to live forever."

"You are still a cynic." Terrel shook his head. He tapped his arm. "There's still something else you haven't told me."

Teal didn't meet his gaze.

"I'm sorry," Terrel said. "I thought everything was all right. But you came back. What happened?"

"There's no such thing as magic," Teal said. "Solve one thing and everything else doesn't suddenly become all right. Nothing went *wrong*, but Terrel, I'm still the same person who slashes his throat and wakes you up screaming in the middle of the night thinking I'm back at Otranadoe and—"

"Hush, Teal," Terrel said. Teal was getting hysterical. Terrel sat him down and talked to him. Teal interrupted him once for no apparent reason to say, "I trust you."

"I know you do," Terrel answered.

Once totally open and trusting, such feelings were rare now for Teal. He could not even have faith that the shell above him might not collapse on him. "Safe as a womb" was grim irony for him. Looking back, *that* had been false security, trusting not to be expelled suddenly into a hostile winter world—not even trusting—never suspecting. Terrel tried to tell him that that was why he didn't trust women.

"I was married once," Teal argued, then dreamed off. "You wouldn't believe how I met my wife." He smiled sadly. Like getting a kitten from a tree. *Her* child had had no safety either. . . . "You know, when I was waving that Caucan head around on a pike thinking how atrocious and vicious I was, I saw a group of women, Royalist and Caucan, catch a Caucan soldier. I guess he was a rapist, because after they'd castrated him they hacked a branch off a tree and used the jagged end to give him the same. And I thought—all I did was kill my man, and what I do now to his senseless head doesn't hurt him. Terrel—*women*. I wouldn't put anything past Earthwomen, but those were *ours*."

Terrel nodded slightly, and Teal knew what he was thinking.

"But I *do* trust women," Teal defended against his silent statement.

"Tell me."

"I trust Nora."

"You know what Nora is."

"What does that have to do with anything?"

"She doesn't play a woman's role. She'll never marry. She'll never be a mother. She's no threat."

That was Earth American reasoning. Teal tried to explain that Royalist psychology was different. They were ruled by different forces; their planetary rhythm, lack of lunar rhythm, the influence of a second sun, lack of seasonal cycle. Their lineage made for totally different influences; their race memory; the Highlanders' line memory; the tight link between father and son and mother and daughter. There was also the influence of the sea; the unity of the Royalist people; their harsh natural law; their freedom from taboos on sex, nakedness, natural functions and states. Teal tried to tell Terrel these were what made up Royalists and that Earth American standards couldn't apply.

"Oh yes they can—you're an Earthman at heart," Terrel said.

Some time, Teal was not certain exactly when, the time had come when he had spent more time among these aliens than at home. So where now was home?

"Are you coming back to *Sovereign*?" Terrel asked him.

"I don't know. I have to talk to Cory."

"He'll give you *Sovereign* back. Our new captain is having real problems. We've had him half a year and we still call him our new captain. It's not working."

Teal looked at the floor. "I don't know where else I'd go—"

"Stop that," Terrel ordered and changed the subject. "Have you seen Calvin? You know that red-headed—you know—his nose is over *here*. I mean it's over *here*, really."

"Really?" Teal said with pseudo-innocence that Terrel saw through at once.

"Guess you settled all your scores, hm, Teal?"

"Tried to."

"I've still got your purple aardvark."

"Funny, I could've taken purple after all. . . ."

Teal had a long talk with Cory, who was genuinely happy to see him. He was even happier to restore his command of *Sovereign*. "Your crew—that's just it—they're *your* crew. They're bucking this other man. He's a good leader; he's proved himself on other ships. But your crew is still yours."

The ousted captain gave him a stoic handshake, and Teal almost felt sorry for him.

The alert came before drilling was done.

"Admiral, my crew is slow; I told you my ship wouldn't be ready for action till after Christmas," Teal objected to the premature call to action.

"Well, merry Christmas. We need every ship."

"If it's that bad, what is it?"

"We don't know."

"Yes, sir."

Teal was told little more en route to the place of emergency in the Taurus constellation. A scientific vessel accompanied *Sovereign* to the disaster scene, a scientist briefing Teal as they went.

"This is all your fault," the scientist said. "You" meant not Teal personally but the entire military division of UEF. "You people have been hushing this up for a long time, hoping it would go away. You asked for it."

Teal waited with sorely tried patience for the man to tell him what had happened and why they were going where they were going.

"Turns out you people have known about this for a while and have been hiding it in a secret file code-named Minotaur. Minotaur is a region in the Taurus constellation that has an unusual propensity for wrecking spaceships for no reason whatsoever. You people call it coincidence, yet you keep a secret file on it. The place is a shiptrap, and you've done nothing to warn anyone about it or to reroute traffic lanes around it, though twenty-three vessels to date have disappeared in that area. Now you've got what you asked for. An entire convoy disappeared in the Minotaur sector, and you've finally called the scientists in to investigate. We're here to give you your answers. I don't know what *you're* supposed to be doing here, though. That's just like the military—solve everything with guns. What do you call that monstrosity you're piloting?" He referred to the giant ship *Sovereign*.

"The largest war machine ever designed," Teal said calmly.

Teal was given the Minotaur file to look over, but it told him nothing. The accounts of ten surviving ship captains, near victims of the Minotaur, all conflicted. One reported spotting a UFO directly before the disaster which it described as an attack; one reported a storm; one reported the stars blacking out; one reported the ship breaking up.

Sovereign added an eleventh account.

The encounter was just as abrupt as the others. What happened happened too fast to be identified.

Everything seemed normal entering the Minotaur sector until the monitor reported losing contact with the scientific vessel. Immediately following that, the internal monitor reported a weakness in the energy field control regulating the energy output of the field that contained the ship's antimatter. "It's critical. The control is going to blow up any minute." Once the control went, explosion of the engines was imminent.

"Evacuate quad four," Teal ordered.

"Done, sir."

"Seal off quad four and prepare to eject."

The man was white and sweating. "It won't go."

"Switch to auxiliary."

"Captain, it's *melted*—the works are fused solid." He was giving way to panic.

Teal ran from the command platform.

"Captain, what are you going to do?" Terrel ran after him.

"I'm going to seal off quad four if I have to do it with my bare hands," he growled, and ran sternward to the control room. If the control failed there would be little if any time to seal the quad and eject the engines safely away from the ship before antimatter met matter.

The engine control room's red door came into view. Teal flew through the door, Terrel at his heels, and the whole control blew up.

IV.

Teal opened his eyes. He was in sick bay, bandaged from head to toe.

Toe. Toe itched. No toes.

Teal looked down. There was a leg and a foot. No toes. No right leg. Toes *itched*.

It was just as well there were no toes to itch, because he hadn't any fingers to scratch with.

He looked over to the next cot. Terrel was either sleeping or unconscious, a bandage over one eye, as well as on arms and legs. There was something on Terrel's pillow. A medal.

The doctor came in, face strong despite wrinkles and a wreath of white hair. He saw Teal was awake, gave him a drink of water, and said, "It's Tuesday, two days later."

That took care of questions two and three but not number one. "How's Terrel?"

"He'll live," the doctor said. Hands that checked pulse were age-blotched but steady and sure, skin stretched taut over long, slender fingers. Teal trusted a doctor who took a pulse by hand. "Whether he can still serve—that's another matter." He shrugged. "Don't know. Probably not." He had to be blunt with Teal. He was the captain. "You caught the worst of it, but we're not worried about you."

"My toes itch."

"That's natural."

Teal frowned. "What happened?"

"You mean after you got blown up?" the doctor asked.

Teal nodded.

The white-haired man folded his hands. "Terrel made a hero out of himself. After he dragged you out of there he sealed off quad four and ejected it. He also put a tourniquet on your leg so you didn't bleed to death before my boys got down there."

Teal looked over at him. "How could he do all that?"

"Good question—he should've been out as cold as you

were. He has been ever since. A merchant ship, *Manuela*, took us in tow yesterday, drifting around in the Minotaur sector. We're orbiting Earth right now."

"Then my ship is safe."

"Your *crew* is safe. Your ship is totaled."

"Will they rebuild *Sovereign*?" Teal asked.

"I don't know, captain. I doubt that too. She's big and old. All the ships they're making now are small."

"The age of the dinosaurs is past."

"Looks that way."

"She was a good ship."

"No one can argue with that."

"What happened? What was it?"

"The Minotaur? We don't know. Science division is working on it. I think they're having fun—they love to see the military begging for answers. I also think they enjoy watching us get blown up."

Teal drifted off for what he thought was a few seconds, but he was surprised when he opened his eyes to find the doctor gone. He was even more surprised to see Terrel walking—stiffly and with great effort. Teal knew on sight that Terrel would not serve again. He tried to call his name but drifted under again.

Finally there were toes (they itched), and fingers to scratch with. Teal was thin and weak but the doctor could not keep him down. He went to find Terrel. (He was just there a minute ago.) The computer had dropped his name from the active list. Teal kicked the machine with his new foot, but it obstinately continued to spit out the wrong answer. *No.* Terrel *was* still in the Fleet. . . .

Teal caught up with his former Sub-second staying at his parents' home in Bloomington, Illinois. The house was on the edge of the city, sheltered by trees and the surrounding greenery. A weeping willow shaded the front lawn. Teal stood outside the gate and a dog came frisking and barking. Not a watchdog because it was wagging its tail and carrying a ball. He stepped inside, patted the dog, a knee-high mutt, and walked up the flagstone path to the porch. He hesitated before placing his hand on the ID panel. *Why don't I go away?*

Vacillating between courses of action, he turned to go—and saw Terrel by the side of the house, the dog licking his hand. He was walking slowly and carefully over the lawn toward him.

"Here it is," Terrel greeted him, indicating the white stone house and lawn and trees around him. "Every bit as middle-class as you expected." He puffed and reached the porch with effort. Teal resisted the impulse to help him up the steps but couldn't keep his face clear of worry. "Don't worry about the leg," Terrel said. "Doc said it would smooth out with exercise. It's good to see you. I swear I thought you were dead." He gave him a welcome hug.

Teal searched his face. One of the gentle eyes he'd loved to gaze into was different. "It's a transplant." Teal touched his cheek below the new eye.

"I knew you'd see that," Terrel said, smiling. "I couldn't tell the difference in the mirror. You're so thin—come in, I'll get you something to eat."

"Why didn't you come to see me?" Teal held onto him.

"You wouldn't have known if I had."

"You didn't," Teal said.

"I've been home hunting. You know they've clipped my wings. I don't have to work but I'd like to. I don't want to rot."

"Did you find anything?" Teal tugged distractedly on his jacket. Two English sparrows in the oak tree were having a quarrel over their lady. Or was it over territory?

"Yes, I think I did. It's a former subject world of the Zhar-aghan Empire. Backward little place, but except for the air pollution in the big cities it's nice. I'm sure I could put my training to work there. They're trying to grow."

"Then you're leaving."

"Yes."

Teal, blinking furiously, took the silver pendant from his neck and pressed it into Terrel's hand. He spoke quickly. "Here, take this."

"But that's your—"

"You're supposed to give it away," Teal said. "Do they speak English?"

"Do who speak English? Oh—where I'm going? Yes, a lot of them do. They still speak Zharaghan in the churches. Every city is built around the church. They have only one religion and they're very devout, but they didn't mind my difference. They just accept that because I'm from a different world of course I'd have a different God. They all go out at sunup and sundown to pray. It's really something to see—the *whole* town comes out."

Teal was facing away toward the willow. "Sunup and sun-down?"

"Yes. They worship the Sun as the visible aspect of the in-visible God."

The Sun. The Sun. Teal could not be concerned with it, seeing the eclipse of his own.

May 15, 2208 A.D. (Tuesday)

Despondent, Teal stared blank-faced over the waters of Lake Michigan, head resting on folded arms, leaning against a window in the stone tower. Voices droned on, ignored, like summer insects. They belonged to some Cleveland engineers, some Chicago officials, and some Luna brass, Admiral Cory among them. Ray was the odd man out, dragged along for the ride. He felt pitying glances on his back. *Poor guy, they're thinking, lost his ship again.* Teal did not care about the Calvin-designed machine referred to as *Sovereign*; he'd saved his crew. What was the strategy here? Teal wondered. Teal was in no way involved or interested in the plans to ex-tend Chicago Base out onto Lake Michigan as they'd done in Cleveland on Lake Erie. Cory was trying to get him involved, not necessarily in this but in anything.

". . . too windy . . ."

". . . average velocity not as great as Cleveland . . ."

Teal yawned and stretched, catlike. He walked to a win-dow at which Cory stood, gazing from the tower toward the coast. Water lapped the base of the tower on this side. Teal stood eyeball to upper arm next to Cory. He looked up at the tall commander. "How deep is the water down there?"

"I don't know," said Cory.

"No idea?"

"No. Why?"

"I feel like Russian roulette," he said, and before they could react he was gone.

The admiral found out how deep the water was—fatally shallow close to the tower, sloping quickly out to a treacher-ous depth that only Teal Ray might survive. And since no body was found, where was Teal Ray?

Cory thought it was a bad joke and waited for Ray to show up. He did not.

Four years and the legends sprang up:

Ray was alive and well and living in the sea.

He had returned to his still-unknown home.

He had defected to the Gerens and would show up next Armageddon.

There were reports of some very unusual dolphins.

And so on.

Cory did not know if he should arrange a funeral. He suspected not, and past experience said no. Admiral Orestes Peralta was hurt that Teal hadn't said goodbye. To him that was proof positive that he was still alive. He sailed out to the tower and, in the red-washed twilight of the setting sun, let fall a red rose into the gray waves of the lake.

The Voyager sped toward the sun, programmed to swing around the yellow inferno and on to its destination. The Sun. The Sun. Teal switched to manual. Into the sun. *Is this what it was all for? Is this all?* The Sun loomed large, swallowing the monitor screen, and Teal stared into yellowness in sour triumph. Yellow sun.

Red emergency lights lit up all over the monitor board. Into the sun. He closed his eyes.

A rosette, a circle, a fish, a cross, the Sun.

The Sun. *This Sun is too white.*

The ship swung around.

Twelfth Sunrise 1089

Scenic hills thick with foliage and wild flowers on open meadows lost their charm for the star-age man thanks to the bumpy roads and slow noisy vehicle in a pre-space-age world. He got lost. (He knew he shouldn't have taken that red-dog road.) Lacking a radio to call road assistance, he was left to local advice. He asked a little girl. She spoke with completely toned sounds, unable to produce aspirates, so *k*'s became *g*'s, *s*'s became *z*'s and *t*'s became *d*'s (as did *th*'s) in the Zharaghan way. "Dage de virzd levd . . ." It was English yet almost unrecognizable. He thanked her and she smiled brightly. He harumphed and tugged on his mustache in agitation.

The road sloped down into a shaded valley, and he almost missed the house behind its leafy screen. Getting away from it all was one thing, but this was barbaric. The house rose three stories and commanded a large spread of land. He noticed a lake in the back and what looked like an old mill.

He shut the car door and followed the flagstone walk to the door, which supported no metal hand panel but a knob and keyhole. Neither was there intercom or ID panel, but there was a bell, almost grown over with ivy climbing up the side. He breathed in chlorophyll and the scent of damp soil. Almost embarrassed, he touched the doorbell.

The door opened to the UEF officer.

Ray's first impulse was to slam it shut but he swallowed his anger and waited in the doorway.

Children ran across the backyard to the lake. "Whose are those?" the officer asked. He took it all in. How bourgeois. How normal. Wonderfully normal.

"Neighbors'," Teal said curtly. "How did you find me?"

"It was disgustingly easy. We didn't look for you. We just traced Richard Barret."

Teal started to close the door on him.

"Don't be angry with me. I'm only a messenger."

"Whose?"

"Cory's." The officer handed him a letter. "That's all I came for. I'll leave you alone, sir," he said and left.

Teal stood some minutes deciding whether to tear it up or read it. Curiosity won out and he opened it.

Captain:
My first thoughts after you dived shocked me even more than your plunge itself. As I stared at the empty window I thought: My son! My son! Now I wonder why I didn't choose some six-foot American to "adopt," but since I didn't, and since you didn't destroy this unopened, these words are for you. Some Polonius-type advice and assurance that you are welcome here whenever. If you are trying to hide, and I assume you are since you covered your tracks so thoroughly, I suggest you have Terrel cover his as well. A great many people are hunting you; and if one knows that two sets of tracks lead to one end and one trail is obliterated, all one needs to do to find the first track's maker is to follow the other trail. If ever you need anything I am not hard

to find. For my own peace of mind let me know if
you ever found what you were looking for. I'd sleep
easier knowing you'd stopped running and finally
found your port.

                    Admiral Robert M. Cory UEF (ret.)

There was a hastily added postscript:

Congratulations are in order for my successor, Fleet
Admiral Orestes Peralta. He wants to know if
you're coming back.

Teal sat out on the porch, letter in hand, reading, glancing
up at the children, rereading. He looked up again to see children splashing in the water, a young woman watching from
the steps of the mill house—the one who had had her eyes on
Richard; the woman that Teal used to be afraid of. He
looked back to the letter. He sat, lazy and long. The sun began to sink and he heard footsteps behind him. He kissed the
hand on his shoulder and composed a reply as the light
dimmed and the evening quiet of people come out to pray
settled on the town.

This ship is home. When they haul me out of this
port it will be as scrap.

Rebecca M. Meluch graduated from the University of North Carolina at Greensboro with a B.A. in drama. She has worked as everything from a control clerk and key-punch operator to an assistant in the Classics department at Greensboro, and she has been active in nonprofessional theater. Miss Meluch lives in Westlake, Ohio.

Ø

SIGNET Books by Robert A. Heinlein

- ☐ **ASSIGNMENT IN ETERNITY** (#W8443—$1.50)
- ☐ **BEYOND THIS HORIZON** (#W7599—$1.50)
- ☐ **THE DAY AFTER TOMORROW** (#W7766—$1.50)
- ☐ **THE DOOR INTO SUMMER** (#E8574—$1.75)*
- ☐ **DOUBLE STAR** (#W8188—$1.50)
- ☐ **THE MAN WHO SOLD THE MOON** (#J8717—$1.95)*
- ☐ **THE MENACE FROM EARTH** (#Y6383—$1.25)
- ☐ **METHUSELAH'S CHILDREN** (#W7591—$1.50)
- ☐ **THE PUPPET MASTERS** (#E8538—$1.75)
- ☐ **REVOLT IN 2100** (#E8674—$1.75)*
- ☐ **WALDO & MAGIC, INC.** (#W7330—$1.50)

* Price slightly higher in Canada